The barbarians are co[ming] . . .
In tranquil, prosper[ous . . .]
Curram holds a glitteri[ng . . .]
heiress learns of the t[. . .]
will change everything[. . .]

The barbarians are co[ming . . .]
In Escaly, a distant, arrogant nation, an elderly
Imperial Geometer receives an unexpected and
frightening command.

The barbarians are coming . . .
In the dank and feverish jungles of Belanesi, a
strange, half-human people wait for a season of
rain and the call of a mysterious piper.

*Who are the barbarians, and what do they
bring?*
Colin Greenland's vivid, turbulent novel follows the fates of two very different people in a
land that is not their own, drawn together at
THE HOUR OF THE THIN OX.

It is never,
in life,
three lines.

                Nicolas Roeg

to Andy with best wishes

THE HOUR OF THE THIN OX
Colin Greenland

colin greenland

London
UNWIN PAPERBACKS
Boston   Sydney   Wellington

First published in Great Britain by Unwin Paperbacks 1987

UNWIN ® PAPERBACKS, A Division of Unwin Hyman Ltd.,
40 Museum Street, London WC1A 1LU, UK

Unwin Paperbacks, A Division of Unwin Hyman Ltd.,
Park Lane, Hemel Hempstead, Herts HP2 4TE

Allen & Unwin Australia Pty Ltd.,
8 Napier Street, North Sydney, NSW 2060, Australia

Unwin Paperbacks, A Division of Unwin Hyman Ltd.,
with the Port Nicholson Press
PO Box 11-838 Wellington, New Zealand

© Colin Greenland 1987

ISBN 0-04-4400020

Printed and bound in Great Britain by Biddles Ltd,
Guildford and King's Lynn

Contents

To Sally
on a different mountain

— 1 —
From the Oriel

They came at first light in their glorious barges, painted with the bright unfamiliar colours of the Seven Realms. All the servants ran up and down the gallery, jostling for the best view. Jillian Curram buried her head under the pillow and wouldn't come out.

'Come quick and see! Come quick or you'll miss them!'

She didn't move. Her nurse thought she was playing.

'Well, wherever can she be? Upon my soul there's no sign of the girl. No sign of the little mistress. Where is she now, I wonder? And such a fine sight to see from her own window – all the noblemen in their fine array – scarlet and emerald and cloth-of-gold – which is the Prince, do you think? There's a barge all full of horses. Beautiful snow-white horses . . .'

Jillian Curram was not to be tempted, not even with horses. Angelica swished across the room and pounced on her.

'Who's a sleepy-head this morning?'

She snatched at the pillow, but Jillian clung tightly to it. Angelica whisked back the quilts and tickled her, without so much as a muffled giggle by way of response. Jillian could decide, when she put her mind to it, not to be ticklish. That meant trouble. Angelica grew plaintive.

'What will you do? You can't keep your bed this morning, Miss Jill, that's for sure. You know what day it is. And with the beautiful boats all sailing by beneath your very window . . .'

And so on.

Bethalie Beavon came clattering upstairs with Robbie. They stopped, uncertainly, outside the door. On a special occasion for excitement children would be children, even in House Curram. If Jillian had been kneeling on the sill in her

1

nightdress, all the maids and pantry boys would have come in and joined her to ooh and ah and make smeary marks on the window. But Jillian was still in bed.

'What's wrong with the little mistress, Angelica?'

'Is she sick?'

Angelica left her to shoo them away, and Jillian took advantage of her departure to bundle the quilts back over her.

'Now come, Miss Jill, you can't laze abed today and you know why. The whole house has been up and hard at work for hours, and I've plenty still to do without wasting my time on a wilful child who won't get up when she's told.'

There was more in the same vein, but Jillian Curram was indeed a wilful child, and not to be cajoled or scolded out of her humour.

She was not actually sulking. To be sure, she could not have said why she loathed the prospect of the day, the banquet and the ball and the grand, stiff costume with the ruffles in the Luscan style, in honour of the Prince of Luscany, and all the pleases and thank yous and the rest of the grim rigmarole of obedience – all she knew was that she loathed it, and would do anything to forestall its arrival. To that end she remained buried, and held her tongue, which bothered Angelica out of all patience.

'Must I fetch your lady mother to you?' she demanded, and when Jillian didn't stir, strode out in high dudgeon.

Jillian reckoned it was time to shift the battleground. She jumped out of bed, neglected to put on her robe and slippers, and ran out into the gallery. Bethalie and Robbie turned from the window.

'Aren't you dressed yet, Miss Jill?' asked Robbie superfluously. They both frowned, but Jillian knew they wouldn't interfere. She tossed her head disdainfully and tried not to glance out of the window as she scurried by. Even so, she caught a glimpse of that great procession coming stately and slow under sails as yellow as the prairies.

Jillian bounded down the back stairs, almost bowling over Dickon Troke, coming up to watch from the gallery. The back stairs were his territory, not hers, so he shouted a rude word at her, and she put out her tongue as she turned the corner and hurtled on down.

Her nurse and mother eventually found her on her favourite high stool by the kitchen fire. She had had time to charm two doughnuts out of Matt the cook and steal a third. Matt was up to his elbows in flour and trying to oversee all the crew who were chopping and peeling, fetching and carrying: he was in no mood to tangle with Jillian too. Chewing unconcernedly, she gazed at the fat logs as they crackled and blackened.

'There you are, you naughty child!'

'Jillian Curram, you are a bore,' said her mother, squeezing between vats and trestles as she swept down on her. 'I don't know how Angelica has patience with you.'

Matt, embarrassed at having harboured and fed a fugitive criminal, was bobbing his head and wiping his hands on his apron. 'You're a very naughty little girl,' said Angelica, 'and a trial to your mother,' but Curram ignored them both, picking her daughter up from her perch and hugging her briefly to her padded and perfumed bosom. The Seal of Curram dug painfully into Jillian's ribs. Carefully avoiding the sticky mouth, her mother kissed her and delivered her to her guardian, who shook Jillian's hand crossly and led her away.

'Jillian,' her mother called, 'I'll have no nonsense from you today, please. You're the jewel of House Curram, you little barbarian, and if you don't sparkle tonight I'll sell you to the soldiers.'

Jillian Curram was nine and three-quarters. Her mother had always talked to her like that since she was a baby, never condescending for a moment. Jillian was her heir, and would be worthy of her, or not worthy of her attention. Whatever Jillian did she loved her with a fierce devotion, which was barely noticed and never acknowledged. Another girl might have transferred her affections to Nurse, who was at least available; but Jillian was not to be satisfied with surrogates, and treated Angelica quite cruelly. She had seized upon the terrible truth that Angelica, when it came down to it, was not *important*; and Angelica perhaps sensed this, without understanding it. She thought it was the arrogance of childishness, and treated Jillian as the baby she took her for. She towed her away now to be scrubbed, confined in a plain frock until the evening, and sent with a mug of tomato juice to the schoolroom. There was no further breakfast, because of the doughnuts.

3

Morelio her tutor, predictably enough, talked about the Cathills. Jillian had often suspected he was a Cat himself – he was certainly a foreigner – so she said, to provoke him:

'They don't have a Sovereign Assembly, do they, sir, the Cats I mean?'

He bridled. 'You must not use that word, Jillian.'

'Which word, sir?'

'Only rude and vulgar people call the natives of the Seven Realms Cats. It's most improper.'

'But why, sir? They come from the Cathills, so they must be Hillcats, sir; and they're always fighting each other, you just said so.'

Jillian had heard her mother call them Cats, but would never have betrayed her, even to embarrass Morelio. He grew impatient, and spoke rapidly.

'Prince Dolo of Luscany and General Hargon of Mohan-Mandevale will kiss your hand at the ball tonight, Jillian, and what will you do then, scratch them under the chin and offer them a saucer of cream, hm?'

Jillian giggled.

'Now sit up straight and pay attention, please. There is nothing whatsoever of the feline about the people of the Cathills. They are human as you or I, as you could have seen by studying them as they sailed by earlier this morning. Observe and learn, Jillian, observe and learn. It will be useful to you later. And to answer your question, no, the Seven Realms do not enjoy the benefits of rule by a Sovereign Assembly as we do in Bryland. Each realm is governed by its own ruler, in a pattern of alliances which has changed remarkably throughout history.'

He was reading covertly from the book. Jillian said, 'Is that why there are eight of them, sir?'

Morelio raised an elegant eyebrow.

'Harmont, Perimont, Luscany, Ducros, Bathista, Broken River, Mohan-Jaspa and Mohan-Mandevale,' she recited.

Morelio blinked.

'Page 51, sir.'

'Ah. I am glad to see you *are* paying attention, Jillian.' Hastily he caught up. 'Yes. If you now turn to page 54, Jillian, you will note that the Treaty of Dead Rock, 1052, though

4

nominally granting jurisdiction over the territories of Harmont and Perimont to Count Carl IV, effectively split Perimont into three counties, one of which at least was the tribal land of the Veniak of Bathista, or Bandu as it then was, while the Partition of Mohan, 1069, notwithstanding the so-called Woodcutters' Charter of the previous year . . .'

A bar of sunlight crept silently across the green baize table-cloth. Through the open window Jillian could see the swifts spiralling in the soft air, and hear the distant fanfare that announced the arrival of the seventeen state barges from the Seven (or Eight) Realms of the Cathills to the city of Hovenstok in Bryland. A reception committee of the Sovereign Assembly waited, ruffled but dignified, in the brisk wind on the Hovenstok waterfront; and tonight they would all be coming to dine with Jillian Curram's mother.

Luncheon, meanwhile, was horrible. Jillian mashed the stewed sish into a mess, then sighed and stared at it glumly.

'I don't want it.'

Angelica glowered. 'There's plenty of little poor girls over in Neath who'd say thank you for a nice dish of fruit and custard.'

'Let them eat it.'

'There'll be no tea today, you know that.' Angelica rose bad temperedly and swept off the offending junket. 'Nor any banquet either, if I had my way! One word from me – !'

She sent her recalcitrant charge back to the schoolroom.

Jillian hesitated on the stairs, watching two flies flick in and out of a shaft of sunlight. The sun was warm on her cheek and shoulder.

She suspected everyone would be too busy to notice her, but it was a risk. She couldn't just loiter about the grounds. There was, however, one place she could go.

In the greenhouse it was hot and dank as always. Jillian sat under her bush and pretended she was in the jungle. She thought of a plan: to steal a Hillcat barge and run away! She wished her father would come and take her off with him.

Jillian had seen her father three times, though she no longer remembered the first with any certainty. He did not live in Bryland. At Mospher Quay Jillian had seen big red tree trunks, skins of strange animals and vats of sticky oil as tall as a man, being unloaded from enormous creaking ships. All those ships sailed in obedience to her father's word. He himself lived in Tarquia, in Tarnosh, where it was always sunny, and sent her exorbitant and inappropriate presents once a year.

Morelio had shown Jillian where Tarnosh was on the map. She had looked at it again since, several times, wondering. In the blue water was drawn one of the giant fish that eat people; and in the green jungleland just below, a fearsome animal with horns and long teeth. Angelica had told her that these animals could talk. Jillian refused to believe it.

There were footsteps on the gravel.

Jillian Curram sat huddled in the green shade. Her heart was beating quickly, but she took no notice of it. Go away, she thought.

The greenhouse door opened, and closed.

'You can come out now, Jillian Curram. I saw you.'

It was only stupid Dickon Troke. Jillian did not move. Catching her and marching her off to Angelica was just the sort of thing he would love to do. Dickon Troke wanted to be a soldier when he grew up.

'Come out, Miss Jillian.' He began poking the plants on the other side of the room, with occasional kicks and muttered cries. 'Ha!'

Jillian sat as still as a toad, despising him. She had no great opinion of little boys, or of soldiers either. There were lots of women soldiers, she knew that, but all the ones who came to House Curram, all the *important* ones, they were always men. Jillian was most suspicious of this. She knew it was not her fate to be told what to do by men. She would not come out for Dickon Troke.

Suddenly his hand was on her ankle, jerking her over backwards and dragging her out into the open.

Dickon leaned over his captive. Jillian spat at him.

'Ugh!'

He scrubbed at his face. She scrambled to her feet and hit him on the side of the head.

Dickon Troke went bright red. He came at her, arms outstretched, fingers clawing. Jillian lashed out again and hit him in the throat. His foot slipped, and he went down on his back. His shoulder caught a bench, and it toppled. There was a cascade of plant pots. One of them smashed a pane. Dickon sprawled, choking, trying to rise.

Jillian fled with complete satisfaction. Now the glass was broken, Dickon would be thrashed, which she never would be. And she would arrive back too late for lessons, but in plenty of time to wash and dress for the banquet.

Angelica, of course, began to screech when she saw the state of her frock and stockings. 'No banquet for you!' she said again as she grappled righteously with the tangles of Jillian's thick brown hair.

'In that case I won't have to wear this stupid dress.'

It was starched, and flounced with Luscan frills, for the sake of the visiting Prince.

'You be quiet. I'll tell your mother what you've been about, you see if I don't.'

She didn't. Angelica was past the point of reporting all Jillian's misdeeds. Jillian knew that too. Angelica marched her into the east wing, knocked on the door, mumbled, curtsied, and disappeared.

'Daughter,' said the Matron of House Curram. She held her arms out stiffly, though Jillian knew she would not actually be embraced, because of the frills.

In Curram's office stucco vines dangled plaster berries over the hideous redwood bureau. The room was cold whatever the season, and even Jillian had never felt any desire to pry into the contents of its cabinets and pigeonholes.

'Humour me, Jill,' said Curram, offering her a sliver of dried fish. 'Treat these peculiar people as if they impressed you. Curtsey before their ridiculous dignity. Preen their self-import-ance. Don't ask them why there are no women in their army, don't ask them anything without asking me first, and don't whatever you do mention cats.' She smiled bleakly, and paced away across the uncomfortable room to seize a sheaf of papers from the counting-table. She scanned the top sheet and rattled it in Jillian's direction as if it should mean something to her. Jillian watched her apprehensively, her hands behind her back.

'Everyone, *everyone* in Hoven is queueing up to take money off this new "alliance",' said her mother. 'We are the first in line. Remember that. It will mean much to you in years to come, when *you* are Curram.' She tapped the Seal with an imperious finger.

'Yes, mother,' said Jillian.

Curram cast her eye over the young girl, reading her just as she had read her paper. 'You look perfectly adorable in that outlandish style,' she said. 'Do you think it's an honour that you'll be the only child at the banquet?'

'Yes, mother,' said Jillian.

'Well, it isn't,' said Curram. 'It's a duty, daughter.'

She flicked a hand towards the door and Jillian left, closing it gently behind her.

Jillian's resentment of that morning was still entirely intact, but the mechanical inevitability of the event had taken over, together with a growing curiosity. On the way to her mother's office she had looked through the banisters and seen the first Cats arrive, servants checking the preparations for their masters. They had looked human enough from above.

She ran noiselessly downstairs in her morganine slippers and stole into the conservatory. Here, secure in the confidence she was behaving with a propriety that even Morelio might approve, she could watch all that was going on in the dining room (provided she pulled the curtain back a little first) while practising on the clavichord. *Observe and learn, Jillian, observe and learn.* She marched virtuously up the scales and down again. Robbie was rushing around with his arms full of candles, while the gardener's girls tidied the potted alianzas and organised imposing centrepieces. She plodded through 'The Happy Skylark'. Sharp-featured Cats in fantastic turbans brought in a sling of kegs, and Dickon Troke, looking no worse for his defeat, leaned on his broom muttering remarks to Bethalie Beavon, who giggled. Jillian thudded into 'The Reaper's Lament'.

'And this is my daughter Jillian,' said her mother to the Prince of Luscany.

Startled, Jillian slammed the lid down over the keys, catching the tip of her little finger. She jumped up, stifling a cry.

Prince Dolo was a slight man with the face of a falcon and a suit of deepest crimson. 'Enchanted,' he said, without a trace of an accent, and, just as Morelio had predicted, brushed Jillian's tingling hand with his moustache. 'Such talent in one of so

8

tender years,' he observed. 'Curram is rich in gifts of harmony and concord.'

Jillian goggled at her mother, who received the transferred compliment with courtly grace, and glanced at her expectantly over Prince Dolo's head. Jillian stood gazing helplessly at the Luscan royal party in a state of utter panic.

Beaked faces swathed in cloth regarded her. A little girl, no more than five years old, clutched a servant's hand and stared at her in profound suspicion. Seeing Jillian struggling, the Prince ventured to help.

'I see you like the pretty dresses of our women. Do you know any of the musics of Luscany also?'

Jillian nodded desperately. 'I'm learning to play "Manori Ro",' she said. Did that sound enthusiastic enough? 'It's my favourite,' she added. There was a slight pause while she realised she would now have to go through with it. Dredging up memories of a lesson months previous, she opened the clavichord again and pecked out a few faltering bars, her damaged finger limping.

The Prince's daughter wrinkled her nose and said something to her guardian, who hushed her. Prince Dolo's smile was a little tight.

'The musics of Mohan-Jaspa are also most pleasant,' he agreed, with some visible difficulty. All the Cats bowed slightly once more and the party moved off into the library. Jillian's mother favoured her with a look of affectionate contempt, and sailed after.

Too late Jillian remembered the Treaty of Pangorian, 1070 – or was it the Battle of Mertha's Ford, 1071? Were the Mohan-Jaspans barbarians or allies? Wasn't General Hargon of Mohan-Jaspa here with Prince Dolo? Or was he from Mohan-Mandevale? She glared accusingly at the clavichord which had betrayed her, and kicked the stool in disgust. It fell over with an echoing crash, scattering sheet music across the parquet. Jillian fled.

Upstairs, the gallery was deserted. Jillian went to her room, but found no comfort in the old toys heaped in the corner. The daylight was fading. She climbed on a low shelf to reach the matches from where Angelica always hid them, and lit the candles on the dressing-table. In the mirror, chin propped on her hands, her face looked morose and unfamiliar. She thought of the little Princess of Luscany, and suddenly felt older, much older than the girl Angelica had chided that morning, the baby hiding under her covers. Tears pricked her eyes, and blurred the candlelight in the glass. She tried to see herself as a rich young matron, wearing a golden net upon her hair.

Downstairs in the hall strings and a pompous bassoon began to play. Jillian blew her nose, smoothed the ruffles of the Luscan dress and went back slowly along the gallery.

At the oriel above the porch she stopped, loitering, irresolute. A pink sunset lay across the fields and tinted the roofs of Hovenstok three leagues distant. Some coaches were making their way towards House Curram, bringing her mother's colleagues from the Market Chambers, and there were folk on horseback too. But it was a man on foot who caught her eye, standing in the gateway looking up the avenue. For an instant Jillian felt he was looking directly at her, though she could hardly have been visible in that darkened oriel, with all the windows alight downstairs. He was alone, and even in the dusk looked slightly out of place, standing with his arms akimbo and his cloak thrown back, as if confronting the House. He seemed to be hesitating outside as Jillian was hesitating inside, both of them reluctant to make their separate entrances.

2
The Geometer's New Home

The stars were fading as the sky grew pale over Consolation Bay. Out of the east a silver light crept across the iron sea, starting a slow clamour of birds. Finch and junco skittered in the brake, and a lapwing flicked into the air.

Ky varan, in a plain coat for travelling, was on his way back to One City. He stood and looked out for the last time over the glistening mudflats. The grey waves began to break with a glint of icy green.

Ky varan made the appropriate valediction, then adjusted his muffler and rode off carefully down the long and bumpy track from the headland. Along the margin of the sea, where the sand was smoothest, fans of spray hissed from his wheels. He hummed to himself, enjoying the simple exercise, while the kittiwakes cried overhead.

The morning was almost past before anything interrupted his reverie. He heard a shout, saw somebody waving to him. It was Gen thiri, out with her dog. He turned and coasted towards them with a surge of pleasure that was all the greater for his three weeks' isolation. Gen thiri's dog, a red setter already dripping wet, frolicked round and round him, dashing through the shallows and barking enthusiastically.

'Gen thiri! How good to see you.'

Ky varan came to a halt and partly dismounted before the dog could knock him over.

'Welcome, stranger,' said Gen thiri, making no attempt to restrain it. 'What are you doing all the way up here?'

'My grade posting,' he reminded her patiently. Ever since the days when she had been his tutor, twenty years before, her memory had impressed him with its ability to retain and co-ordinate essentials, and infuriated him because it classified everything to do with him as dispensable. 'Three weeks at the Observatory over Consolation Bay.'

'Peering through glasses at the stars and the birds.' Gen thiri managed to make it sound like a fatuous pursuit. 'What did you learn?'

'Patience,' said Ky varan.

She gave a short, derisive laugh, but looked at him fondly, fishing in the pocket of her smock for her pipe. The dog, losing interest in the conversation, padded off to nuzzle an inert starfish.

'What's been happening in College?' he asked.

'Don't ask me,' she said. 'The Councils debate half-inches with great solemnity and prudence. The Middle College is all factions and gossip. This year's initiates have proved exactly as stupid as last year's, to within two or three degrees of mental arc. I've been fishing.'

Ky varan smiled, not believing half of it. The cynical green eyes, the rough clothes, the stubby fingers pressing mundungus into the pipe bowl, all concealed the shrewdest sensibility in the Upper College of Geometry. Without possessing any of the matter or manner of her in himself, Ky varan had learned a great deal from her offhand tuition. He suspected she had a low opinion of him, but he valued the brusque familiarity with which she treated him. Certainly, with no other Upper Collegian could he converse so informally, strolling along the beach. There was some significance in her being the first person he had met on his way back to civilisation.

Gen thiri breathed expansively, filling her mighty lungs. 'You should live by the sea,' she said.

So there it was.

Ky varan stiffened, alert for her next word or sign, but she said no more. The dog trotted beside them, trailing a hank of purple seaweed.

'Is that your advice?' he asked cautiously.

She answered only: 'Sea air is invigorating. I come here as much as I can.'

'You live by a lake,' he pointed out.

'It's not the same,' she said. 'Two completely different elements,' and as if to illustrate it, a great wave broke just beside them and flooded their feet. Ky varan gasped and pranced awkwardly up the beach, dragging his bicycle, his shoes full of water; but Gen thiri just gave a loud snort and strode on, puffing at her pipe.

Was she teasing him, being brutally vague, or had he been adjudicated in his absence? As a Middle Collegian, supplicant this term for promotion, Ky varan would be given permission to move out of College chambers only with the granting of his licence to enter public practice. Where he set up house would determine the nature and extent of his future career.

'Is there word for me from the Adjudicating Council?' he asked.

Gen thiri, however, was not to be drawn. 'You know I never read the notice-boards,' she said.

'You have no need!' he protested.

'I'm past the age of seeking to see my name up on a wall,' said Gen thiri. She picked up a stick of driftwood and flung it end over end out to sea. The dog splashed out eagerly to retrieve it, then shook itself, making Ky varan's trousers even wetter.

'I mean you draw your information from higher regions,' he persisted.

Gen thiri looked enquiringly at the clouds. 'The birds and the stars?' she said. 'I leave that to you. I prefer fish.'

Hitching her trousers up at the knees, she squatted slightly and began writing in the wet sand with the stick.

Ky varan waited patiently. It was true: to secure the last grade of his promotion to the Upper College, he would have to discourse on the recondite harmonics of the astral and avian orders before the Council of Adjudicators. But it would not be the first time a premature judgement had been secretly arrived at, and privily communicated to an anxious candidate.

'There,' said Gen thiri, straightening up and pointing to her handiwork with the stick. 'I've written your name for the fish to read – just in case it's not on the notice-board.' She clapped him on the shoulder with hearty reassurance; then put finger and thumb in her mouth and whistled her dog so suddenly and loudly Ky varan stumbled backwards and collided with his own bicycle.

A wave rushed up to lick at the crumbling letters of his name.

In the event Ky varan took a house in the Shuan Hills, three or four miles outside One City proper. It was a district not unlike Gen thiri's own, inhabited only by senior ministers and those who earnestly sought to emulate them.

From his walls Ky varan could look down, not on to the sea, but at the Foxchiver outskirts, all red roofs and cobbled yards scattered down the hill. He was so far above their streets that he could expect none of the routine Geometer's work, of advising on the correct site for a house, or a propitious route for a journey, on which his city colleagues were building their careers. Instead, he was determined to maintain a larger view. In addition to a heavy burden of discourse and tuition, Ky varan would work at gaining nomination to the Upper Collegiate civic councils. He would become involved in consultations for the refurbishment of a bridge or a thoroughfare; report to committees on forestry or quarrying; even seek appointment as a regional representative at the Escalan national synod. He was convinced that his elevated situation in Shuan, with the yellow hills behind him, the Foxchiver Cemetery on his left and the quince orchards on his right, would make manifest his capacity to comprehend One City at large, balancing its ancestral traditions on the one hand with its fruits for posterity on the other.

As a concession to Gen thiri's advice about running water, he had a pool sunk in the main concourse, and a fountain set in the middle of it. Around this grew a splendid array of potted plants, brought by his third uncle, back from the jungles of Belanesi.

Women of all ages toiled up the hill from Foxchiver seeking employment. Many of the younger ones, after meeting the minister and learning that there would be no mistress of the house, withdrew politely and left, anxious to avoid any possible breach of propriety. One who did not was Mo tai.

Mo tai was perhaps twenty, a scant half Ky varan's age. She was short, and compactly built, her black hair agleam with old-fashioned goose grease and her orange skin turned a dark tan by much outdoor labour from an early age. Her parents kept a smallholding in Foxchiver. She was the youngest of four, with small hope of inheritance and none of education. She stood round and stolid as a jug in her brown apron and her worn old button boots and did not blink when the gaunt Geometer told her he would be living there alone. She was properly humble, but self-possessed: she answered him in monosyllables, neither stammering nor striving to ingratiate herself with pleasantries. She held her hands behind her back.

Ky varan interviewed her in the study, where he was unpacking his books and arranging them on the shelves according to a brief catalogue he had prepared for the purpose. Setting this aside, he took her on a tour of the house, to acquaint her with the disposition of the rooms and furnishings, and with what her duties might be in each. Finally he left her to investigate the larder and prepare a meal for him on his return from College. If the meal was satisfactory, he told her, the position would be hers. Privately he had already made up his mind to employ her.

When he arrived home that evening she met him at the gate and relieved him of his bicycle. As she wheeled it away under cover, Ky varan went upstairs to check a reference in a book of geological tables. He was astonished to find the unpacking completed, and every book in its place on the shelves.

'Who did this, Mo tai?'

'I did it myself, minister.'

'But can you read?'

'No, minister; but I compared the marks on the edge of each book with the ones you had written down, and sorted them that way.'

She did not seem especially proud of her achievement. The untutored intelligence, said Ky varan to himself, does not know its own face. It was more than fitting that he should take Mo tai into service: it was his duty, to provide her with a place in which she might have the privilege of absorbing the rudiments of intellect, in return for performing some simple chores, appropriate to her status.

He permitted her to eat her meals with him, for the benefit of his conversation. He would attempt to extract from his day's work a few simple illustrations to show how he arrived at a measurement or a divination. Mo tai would listen, chewing rhythmically at her okra or celery or squid. If she did not flatter or venerate him, as he had secretly hoped, she always paid him undeviating attention, letting his words suffuse her like water

15

flowing over a stone. Her passivity pleased him. He took it for a kind of natural wisdom, instilled by a life-long immersion in the verities of existence, sensitised by poverty, and now enriched with the learning he, a minister of the Upper College of Geometry, could impart. There was much that he could give little Mo tai.

As for Mo tai, she seemed contented enough. She had secure employment, comfortable accommodation and regular meals. Her time was taken up. If her employer liked to lecture her on the strange notions that occupied him and his colleagues, that was no particular hardship. All she had to do was nod her head when he called for a response, or, from time to time, venture an opinion of her own, which he would smilingly correct. Ky varan was a kind man, as men go, and if all men were fools, his folly oppressed her less than others she had known, men – boys – of less dignity, less culture, and considerably less wealth. It perturbed her not at all when Ky varan developed a habit of calling her at night, to fetch him some book or straighten some misplaced article which he could not reach from his bed. This fancy of her master's inconvenienced her only inasmuch as it obliged her to get out of bed herself; so she resorted to visiting him routinely, last thing.

'Is there anything you want, minister?'

'Nothing tonight, Mo tai, thank you. You may retire.'

Every month Mo tai went home to spend two days with her family in Foxchiver. On these nights Ky varan would miss her appearing silently at his door in her pyjamas with a lamp, like some luminiferous angel of the nocturnal ether.

—3—
The Prince is Gracious

A surge of laughter and loud voices announced the arrival of another party of guests. Jillian Curram watched from the top of the stairs, hoping the curly-haired stranger might be among them; but it was only more relations. Her heart lifted, though, for after the gaggle of aunts and cousins, in came her Uncle Lorenz, who at once caught sight of her clinging to the banister and roared, 'Jilly my love!'

She scurried downstairs to give him a kiss; and then she was in the hall, waist-high to more people than she had ever seen in one place, inundated with the light of every chandelier blazing, and awash with noise and merriment and triumphant music. For it was a triumph. The latest alliance in the Seven Realms was raising an army to repel the barbarians, and they had come with gold and silver down to Bryland, and first to House Curram.

Jillian went with her Uncle Lorenz and the others to seek out her mother, unrecognisable in her glory as she always became to her daughter on grand occasions. Jillian was presented to the dignitaries who surrounded her, then passed smoothly aside into the care of her uncle. Him she liked immensely because he would play with her and spoil her with attention as no one else ever did.

A waiter offered her uncle wine, a great delicacy shipped all the way from Belanesi. 'Let me have one too,' Jillian ordered, but her uncle waved him away. 'Let me have some of yours, then,' she persisted.

'When you're older, Jilly,' he said. 'It makes little girls sick.'

17

'It won't make *me* sick.'

'It will so,' said Uncle Lorenz, 'and then you'll take a great dislike to it, and refuse to try it again; and that would be a pity.'

'Why is everything only for grown-ups?' she demanded.

'Because grown-ups lead very boring lives, and have to work hard and make money, so they keep special pleasures for themselves to make it all worthwhile.'

He winked at his wife, who said, 'Don't tease the child, Lorenz.'

Then Aunt Clotilde and her sisters had Jillian answer the customary juvenile catechism of what she had learnt at her lessons, which inspired Uncle Lorenz to a delightfully disrespectful impersonation of Morelio. Aunt Clotilde reprimanded him again. By the time the dinner horn was blown Jillian had quite forgotten she was dying of hunger.

Angelica, pink-cheeked and rather flustered, claimed her and steered her back to her mother before disappearing to sit with the other servants. Her mother took Jillian by the hand, as she never did normally, so Jillian knew at once it was a public gesture and nothing for her comfort. She led Jillian to sit beside her, the daughter of House Curram, nine and three-quarters or no.

Next to her Prince Dolo of Luscany greeted the grave little girl with a smile rather more genial than his last. Jillian noted that his own daughter was nowhere to be seen. Tonight, Jillian was a grown-up, whatever Uncle Lorenz had said; but they did not serve her wine.

'Prince Dolo, what's your daughter's name?'

Her mother touched her hand and smiled. 'You must say, "Your Highness",' she told her.

The Prince gave an indulgent wave. 'Not at all, Curram. I like to be reminded that I too have a name and am not just a crown, yes? And my daughter's name, Jillian, is Nette.'

'That's a funny name.'

'Jillian!' said her mother; but the Prince was eating and affected not to have heard.

'Where is she?' Jillian wanted to know.

'Tucked up in bed, of course,' said her mother, 'where you were when you were only five.'

18

'Little children must have their sleep,' said Prince Dolo, 'or they will not grow up to be intelligent and so accomplished young ladies.'

Jillian understood he was complimenting her, and thought to acknowledge it with an apology. 'I'm sorry I made a mistake about "Manori Ro",' she said. 'I get muddled sometimes. This morning Morelio, he's my tutor, was telling me about the Seven Realms and I counted eight!'

'Sometimes it *is* difficult, even for us in the Cathills, as you call them,' said Prince Dolo, 'to remember exactly who is on which side today.' And he caught the eye of General Hargon of Mohan-Mandevale with a confidential smile.

Tomorrow I'll tell Morelio *that*, Jillian thought smugly.

Bethalie came to change their plates and bring the next course. Jillian had noticed the Prince had a turbaned servant standing motionless at his shoulder, a boy no older than herself. As Bethalie spooned baked calibac on to his plate, the Prince summoned this boy forward with a curt gesture. Puzzled, Jillian watched him take a morsel of the Prince's food, put it in his own mouth, chew and swallow it. Prince Dolo looked at him expressionlessly for a moment, as though waiting for something to happen. When nothing did, he turned back to the table and began to eat the calibac himself, with every appearance of polite enjoyment.

Before Jillian could ask the inevitable question, her mother stopped her with a warning look. Evidently this was a mystery not to be probed aloud. She would have to consult Morelio or Angelica tomorrow, or Uncle Lorenz later, if she saw him again that night; though Uncle Lorenz's explanations were not always to be trusted.

Minutes later another servant appeared with fresh wine. He filled Curram's glass, and then Prince Dolo's. Again the Prince beckoned his servant.

Jillian was quicker off the mark. 'Let me try that for you, Your Highness,' she said, and before the boy could reach it, she seized the goblet and took a swift mouthful. There were gasps and chuckles, and Jillian knew at once that her mother was displeased; but she was concentrating.

What was the secret of the purple drink? Did it really have the occult power to discriminate between grown-ups, whose onerous lives it made cheerful, and little girls, whom it merely sickened? Jillian was determined to master it.

It tasted fruity in her mouth and suddenly sharp as she swallowed, almost making her splutter; but she controlled herself, with eyes watering. As she gave Prince Dolo back his glass, she wondered whether she should say anything, and whether she had liked it or not. But Prince Dolo was speaking already, brushing aside Curram's apologies.

'Curram, this daughter is a brave girl,' he said. 'Her confidence does her credit, and you also. Her courage will bring only honour to your House.'

With that he turned and dismissed the young boy, who melted away into the bustling crowd of servants bearing salvers and tureens.

Jillian blinked and looked around the table, observing amusement on every face. Even her mother was looking at her fondly. Whatever she had done, it had been good – not good enough for anyone to award her a glass of wine of her own; but for that she now thought she was probably grateful.

Somewhat overawed by the unanticipated compliment and her mother's reaction, and not wanting to do anything to spoil it, Jillian kept quiet for the rest of the meal, and ate many things that Angelica would have been astonished to see her even consider. Jillian was proud of her onrushing maturity.

In the ballroom the orchestra measured out the official merriment, while formalities and indiscretions were exchanged over cups and behind fans. The mirrors multiplied the crowd: everyone in the world was there, dressed in jewels, and everyone was happy. Curram danced with Prince Dolo, somehow contriving not to dwarf him, so that he seemed to lead all the while she waltzed him around the floor. General Hargon had acquired a crowd of admiring young people who marvelled as he spoke and flourished an imaginary sword.

'Uncle Lorenz, I drank wine and I wasn't sick.'

'My goodness, what a supernatural young woman you are. I don't suppose you asked your mother first, did you?'

'It wasn't mother's wine, it was Prince Dolo's.'

His eyes widened in amazement and he clutched his niece's shoulder. 'But you're still here. How is it you were not arrested at once for high treason?'

'He said I was very brave.'

'To steal the royal wine?'

'I expect he said I was brave because it might have made me sick but I drank it anyway.'

Aunt Clotilde looked disapproving and fanned herself briskly, but Uncle Lorenz seemed amused. Everything amused Uncle Lorenz. 'I expect so,' he said.

'Doesn't wine make boys sick too?'

'It certainly used to, Jilly,' he said, 'when I was a boy.'

'Prince Dolo's boy was trying all his food. Prince Dolo was going to give him the wine to try too, but I got it first. He would have been sick, wouldn't he?'

'He might well have been – especially if there had been anything *in* the wine.'

Jillian saw her aunt frown again and sensed the presence of adult secrets.

'What sort of anything?'

Uncle Lorenz looked over his shoulder, then bent and whispered dramatically in her ear: 'Poison!'

'Lorenz, hush,' said Aunt Clotilde. 'You must take no notice, Jillian dear: he's being very silly.' She waggled her fan.

'Poison? What for?'

'The Prince has many enemies. All Princes do.'

Jillian thought of the confusing history of the Seven Realms. 'The Cats are always killing each other, aren't they?'

'Jillian!' cried her aunt. 'You mustn't say such things.' She tapped her husband on the arm. 'You see what nonsense you're putting into the child's head? Jillian, your uncle is telling you fairy stories. All the Cathill people here are friends. See for yourself.' She indicated Prince Dolo, who had joined General Hargon's group and was smiling with some satisfaction. 'They are allies, Jillian. That's another way of saying "friends".'

'They may be allies, my dear,' said Uncle Lorenz, 'but are we? Can we be trusted?' He drank deeply. 'For all Prince Dolo knows we may be barbarians.'

Jillian laughed at that. 'Of course we're not *barbarians*, Uncle Lorenz. You are silly. We're Brylanders. The barbarians live a long way away, over the mountains.'

But he shook his head sadly. 'Would that they did, Jilly.

21

Nowadays the barbarians keep coming over the Cathills. The barbarians are everywhere. Prince Dolo has to fight them. That's why he's here.'

'Why?'

'To ask us to help him.'

'Oh. I thought he'd come to buy something from Mother.'

'Indeed he has, perspicacious child. He has come to buy guns for the alliance. And there, unless I'm very much mistaken, is the man who'll provide them.' He nodded in the direction of Prince Dolo and General Hargon, now deep in conversation with the matron and a man – the man Jillian had seen from the oriel, standing staring at the House in the dusk.

Now that she could see him plain, she realised he was quite young, much younger than her mother or the Prince, and coarsely dressed, not in finery like everyone else, but in shabby work clothes. His curly hair was unkempt, unprinked. Jillian turned to her uncle. 'Who – ?'

But Aunt Clotilde had intervened. 'Lorenz, enough. Jillian, I think I see Angelica looking for you. And this is positively my favourite dance. Do excuse us, Jillian dear.'

Real or imaginary, a summons from Angelica was the last thing Jillian wanted. As Aunt Clotilde led Uncle Lorenz firmly on to the floor, their niece slipped between a Luscan soldier and a potted plant, and found a corner where she could observe the conference unseen. Something told her that, jewel of House Curram or not, this was not a moment for her to put in an appearance.

'And can you confirm,' General Hargon was saying, 'the reports we have heard of the new weapon?'

'Depends,' said the stranger.

They all looked at him.

'What you've heard,' he amplified. He put his hands in his pockets.

'Your Matron Curram has suggested that it reaches farther than any pistol, but can still be carried and worked by one man,' said the General.

The young man nodded.

'Also,' Prince Dolo added, 'it can kill many at one firing.'

'Depends,' the young man said again.

There was another pause.

'A remarkable effect, Karel,' said Curram. Jillian's stranger now had a name. 'Is it too fearfully complicated to explain? – roughly,' she stressed, putting a hand on his arm and staring intensely into his face.

'Well.' Karel freed his arm and held up a finger and thumb. 'Handgun fires a ball so big. With this –' He brought finger and thumb closer together. 'You can fire smaller shot. Handful of it.' He cupped his hand and looked at each of them to make sure they understood. 'The shot – spreads out.' He spread his hands to show them. 'That's one kind.' Almost with a shrug, he replaced his hands carefully in his pockets.

The allied ambassadors looked at one another. Neither spoke.

'How dreadful,' said the matron, with considerable relish. 'Tomorrow, Karel, we must all come to the forge and see you demonstrate this horrible device.'

She shut her eyes and gave a perfectly executed shudder.

'Will this be convenient?' asked Prince Dolo.

Karel nodded. 'When you're ready.'

General Hargon was ready. With an effort he relaxed and took another mug of beer from a passing tray.

The Prince asked, 'And Karel, tell me: can you produce hundreds of these, if need be?'

Karel considered briefly. 'We've other work,' he said, 'da and me.'

'None so potentially rewarding, I'm sure,' said his matron.

'Depends,' said Karel a third time.

Hidden in her corner, Jillian was absolutely captivated.

'Find the workers,' said the smith, 'and the iron, and I'll tell them what to do.'

'Just to think of you toiling at the furnace makes one faint with thirst,' said Curram, who had never been known to faint and seemed extremely unlikely to now. 'Karel, will you drink?' She snapped her fingers to call back the beer.

'No,' said Karel. 'I don't drink. Thank you, ma'am. I'll see you gentlemen tomorrow.' And he turned swiftly and walked away across the floor, ignoring the dancers and the soldiers and the merchants as if they had been so many noisy and colourful farmyard birds.

'What a delightfully shy young man,' said Curram. 'But –

23

believe me – so *clever*. So *dependable*. These artisans: they live and die for their work.'

Prince Dolo cleared his throat, and stroked his moustache with his thumbnail. General Hargon was pensively watching the young man leave; so was their hostess; and so was the heiress-apparent to House Curram.

——4——
The Nuptial Day

In the Shuan Hills above One City spring came suddenly, speckled with shy flowers, and summer with violent thunderstorms that bruised the earth a sodden, livid green and left the air breathless and tingling. A deputation of local landowners with polished buckles and stout woollen coats arrived to seek the Geometer's approval of the site for the Foxchiver fair. Ky varan graciously waived his customary fee and returned home instead with a gift, a roan mare of fourteen hands. At liberty he would ride around the hills to dine on glazed pheasant, succulent pumpkin and quince condé with his neighbours, the tax assessors, architects and antiquarians. In the lengthening evenings they reclined, presiding over the dim valleys and marinading the glories of the past and the grandeurs of the future in mellow red brandies. At home Mo tai waited, sitting up with her mending basket, and tending the porch light.

Iot tregar had been a harbour warden in the Stone Eye colonies, where Shas don his wife had done such sterling work retraining native musicians in the modes of Escaly. Pra veo, the daughter of their middle age, was accomplished in the artistry of herb and shrub. Late one evening Iot tregar sat pushing a mess of curds absent-mindedly around his plate while his wife and daughter waited patiently to clear away. Ky varan, their guest, sat facing the window, somnolently contemplating the white blossom glowing on the dusky hillside. Then Shas don suddenly demanded: 'Will you tell him or must I?'

'What – oh, what's that, my dear?' havered the old Marine. His military background still made him uncomfortable with Collegians.

While Pra veo blushed and looked at the tablecloth, Shas don frowned reproachfully at her husband. Iot tregar dropped his tardy spoon with a clatter and shifted guiltily from one buttock to the other. 'I – ah – Ky varan – ahem . . .'

'Ky varan,' said Shas don, quietly but clearly. 'This week our beloved daughter was engaged to be married.'

'Pra veo, my congratulations!' cried Ky varan. 'Who is the man I must envy, may I know?' The Perigian wine made him animated and gallant.

'His name is Ben etia,' Shas don answered for her bright-eyed daughter. 'Ben etia is a herald and overseer of the Messenger Guild, from Under Chaylo, now serving the Emperor in the province of Salt Fan.'

'First-class credentials . . .' rumbled Iot tregar. 'Excellent prospects . . .'

'A harmonious match, then,' said Ky varan, bowing again to Pra veo over the empty beakers and biscuit crumbs.

'Thank you,' she said.

'We hoped you would think so,' continued her mother. 'We decided to tell you privately like this, before the public announcement, because we hoped you would honour us further by selecting the wedding site.'

'Great honour . . .' mumbled her husband.

For such a conjunction of meritorious lines as Pra veo's and Ben etia's there were in fact only seven or eight acceptable locations in One City and its environs. It would have been perverse of any Geometer to recommend anywhere else, even if the auspices seemed to demand it, and Ky varan had not been selected for his reputation as a freethinker. Accordingly he took the bag of natal earth that Pra veo brought him, and its companion bag delivered by the messenger from Salt Fan, and spread their contents side by side on the appropriate dish on the appropriate day, and combed them both with the wooden comb, and treated them both with the water and wax, and thereafter informed Iot tregar that his daughter and her fiancé should be brought together in the Bee Meadow on the fifth day from the next full moon after Ben etia's return from the west, at the sixteenth hour.

Mo tai washed up the dish and the comb. At supper she asked the Geometer: 'Why must she not see him until the wedding?'

'Their affections might lead them to dishonour one another,' said Ky varan.

His housekeeper was looking at him uncomprehendingly.

'They must keep themselves pure for the ceremony,' he said.

Still she seemed not to understand.

'Bodily,' he explained, somewhat distantly.

Mo tai sipped her broth. 'My sister An mo loved a boy from Trysk,' she said. 'He was apprentice to a cobbler. He had no money, no more than us. They were saving up for the wedding, then the boy was sent for a soldier to the fighting at Broken Cap. He knew he wouldn't be back less it was in a box.'

'Our soldiers make many brave sacrifices for us every day,' Ky varan told her, thinking the story was over.

But Mo tai shook her glossy head.

'She said to me, Come round behind the barn. She wanted to ask me something private, she said. She said would I let him have my half of the bed tonight. I slept in the straw and a mouse ran up my leg.'

She raised the cup to her lips again. This time Ky varan did not interrupt.

'The next day he went for a soldier. No one's seen nor heard of him since, not a hair of his head. Red hair, he had,' she added. She looked at her master with patient, searching eyes. 'Was it wrong, minister?'

'No one could blame you for what you did,' said Ky varan gently. 'If you had said no, they would have found another way.'

'But my sister and her man, were they wrong?'

'The young man should have sent to the Emperor for a postponement of service,' said Ky varan. 'The Emperor is a very clement man.' He rose from the table.

But Mo tai was unmoved. 'He was a cobbler's prentice,' she said again. 'My sister An mo works at the washing. It can't be wrong, surely, if two people love each other, if they mean to wed.' She looked up at him unsatisfied, her small fists on the table before her.

Ky varan shook his head. 'Return to your chores now, Mo tai,' he said.

The bridal day was overcast, but that did not detract from

the splendour of the ceremony. In plain sight (but out of easy reach) of the gawping crowds on Arbo Bridge, the Bee Meadow made a perfect setting for the nuptials of a family with the status of Iot tregar's. The tents were decked with bunting and paper lanterns, and the brown and yellow of the Messengers' Guild made a striking contrast with the imperial silver and turquoise of the Colonial Marine. Shas don's sprucely uniformed ensemble played cheerful arrangements of Escalan and western tunes, and the crowd, to Ky varan's discerning eye, was a most felicitous mixture of Iot tregar's distinguished contemporaries and Ben etia's shining and ambitious young colleagues. Not that any of them wanted to talk to him, of course. Collegians were not welcome in such worldly gatherings. His own presence was, he knew well, symbolic. He stood a little apart, nibbling a macaroon.

Whenever he ventured to start a conversation, he seemed to make people nervous. The father of the bride, for instance, bustling around dispensing bonhomie and sweet Oxignon with a generous if unsteady hand.

'Couldn't wish her a finer fellow,' Iot tregar enthused vaguely, gesturing towards his daughter and son-in-law now waving and smiling rather palely as they withdrew into the nuptial tent. He nudged Ky varan. 'What have you celibate types got to make up for that, I'd like to know. There she goes, eh? There she goes!' He grappled with his nostalgia. 'Drink up!' he exhorted; but his mind was elsewhere.

'I seem to have mislaid my cup . . .'

'I'll tell you something, Ky varan,' said Iot tregar, putting his arm around the Geometer's shoulders, 'something I've never told another man. If you go into the College of Jurisprudence by the Rye Lane Gate, and upstairs to the lecture room, about a third of the way along the back bench, you'll find my name carved.'

He gazed emphatically into Ky varan's face. '*My* name. *I* wrote it there. Here, do you want some of this? Give me your cup.'

'I can't find it.'

'Carved it myself. That's true.' He nodded. 'Some of the people they had there: talk your ears off for an hour and a half – never say a thing!' Iot tregar seemed to have forgotten he was

28

talking to a Collegian. He thrust his bottle into Ky varan's hand.

'Is there a clean cup?'

His host chortled. 'What? Never stopped us in the old Stone Eye, did it?' He was now under the impression that the Geometer was an old crony from the Colonial Marine. 'You can drink from a bottle, can't you? Well, can't you? Even a baby can drink from a bottle, Commander!'

Reluctantly Ky varan raised the bottle to his lips. To his surprise he was able to take a mouthful from it without choking.

'So, you were a commoner at Jurisprudence, were you?' he said gamely.

'Five years I was there. Failed Pon. Pos. Threw me out. Father put me straight in the Marine. Best thing he ever did for me. But there – I was in College before I was ever a soldier. I've never told that to another man. I'm not ashamed of it, mind.'

Iot tregar embarked on an illustrative anecdote. Ky varan practised drinking from the bottle. He wondered why it had always seemed so difficult before.

'That's the spirit, uncle!' crowed the father of the bride.

It began to rain.

Ky varan looked around. Empty cups and broken food lay strewn across the muddied grass. Banners flapped sulkily in the chill. Time seemed to have passed, somehow, without his noticing. He found he was wearing a wreath of battered peonies about his neck. His coat was soaked. The Bee Meadow was utterly deserted. As if by some freak of acoustics, he seemed to hear wild moans and frenzied panting emanating from the nuptial tent. He turned and fled back towards the Shuan Hills, spinning mockingly around beyond the rooftops.

It was dark by the time he arrived home. The porch light was burning, but no one answered his knock. The gates were unlocked. He left them open behind him as he stumbled across the courtyard.

The house was as silent as a vacant property. Mo tai was not in the gatehouse, the reception room or the kitchen. Conceiving a mighty thirst, Ky varan sought the fountain playing in the empty concourse and plunged his head into its cascade. It sobered him somewhat. The bedraggled lei finally fell apart.

Black petals swirled in black water. In the shadows the Belanesi plants seemed like giant spiders, watching him.

Gasping, Ky varan wiped his face on his sleeve and started upstairs to bed.

A light shone from Mo tai's door. In his fatigued and poisoned state, Ky varan felt it was pulsing, warm and inviting on his clammy skin. He pulled off his stained coat and dropped it on the floor. It occurred to him that Mo tai should have been waiting up to receive him. Anger swelled in his breast and he strode into the light.

Mo tai was asleep in her chair, her hair loose about the shoulders of her nightclothes, her sewing still in her lap. Beside her bed the long flame of a neglected candle bobbed and settled, making the shadows lurch madly up and down the walls. Dizzy, Ky varan shut his eyes for a moment and watched the whirling coloured patterns dance around his brain. He opened his eyes again, crossed to the bed, sat down and removed his shoes. Then, moistening his finger and thumb, he carefully pinched away the snuff from the elongated wick of the candle.

The candlelight steadied, dimming, but making the room seem warmer, more comfortable. He looked at Mo tai, breathing quiet and shallow in her chair. The candleglow on her orange cheek was the most beautiful, comprehensible thing he had ever seen. He reached out to touch, but pulled away. Then he got to his feet and took off the rest of his wet clothes. He leaned over the sleeping woman. His fearsome breath woke her a moment before his kiss.

Mo tai shrank back with a cry, throwing an arm up in front of her face. He began to murmur endearments and fumble with her buttons. She seized the sewing from her lap and thrust it up at him. Clumsily he knocked it from her hands. The needle rattled distinctly on the floor.

'Mo tai, Mo tai, I sha'n't hurt you, indeed I sha'n't. I'd rather die than ever hurt you,' he crooned. 'Am I not your master? Do I not feed and protect you, yes, and love and cherish you too, in my own way? Come, come, come . . .'

With a little cry Mo tai flopped back in her chair, her resistance abruptly over. She seemed to withdraw behind her stricken eyes, unnaturally calm, disquietingly limp. In his giddy hunger, Ky varan noticed nothing but compliance. He chuckled softly, lifted her to her feet, and slipped her arms out of her jacket. Then with some difficulty he raised her up, cradling her to him and laying her gently down upon the bed. He drew off her trousers and opened her legs.

In a moment, he was done. He wept and she stroked his head, calming him. She did not speak, nor did she return his kisses. He got up, gathered his clothes, and went unsteadily to his own bed.

In the early morning he rose, washed, shaved, dressed and went down to the kitchen. She stood at the stove in her robe, looking no different from any other morning.

'The best of the day to you, minister,' she said.

'Mo tai,' he began, 'you think I did you a great wrong last night, when I was not myself. But I tell you, I was more myself then than I have ever been. I was subject to a great revelation, and what happened was a wonderful thing, wonderful, dearest Mo tai, my love . . .'

He told her he had always loved her, unknown to himself, but that last night he had had a vision, and come to his senses. He said he knew she would come to love him too. He did not attempt to touch her, and she made no reply.

When his nervous rapture had run its course, she set his breakfast on the table before him. He gazed at her, haggard and frenetic.

'Will you come to my bed tonight? Say you will.'

'You are my master,' she said.

'Ah, the wisdom of woman! Until tonight we shall be as ever before, master and servant. Only by night we shall meet as lovers. The night-time and the daylight of the human heart, that secretive complementarity . . .'

Mo tai inclined her head and left him to the food cooling on his plate.

Post-alcoholic gloom struck him down before midday. He was a criminal, a monster. He wanted to tear his unnatural flesh to pieces with his bare hands. Guilt and despair made him loathe and shun her. He fled to the stable and galloped off into the hills, not returning until night fell again. Scarcely pausing to tend his mare, he crept indoors like a thief, up to his room, undressed without a light, and flung himself into bed.

There was a knock at the door.

Ky varan froze, unable to speak.

The knock was repeated. Then the door slowly opened. Mo tai stood there in her pyjamas with her lamp.

'Is there anything you want, minister?' she asked.

'No. Nothing,' he forced himself to reply. 'Go to bed.'

She did not.

'Why don't you go?'

'This morning you asked me to come to your bed.'

'It is forbidden! We must not! Go away!'

Mo tai set down her lamp. She unbuttoned her pyjamas. Ky varan gazed again at her plump, ripe body. He caught the scent of a cool perfume. Expressionless, purposeful, she climbed into his bed.

At breakfast they did not speak. Ky varan left immediately afterwards to cycle into College. He did not return for three days.

When he did return, Mo tai opened the gate to his knock and wheeled his bicycle away for him, just as before. All day there was no exchange between them that was foreign to a minister's dealings with his servant. That night she found his door locked against her. She knocked but he did not respond. Neither spoke.

Ky varan slept alone for thirteen nights. On the fourteenth, at three o'clock, he walked naked into her room, without a word, and spent himself copiously across her breasts. She stared up at him, her eyes pale as the moon.

After that they slept together every night, the gaunt Geometer and his silent housekeeper. By day their conduct was irreproachable; and yet soon Ky varan noticed that Collegians in the cloisters stopped talking when he went by. Following a council discussion of social and family mores in the primitive north-west, Ky varan, hollow with duplicity, sought to speak to the chairman, the wizened and amiable Go thal. Looking into those gentle eyes of pale yellow, however, Ky varan felt his resolve evaporate and heard his tongue lead him away to commonplace topics.

Gen thiri had her study under the dome of Upper College, though she was rarely there. The third time Ky varan climbed the cool spiral staircase, he told himself that if she were still not in, this would mean that he was not meant to see her, and he might go home with a clear conscience. But it was not to be. This time he heard music, and when he knocked, her voice: 'Come.'

From the bay window of Gen thiri's study one could see across the Avenue of Constancy to the Nightingale Library, and along the alley that wound eventually down to Arbo Bridge. In front of this placid vista sat a puppy-eyed teenager in a surplice of primrose yellow, playing a dulcimer. Gen thiri reclined on a cushion.

'Ky varan. Dear man. Wait until the end of this passage, then we'll ring for tea.'

Ky varan sat respectfully at her feet and attended while the roulade meandered to its nostalgic interval.

'Perfectly lovely, Fi tenai. Ky varan, have you met Fi tenai?'

Gen thiri's brother worked as an Arranger at the Music Gardens. His more able pupils and his ensigns were often sent to present his compliments and entertain her for an hour or two. This one rose and bowed.

'Your playing is very sympathetic, Fi tenai,' said Ky varan.

'Perhaps the composer would not think so, minister,' said the boy modestly. He looked to Gen thiri for her approval.

'Isn't he delicious? I swear he has even assuaged the agonies of this afternoon's Protocol Council. Fi tenai, you may take tea with us before completing the piece.'

'I would speak with you alone,' Ky varan told her.

'Fi tenai will be most discreet.'

'Even so.'

Gen thiri gave a theatrical sigh. She waved her hand. 'Go to the pantry and order apple tea for us, Fi tenai. Walk in the grounds awhile. Return when you see my colleague leaving.'

When the minstrel's footsteps had died away, Ky varan said, 'If someone had a dream – '

'A dream? What sort of dream that cannot be discussed before fourteen-year-olds?'

'It would be indelicate to – '

'Oho! An indelicate dream! Let me hear it at once.'

'I say, *if* someone had a dream – '

'Then I should send him to the Oneiromancers. But if *you* had a dream, especially an indelicate dream, I should advise

33

you to tell me it at once.' Gen thiri sat up and rearranged a cushion.

'How can I tell you at all if you constantly interrupt?'

'Proceed!' She lay back.

'There is a man,' said Ky varan. 'A minister, let us say.'

'Let us.' Gen thiri sat up again, reaching for her smoking kit, though her amused gaze never left Ky varan.

'The man has a dream. An incubus comes to him in the form of a woman, one he knows well. She comes many times. He tries to resist her, but she has him in thrall. What should he do?'

'Wake up as soon as possible.'

'Yes.' Ky varan looked at the carpet, dispirited. He mused for a moment. 'What is your opinion of celibacy, Gen thiri?'

'If by celibacy you mean abstention from marriage, I am greatly in favour of it. But if you mean abstention from sex, that's another matter.' She scraped the bowl of her pipe. 'A minister must not marry an inferior.'

Ky varan blinked. 'A man cannot marry an incubus,' he said, guardedly.

She stared at him, all her good humour gone. 'If he has any sense at all, he will put himself out of reach of the incubus. If he has any strength at all, he will dismiss the incubus altogether.'

'May he seek help from his colleagues and friends?'

'If he has any sense, he will not want to. If he has any strength, he will not need to. If he has neither, he is past help.' She closed her eyes. 'Did you interrupt my recital to ask me about a dream?'

Ky varan realised that she knew.

'Perhaps it is not a dream,' he said, unhappily.

'Why, then, the man is awake and behaving like a fool,' she said angrily, throwing down her pipe. 'And I shall have my musician back.' She whistled piercingly from the window, just as if the boy were her dog. 'Come back when you have made up your mind which it is,' she told Ky varan, not turning.

Fi tenai knocked.

Gen thiri went and opened the door, admitting the boy and dismissing Ky varan. 'You should get yourself an ensign,' she said in parting. 'Young people are always in need of instruction, and some of them can be most entertaining.'

34

As Gen thiri closed the door, Ky varan saw her wink at Fi tenai. He cycled home, feeling cold and sad.

Mo tai met him at the gate. She reached as usual for his bicycle, but he moved it away and leaned it against the wall.

'Leave me,' he said.

'Minister?'

'Go away,' said Ky varan. 'Purify yourself. Tempt me no more.'

He held out a purse to her. Mo tai made no move to take it. The Geometer dropped it at her feet and strode on by her into his house.

—5—
Negotiations

Prince Dolo of Luscany never came back to House Curram in Hoven, but his daughter Nette once did, fourteen years later, very late in the year.

Jillian Curram was in her office, shuffling abstractedly through a sheaf of unpaid bills. Dickon Troke appeared at her door in his cellarer's apron, wiping his hands on a dusty rag.

'Excuse me, matron, Beth says there's a rider near.'

'From the city?'

'From the north.'

'What's he look like?'

'Young man.' Dickon shrugged.

'Go and meet him, Dick. See what he wants. See if he has news of the war.'

'Yes, matron.'

'Take care. If you don't like the look of him, come back.'

'Yes, matron.'

Everyone that came from the north these days had news of the war, but for months nothing much had changed. Still the barbarian advance across the Cathills, still the allies' resistance, or what was left of the allies, anyway. Jillian had virtually stopped paying attention, she had too much else to think about.

She heard Jek come running to find his father. 'Can I come, Da? Oh, *Da*!' And Bethalie calling the boy to her. With strangers about it was as well to be careful.

Jillian yawned.

It was five months now since her father's message had come. There were pirates in the Elgoe Strait, orange men who wore their hair in manes, like horses. He had had to pull in the fleet.

36

He would make other arrangements.

Jillian had waited. Nothing had happened. Rumour said her father had been shipwrecked; or that he had cut his losses and fled south to Belanesi. Suddenly her sheds were empty. She laid off one in three of her wharf crew. In retaliation, when fruit did arrive, they refused to unload it. The spices had not come at all, nor the oil. By the time the sish had reached market, most of it had spoiled. In panic she had bought in from House Olbain and put it back on sale at a higher price. Her pursiers had been expelled from the Chambers, amid angry shouts and jeers. It was malpractice, they said. The fruit was forfeit. Everything hung on her father, and the next shipment. It did not arrive. Creditors did, respectfully at first, then with barely concealed contempt.

Even with expenditure cut right back, Jillian could feel the money running through her fingers. Many of the stipends she was saddled with were going to people whose services she no longer needed, whom she never saw from one month to the next. But if the war came to Bryland, some of those might be the very people she would need to call upon. Three-quarters of her barges were lying idle, rotting on the wharfs of Hovenstok and Neath. She had had them on half wages most of the year. When she rode one day past Haker's Mooring a sallow woman had spat at her from the peeling deck, clutching her baby to her as if she thought Curram might be taking that from her next. Another of her children had thrown a stone from the towpath and caught Pedr on the rump. Certainly there was an obligation. But what she was paying them was a charity she could ill afford.

What if she let them all go?

Then, of course, the barbarians would come. The army would get itself organised; the canals would thrive again, and House Curram would not see a penny of it.

Dickon was back. Jillian heard the murmur of his voice, speaking to Bethalie, and Bethalie's laugh. She laid her pencil aside and went to the stairs. Jek was running up to give her the news.

'The Princess of Luscany!' he said.

For a moment it meant nothing to her. Then, absurdly, she remembered the face of the little girl with pearls in her hair, scowling at her in the conservatory when she fumbled at the keyboard. But that was fourteen years ago.

'Where? Is she here?'

Jek shook his head, at a loss. The matron hurried past him and he followed her back down to the kitchen, where his mother and father were talking.

'Princess Nette, he says,' Dickon reported, 'and three days away.'

'Where?'

'In Barlay, Towstok, somewhere up that way.'

'Have we room, he says!' laughed Bethalie.

Jillian gave a brief smile. 'She can take her pick of sixty rooms, tell him.'

'Didn't I say so?' said Bethalie to Dickon.

'But none ready,' Jillian went on, 'and no provisions.' She turned to Dickon. 'How large a party?'

'Small, he says.'

'Small, small. How small? Ten? Twenty?'

The steward shook his head.

'Where is he? Did you not bring him in?'

Dickon pointed. 'In the yard, matron. I thought best – what you said – '

She hesitated. 'Is he a Luscan?'

'No, of Towstok, he says, and just a boy.'

She came to a decision. 'Bring him in, then, Dick. Jek, go see to his horse. Beth, food and drink.'

Dickon looked worried, Jek excited; Beth, capable as ever, was taking it in her stride, fetching bread and ale. 'There was a horseman in the cards,' she told her mistress, as if that confirmed the boy's existence. 'Is it good news at last, ma'am?'

'How do I know until I've heard it?'

But the prophesied equestrian, a red-faced lad from the sheeplands of Barlay, could tell her no more than his father had told him to say. At first he was overawed, to be speaking with a great Matron of Hoven at her own kitchen table; yet he had not seen the foreign princess, and she had not told his father what she wanted in Bryland.

The great Matron of Hoven thought she probably knew; and if she were right, the royal visit could be the saving of a once great House of Hoven. First, however, she would need to pay a

38

call on one of those unprofitable retainers that were troubling her, to verify a report she had heard weeks ago and should have followed up at once. Now she had three days to do it in. Yet the afternoon of the third found her down by the sea, riding around aimlessly, lost in thought.

As she cantered unaware the clouds built up above her. The mindless boom of the sea receded beneath a greater stillness, presaging storm. Suddenly the air was filled with a fine stinging rain.

Pedr snorted, protesting at last. Jillian realised she must have been riding him uselessly up and down the beach for an hour while the sky thickened and the brief day failed.

She had been thinking once more of her father. His absence had never meant much to her before. He had been the invisible provider who made House Curram work. Now she had to accept that he was dead, or lost in the jungleland forever. She wondered what sort of man he had been.

Brooding would not fill the bank.

'Good boy. Home, boy.'

Eager to be gone from the tedious beach, Pedr lifted his head and trotted inland with a better grace; but he was not allowed to go home straightaway. Berating herself once again for wasting time without even peace of mind to show for it, Jillian made a roundabout way back towards the path of duty, going first up by Heykl Street to Inn Farland, where there was good coal burning.

Acknowledging greetings with a general bow, she bought oats for Pedr to appease her guilt and ale to lift her mood. Not that Inn Farland was ever a place of jollity and high spirits, Farland herself being a dogged individual more suited for an undertaker than the keeper of a tavern. Jillian Curram sat at the bar and rehearsed with her mechanically the inclemency of the weather, the proliferation of suspicious foreigners, the uncertainty of the war. Farland's ale was heavy, her house a-reek with smoke.

Far from cheering up, Jillian was drinking herself deeper into gloom when Jek appeared at the door. Uncowed by the stares of a dozen adults, he came in, his oilskin cape spattering them all as he pushed his way through to his mistress.

'Leave your coat at the door, boy,' growled Farland.

'I'm not stopping,' he told her, unabashed, and bobbed his head to the matron. 'Father's compl'ents, ma'am, and to say that the Princess is come.'

That stopped what conversation there still was. Farland lifted her eyebrows, but Jillian attempted no explanation. She abandoned her beer and followed Jek out into the rain.

The boy looked on hopefully as she mounted, and she was about to hoist him up before her when she changed her mind.

'There's a call I must make first, Jek. Run home and tell your da not to wait supper for me, but to give the Princess what she fancies, and to entertain her as royally as I know he will. Say that back to me.'

Rain ran from Jek's hood and splashed his nose as he stood in the mud and repeated the message, not showing disappointment. Jillian nodded, satisfied. 'And you're to have her leavings,' she told him. 'Will you tell him that too?' He smiled broadly and nodded. 'Off you go,' she said, as the thunder broke.

Away he dashed into the filthy dark, while Jillian turned Pedr's head back along the coastway, returning to the errand she had been shunning all afternoon. She wondered how she could put a visit to a freeman artisan before her duty to a royal client, and what her mother would have said.

The glowing windows and dim lanterns of Tarp's Edge were on her right hand, and the leaden sea on her left, as Pedr carried her uncomplainingly towards the harbour. She saw no one on the way; no one else would still be about their day's work on a stormy evening when they might be indoors by the fire. But there were still lights at the Jessups' yard, as Jillian had known there would be.

The high black gates, fantastically wrought in thick blunt spikes and iron filigree, were less for protection than showpieces of the smith's craft. It was the father who had made them: Karel Jessup would never have been so ostentatious. The gates stood open, leaving the defence of the forge to the watchdog who strained at Jillian until she thought his chain would break; but that too was Mortimas's work. The clamour of canine outrage almost topped the next peal of thunder, and Pedr shied back in alarm. Then Mortimas himself arrived with a lantern.

'What is it? What d'ye want?' he demanded, as though it were the middle of the night and she the one making all the noise. Jillian threw back her cowl. He peered at her. 'Curram, is it?' His manner changed not a jot, but it was none of a matron's business to quail from tetchy old men, nor to quarrel with them.

'I'd speak with Karel, Mr Jessup,' she said civilly, 'if he's here.'

'Fine time to be visiting.'

Staring at her from under ferocious brows he jerked the dog out of the road, half strangling it, she feared, and brusquely waved her by. Jillian walked Pedr into the yard and jumped down.

'May I leave him here?'

She pointed to a dripping canopy propped between the wall and the rotted hulk of an old cutter that would never put to sea again.

'Aye,' said Mortimas Jessup, 'or where you will.'

Lightning glimmered in the west as she hitched up Pedr and briefly rubbed him down. In the livid flash she saw some new contraption rigged above an outhouse, turning smartly in the storm-wind. Nothing else she saw had changed in the year since she had been there; but there was little enough she could see. The rain beat senselessly on. Jillian turned up her cowl again and picked her way between the puddles to the red door of the forge, Mr Jessup cursing the dog quiet and stumping after her.

Inside, she hesitated, confused by the wall of heat and the red glare. 'Karel?' But the curly-haired figure at the workbench was someone else, an apprentice, about the age Karel Jessup had been when Jillian had seen him first, at evening, from the oriel.

'He's at the mill,' said his father at her shoulder.

'The mill?' Tinkering with some jammed cog, no doubt, while she had ridden a league in the wrong direction, in the wind and rain. She rounded on the old man. 'Why didn't you tell me at first instead of wasting my time?'

'He's at the *mill*,' he repeated stubbornly, and the apprentice came forward, wiping sweat from her sooty brow and pointing across the yard to the building Jillian had noticed before, the one with the whirligig clattering on the roof.

Jillian followed Mortimas there, wondering why the Jessups

ground their own corn now, on top of everything else. But in the outhouse were no sacks of grain, no clouds of dust, only a string of lanterns, a strange great drum rapidly spinning on a shaft through the roof, and Karel drinking a mug of beet tea.

'Well!' he said. 'What brings Curram down this way in the rain?'

His voice was entirely good-humoured, though there was something insulting about it too. He did not rise and bow. Jillian had known he would not rise and bow; did not particularly wish him to rise and bow; yet his failure to rise and bow made her uneasy. He lifted the mug to his lips.

The lantern light blinked steadily off the spinning drum, which was set about with thick brass posts and nets woven of brass wire. There was a tang in the air, like the smell of the sea that afternoon. Karel's shed seemed about to brew up a thunderstorm of its own.

'I'd have come earlier,' Jillian said, busying herself shucking her cloak, 'but I was detained.'

Karel said nothing, but smiled, undeceived.

'This is new,' she said, nodding at the engine as though it scared her not at all. Karel nodded also, but still said nothing. She pressed on. 'Is it to do with the new gun?'

He thought about this.

'No,' he said. 'Though the trick of both's in the spin.'

Jillian could see he was waiting for a puzzled response, but matrons soon learn the diplomatic art of feigning comprehension to facilitate communication.

The smith reached out and almost touched the drum. Jillian started, fearing for his fingers; but he stopped a quarter-inch away, and gave her a contemptuous smile.

This rudeness was neither more nor less than she had expected. His uncouth manner, she told herself, was the reason she had stayed away from the Jessups' yard since the official tour at her assumption. She looked at Mr Jessup and at his son.

'This is no ordinary mill.'

The old man sniffed. Karel kept on grinning, and swilled the tea around in his mug.

Jillian persisted. 'What does it grind?'

By way of answer he got to his feet and pulled a heavy lever.

Instantly white fire cracked around the pillars, then spat into the net, which hung sparking and shaking for a second or two before the flare died.

Jillian realised she had cried out.

'Karel, you fool, you've let in the storm!'

Still greatly amused he sat nodding his head.

'Maybe.'

Jillian was trembling. There was a vile metallic taste in the back of her mouth.

'What is this,' she asked, gesturing impatiently to cover her fright, 'an exploding lightning conductor?'

'I don't need no lightning,' he said, 'not for this. Makes its own lightning, you see.'

'Then why are you out here now?'

'The wind I need. The miller must mill when the wind blows, Curram. Even on a stormy night, if the wind blows, he must get up and mill.'

'Well, I'm sure it's very clever but it's absolutely frightful, Karel.' Not for the first time Jillian heard herself speaking in her mother's voice.

He looked at her. 'Is it this you've come after, or the new gun?'

'The gun.' Gratefully she fell back on the speech she had prepared that morning, when the Princess would arrive and this visit could not be postponed any longer. 'Reports have come to us at House Curram that you are at work on a new gun, Karel, the modifications of which – '

He spoke past her to his father. 'Is Myrn still here?'

Mortimas grunted.

'Let Myrn show her,' said Karel, and turned his back on his matron.

She started to protest. 'Karel, I – '

Then Mortimas interrupted, equally rudely but, much to her surprise, in her support. 'You must show her yourself,' he growled.

Karel shook a hand irritably in the direction of the other workshop. 'It's all there. Myrn knows all.'

'You must go yourself, boy,' said his father grimly to Karel, who was thirty if he was a day, Jillian supposed.

'Karel, House Curram cannot draw up agreements with an

apprentice, yours or any other,' she reminded him, as mildly as she could.

'Is there a buyer then?' he asked.

'If our reports are accurate and the weapon performs half as well as predicted,' she temporised, 'buyers will queue from here up to Luscany, don't worry.'

She had spoken without thinking, and regretted it at once.

'Jonal is the great enginer of Luscany,' Karel said. 'Let him make his Princess a gun.'

'If not Luscany then another of the squabbling Cats,' said Jillian firmly. 'Will you show me this latest toy of yours, Karel, or have you had enough of House Curram gold?'

He ran a hand backwards through his curls. All at once she noticed how tired he was looking. He set down his mug, then picked it up, procrastinating. 'Will you have some tea, Curram?'

'Afterwards,' she said, 'thank you.'

Without a word he pushed past her and went out into the rain. In the workshop adjoining the forge he dug out a gun from where it lay neglected under wood shavings and poked it in a desultory way with a wire brush while the apprentice Myrn set up a line of paper targets.

The new gun, Jillian saw, was a cumbersome thing, set with a wide central wheel between the barrel and the handpiece. Karel twisted it open, showing that the wheel had compartments for five balls and turned on a spring. She found it much too heavy to hold up, even with her other hand bracing her wrist, so he swept a space clear on the corner of the bench where she could rest it.

'Each ball is backed by its own powder charge in a pellet, so,' Karel said quietly. 'Takes twenty seconds to load, fires five shots at a loading.'

He took her hands in his to show her the proper grip. She felt awkward, but he was patient. His sudden gentleness surprised her. He had forgotten for a moment that she was his matron, Curram in person. Matrons he had precious little time for; but this girl was holding an engine he had made and learning to use it. He laid a hand on her shoulder. 'Try it.'

Jillian squeezed the lever, heard the blast, felt the kick back and sideways as the wheel jumped round. She screwed up her eyes against the smoke and fired again. The noise of it in that confined space made her head ache. She straightened up, rubbing her hand. Karel took the gun from her and loosed the other shots one by one through a target and into the straw behind. 'That's it,' he said, and laid it back on the bench, not carelessly but without much interest.

Like a true merchant, Jillian Curram tempered her enthusiasm to his coolness, and found what fault she could. 'Can it be made lighter?'

He nodded. 'Maybe. Or I can make it a shotgun, with a tripod to it.' He signalled the apprentice to bring over one he was adapting.

'Have you the plans to construct these by?'

'Aye,' he said. 'In my head.'

Jillian touched his hand. He did not respond.

'Guard them well till I come for them, then.'

They left the workshop. Her ears were ringing with the echo of the new gun, and the clamour of the storm.

'Thunder, and lightning,' she observed.

He looked at her uncomprehendingly.

'Karel, I'm sorry I scorned your mill,' she said. 'To tell the truth, it frightened me. I can see now, it would make a powerful weapon, you're right.'

'Weapon?' he said.

They passed beneath the ceaselessly scything blades.

'To bring down the lightning at will,' she replied, 'isn't that it?'

'For a weapon?' he said, as if the idea had never occurred to him. 'Depends.' His face was turned away.

Mortimas was still there, sitting in the shadows, watching like an ancestral statue. Brown moths flittered urgently up and down the row of lanterns, not knowing a wilder light was imprisoned in the trundling drum close by. Was there some technical reason, Jillian wondered, why all this could not be used to rout a barbarian army with one well-placed thunderbolt? Perhaps it was just too cumbersome to be moved on to the field.

'Karel, you must forgive my ignorance,' she said placatingly. 'If it's not a weapon then what is it for, your storm-mill?'

'Don't know,' he said, irritably. He brushed the bench off,

45

needlessly; and suddenly turned. 'Why must it always be weapons?'

'The war is coming, Karel,' she said.

The expression on his face was unfamiliar, unreadable. He did not seem impressed.

He asked: 'Do you run to meet it?'

The Hoven Canal was rising, turbid and brown, as Pedr gave her his best speed for home. The empty prairie stretched away to either side, a dull void divided by glistening tracts of water.

She came to the lightless hulk of House Curram by way of the orchard. There was no one to help her stable Pedr. She cursed herself for not having brought her keys, which meant a run in the rain all round the shuttered west wing, across the flooded courtyard and up the ornamental stair to the front door. Dickon and Bethalie came in haste to take her wet things and smother her with warm towels. There were still some comforts left in House Curram.

'Did Jek bring my message?'

'He said to set before Her Highness and not wait for you,' said Bethalie. 'There's broth still on the stove. Are you not starved to death, ma'am?'

'I'd have drowned first,' said Jillian, towelling her hair fiercely. 'Is she well? Is she in one piece? What humour is she in?'

'Something perplexed at the empty House,' Dickon told her, 'and a mite fretful, I'd say, at your not being here, matron, begging your pardon. She's in the library. Shall I to her and say you'll come straight?'

'Dick, will you not let the matron sup first?' demanded his wife.

'Bring it me there,' said Jillian. 'Bring plenty, in case she wants more. She'll be too polite to let me eat alone. These Luscans are courtly enough, if I remember.'

Dickon, prompt as ever, had the Seal of Curram to hand, which Jillian disliked to have banging against her breasts as she rode about. She let him set it around her neck as she peered into the speckled mirror and dabbed impatiently at her damp hair. 'Has she brandy? Bring that too.'

Dickon took his candle and hurried off to the kitchen.

'Did you sort out beds for her company?' Jillian asked as Bethalie tied her slippers. 'I saw no lights as I came by.'

'There are only three,' said Bethalie. 'Her coachman asked to sleep above the stable, so I put her secretary and her bodyguard in the chamber next her own. I hope it was all right.'

'Fine, Beth, fine,' said her mistress, assuming a heartiness she did not feel. Then she took the lamp and hurried down the darkened hallway to the library, her shadow leaping at her heels.

——6——
A Petition
in the Music Gardens

It was an absolutely beautiful afternoon and the Senior Geometer, Ky varan, saw no reason to waste it sitting indoors. Summoning his Middle College students, he set off down Imperial Way to the Music Gardens. Not a few citizens bowed respectfully as the little procession passed.

When they reached the Music Gardens Ky varan and his escorts made the customary clockwise perambulation. As well as announcing the arrival of a Senior Minister, this procedure had the virtue of allowing him to choose where he would sit. On this side there was too much loose percussion, on that, a stridently inept ukelele. In one of his favourite spots, beside the great cedar, there was a group of young soldiers with an accordion. One of them called after him, forcing him to walk on round. Finally he lit upon a space where an elderly flautist he knew by sight had managed to elide the public theme into a duet with a particularly winsome waterharp. Here, all was harmony. Nothing jarred, not even the whistle of the girl with the tea-pitcher.

As a younger man Ky varan had been pleased to sit on the grass in the sun, but now it seemed more becoming, not to say prudent, to let Jo aaki and Phrem peli spread a rug and erect an awning for him. At fifty-five he was far from frail, but he allowed his inferiors to make a fuss of him. Their solicitude showed a proper deference. Ky varan lay back and shut his eyes, dissolving himself into the garden full of music.

He reassembled himself abruptly as a shadow fell across his face. He blinked. 'Who – ?' He could not make out a single feature of the figure, dark against the sun, bending over him like an importunate seller of sweetmeats. He waved his hand, as if flicking at a fly. 'Go away.'

Phrem peli leaned towards him. 'Minister, he is a messenger.' And indeed, now that he had moved out of the sun, Ky varan could see that the man wore the yellow and brown uniform of that guild, though with the insignia of a clerk rather than a lowly messenger.

'You have a communication for me?'

The man smiled. To Ky varan's eyes, still dazzled from the glare, there seemed to be something ironic, even mocking, in that smile; but when he spoke his words were polite enough.

'No, minister; but if you will permit me, I should like to offer you and your esteemed companions some refreshment – a melon slice, perhaps, or some tea?'

The gesture was appropriate to one seeking to engage a Senior Collegian for a consultation; but not from a man of such an unremarkable rank. Rather, this sort of demonstrative approach belonged to a Magistrate, say, or a Convener: someone who had something to gain by conducting his business in the public eye. In any case, even in privacy a Senior Geometer was scarcely available for consultation by anyone of common estate. Ky varan would have been justified in reiterating his dismissal, and the pursed lips and protective attitudes of his acolytes already said as much. Nevertheless, he was a generous man, and hoping to help the poor fellow avoid a terrible breach of propriety, he said mildly, 'If it's a matter of a house or a contract, perhaps one of my colleagues here will be able to advise you. All you have to do is attend at the College of Geometry tomorrow morning . . .'

The clerk smiled again, inclining his head slightly. The Geometer could see that he had anticipated these objections and would have none of them.

'My concern is with you, Ky varan, with you alone.'

On either side of him Ky varan felt Phrem peli and Jo aaki stiffen, as if a threat had been uttered; yet the fellow's manner was urbane as ever.

'And your name is?'

'My name is Kam fen, minister.' He smiled self-

49

deprecatingly. 'It will mean nothing to you. However, I think you will recognise the name of my wife.'

'Your wife?'

'Mo tai.'

All around the leafy gardens it was as if the music had suddenly ceased. The blazing sun vanished from the sky. A cold hand brushed Ky varan's forehead and he gave a shiver.

'I present the compliments of Mo tai, my wife,' Kam fen was saying, 'and announce her petition to you.'

'Minister – ' objected Jo aaki.

Ky varan raised his hand. 'I am listening,' he told Kam fen.

'The petition concerns our son, Bi tok.'

'You have a son! Providence has blessed you.'

'Bi tok is our pride and our hope.'

'Naturally.' Ky varan began to warm to the man. All had not gone badly for little Mo tai, no matter how inauspicious a start she had made in his house. 'How old is your son, Kam fen?'

'He is of age to seek apprenticeship and ensignature.'

There was a pause. Phrem peli and Jo aaki radiated offence, but Ky varan retained his composure.

'With your permission, minister,' continued Kam fen, placidly, 'we shall present the boy to you tomorrow morning, at home.'

'Gladly,' said Ky varan.

Kam fen bowed.

'You are welcome to me, Kam fen,' said Ky varan. 'I greet you and your family with all my heart. Tell your wife so. And bring your son to me tomorrow morning.'

Kam fen bowed again. Still smiling politely, he took a step backwards and clapped his hands. At the signal three young women in yellow and brown stepped out of the crowd and knelt before the three members of the College of Geometry, offering each of them a crystal glass of fragrant tea. Kam fen stood for a moment while all nearby heads turned to the tableau, then bowed a third time and walked swiftly away into the shrubbery.

Phrem peli glared after him. Jo aaki made to rise to his feet and follow, but Ky varan said mildly, 'Gentlemen, shall we drink this delicious tea?'

A trifle stiffly, they accepted their glasses from the women, who then rose as one, and left in three different directions. Not another word was spoken.

At the first decent interval in the performance, his companions got up to go, but Ky varan would not accompany them. Instead he sat on alone, lost in thought, until the sun sank down behind the trees and the Music Gardens grew silent and chilly.

Next morning Ky varan stood on his balcony, still distracted. The courtyard had been cleared, as he had instructed. Sun blazed off the red bricks. Into this circle, Experience would receive Youth; here Yesterday would embrace Tomorrow. Which was as it should be. Yet he had been troubled since waking with an unfamiliar feeling which he had finally diagnosed, with some surprise, as nervousness. He had not felt nervous for many years. He had no reason to feel nervous today. The occasion called for the observation of simple symmetry, and that was how he would conduct it.

At last he saw the three ponies climbing up the road from Foxchiver, and called Par soo, his housekeeper, to open the gates. The boy, Bi tok, was in the lead, as he had been all the way up the hill. He looked straight up at the house and saw Ky varan on the balcony.

'The best of the day to you, minister,' he called, loudly and clearly.

Ky varan saw that Bi tok's face was open, that he was ready to learn. In the hot air that hung between them he felt the weight of the years, shimmering.

What Bi tok saw was a man, grizzled but unbowed, in thick full Senior Geometer's dress. He must have been extremely hot and uncomfortable, but he did not show it. He did not show anything, though there was a slight lift to his eyebrows that Bi tok would come to know as an expression of great pleasure and satisfaction; and the hands that gripped the balcony looked strong. Bi tok had been told that the Geometers were masters of formality. He bowed, and wondered whether he should dismount, or wait for his parents. He sat still, holding the pony's reins against its neck.

The boy would do, thought Ky varan.

Kam fen and Mo tai rode into the courtyard. Mo tai looked stunning in high blue, side-saddle on a bay of some breeding.

Blue was not a colour she would have worn when Ky varan knew her. How time separates things, he reflected. He wondered if it was for seeing her again that he was nervous. How would it be, after fifteen years? He suspected he had treated her badly.

Yet she no longer hated him. That she had shown by sending Kam fen yesterday with her petition. She had forgiven him, as the only way she could profit from her position. The petition was one she had no formal right to make, but one Ky varan would be bound to honour. If Mo tai could not benefit from their past association, her son would.

'Mo tai,' said Ky varan.

She did not smile. She had rarely smiled, he remembered. He held her eye a moment, wishing there were some way he could tell her he was happy to be ensigning her son.

'Kam fen,' he said.

After leaving the Music Gardens Ky varan had called upon Ben etia of the Messengers' Guild to inquire into Kam fen's character and conditions. He proved to be of unexceptional family, decent enough provincial folk, all clerical. He worked in Birling, according to his file, with an unusual combination of earnestness and suavity that suggested he might be suitable for a diplomatic post; but, said Ben etia, not every Senior felt he was trustworthy. Ky varan had been impressed by the way he had surmounted protocol at the Music Gardens, but could see the source of his unpopularity in the reactions of Phrem peli and Jo aaki.

Unlike his wife, Kam fen was continually smiling.

'I am glad to see you both in sunlight,' said Ky varan. 'And Bi tok. You are welcome. Enter.'

When he got downstairs, Par soo, his housekeeper, was dusting his visitors' boots. She brought apricot tea to the poolside, where they sat and talked of riding. Kam fen expressed polite surprise that the minister should be such a horseman. Bi tok said little. He was watching the fountain.

'The arrangements are as usual. I take Bi tok into my house, and teach him the rudiments of my art. The first year he may pay you five visits, the second, four visits, and so on. At these times he will advise you of what you owe, and by what arrangements to pay it.'

Ky varan was pleased to find he knew the procedure without checking. Last year, Gen thiri had been much amused to come upon him in the dim recesses of the Nightingale Library, looking it up in the statutes. Taking an ensign was a practice he had avoided for many years, feeling a general antipathy towards the young and alarm at the idea of being responsible for one of them. At last he had acquired one accidentally, inheriting him from a colleague who had died of a fever; a gesture more of sympathy for her widower than interest in the boy's future. Ky varan was not liked by his students. This would all change now.

Mo tai said, 'We will pay you nothing, Ky varan.'

'Indeed you will,' he said, startled, 'or I shall not take him!'

Her husband held his hand to his lips, but Mo tai ignored him. 'You profited well from me, when you had me. I have nothing more to give you – not a penny. You will take our son, or I shall tell your story.' She glanced at Kam fen, who touched his lips again, but she said, indicating him: 'My husband works for the Messengers. He knows how to issue a proclamation.'

There was neither triumph nor venom in Mo tai's voice. She had said that speech over to herself too many times: every night for fourteen years. Now it was simply a statement of the inevitable for her.

Bi tok, listening attentively, did not understand his mother was making a threat. To distract him, Kam fen took his hand and put a purse into it.

'Give that to your patron.'

Unhesitatingly the boy obeyed. Ky varan took the purse and, smiling gravely at Bi tok, opened the drawstring and tipped the contents into his hand. There were three terro, and two quarters.

'Half the fee,' said Kam fen. 'Be reasonable, Ky varan. We do not want to be the authors of your destruction. Calumny is so inelegant. Mo tai paid you and paid you well. Consider that. Take half and be content.'

Ky varan looked at the impassive Mo tai and at her conciliatory husband. His motives would be quite different from hers, of course. Ky varan tried to estimate his ambition. He put his hand on Bi tok's shoulder and turned him to face his parents. Then he said: 'For the half fee, Kam fen, and an hour alone with your wife, I shall ensign your son.'

Kam fen sat back. His glance flew anxiously from the Geo-meter to his wife, and back again.

Mo tai said merely, 'Minister, you disgust me.' Her son looked at her, puzzled.

'So, Kam fen, I have found your price,' said Ky varan softly. 'Mo tai, have no fear. Do you really think I could still love you after you have threatened me with blackmail? No. I shall ensign your son at half-fee. I know you are not rich. I can afford to be generous, for the sake of an old affection. Bi tok, say farewell to your mother and father. Let them depart with honour.'

Kam fen held out his hands for Bi tok to kiss.

'Goodbye, son. Learn what Ky varan has to teach you. Obey him, honour him. Follow him wherever he takes you. And seize the opportunities you find there!'

At the last Kam fen made a convulsive grasping gesture with his right fist, which Ky varan thought out of character and odd. Then Bi tok kissed his mother's hands, her throat and cheeks.

'Son,' she said, 'this is a new life for you now. Be careful with it. Your path is clear to finer things than I've ever done. Don't run before you can crawl. But don't let anybody ever hold you back.'

She looked coldly at Ky varan over Bi tok's head.

Then Kam fen took the boy outside to give him his knapsack, a coin or two, and a keepsake. Mo tai followed after them. As she reached the open door sunlight illuminated her for the watching minister. Her hair was short now, but no less beautiful.

'Mo tai,' Ky varan essayed. 'Your husband should have known that in such conditions he could not have prevented you from publishing my indiscretion – yet he considered the offer!' He threw out his hands. 'Ask yourself: what kind of man have you married?'

But Mo tai said only, 'You meant it, Ky varan. You meant it.'

Bi tok seemed almost impatient for his parents to go; but when his father mounted up and took the reins of the pony Bi tok had ridden, he said, 'Can't I keep him?'

'Perhaps later we may find you another horse, if you do well,' said the minister. 'But now say a last goodbye and come with me, and I shall show you something better.'

As the two riders and the three horses disappeared down into the lanes of Foxchiver, Ky varan looked at the curly-headed boy, at his olive eyes and pointed chin.

'Bi tok, I shall say this once, and not again. It is well for you that you do not remind me of your mother.'

They went back inside then, and Par soo shut the gate behind them.

'Bi tok,' said Ky varan, 'this is Par soo. She will look after you – your clothes, your bedroom, your food and so on.'

'You must tell me what you like to eat, Bi tok,' said Par soo.

'If you have any problems or questions about those things, you must speak to her. I shall expect you to be clean and neatly dressed at all times. Your room must be kept tidy. I know you will not disappoint me. Do you have any questions now?'

'What is better than a horse?' asked Bi tok.

Ky varan smiled. What had he been like at fourteen years old? He could not remember. His parents would have been entirely unable to afford ensignature for him, even to the lowliest clerk: there too was a symmetry between himself and his new charge. He said to the boy: 'Come and see.'

There in the shed behind the gate where Ky varan kept his ministerial bicycle was a second, rather smaller machine. 'This belonged to my second ensign. He left it behind when he went abroad in the colonial service. Now it can be yours.'

Bi tok beamed.

It was apparent that the frame was chipped in one or two places, and rather warped, but that did not seem to affect its steering as Par soo wheeled the bicycle out of the shed. She dusted the saddle with her hand.

'Can you ride?'

'No,' said Bi tok, amused. 'There are no *bicycles* in Birling!'

The Geometer noted how ready the boy was to disparage his hometown.

'Then that will be among your first lessons,' said Ky varan.

'I think this will be a little large for you yet,' said Par soo. 'But we can paint it straightaway, whatever colour you like.'

'Today?' Bi tok seized the bicycle and pressed its horn several times, loudly.

'Please!' cried Ky varan, laughing. 'Exercise your father's instructions with discretion.' He was glad of the boy's enthusiasm, but did not wish to encourage him to begin at a rush and stumble on the threshold. So he gave him only the plainest answers and introductions as he showed him around the house, and then, to consume his energy, sent him out to chop wood.

Par soo came to consult her master about luncheon.

'He says he likes calota root.'

'To start at the root: a suitable beginning.'

'But I think he will need no spice, minister.'

'Quite so, Par soo.'

──7──
Milling the Storm

There was no one in the library. Many of the high windows were unshuttered and the vast room was clammy and cold. With the rain coursing down the panes and the green gloom of the storm, it was like some undersea grotto, lined with dark ranks of books like shelves of stalagmites. Two lamps by an empty couch and the wood fire in its deep grate made no impression on the shadows. Through an open door from a neighbouring room came a chime of little bells. Jillian Curram arrived and recognising it nearly laughed aloud. She pushed back the curtain.

Princess Nette of Luscany was in the conservatory, seated at the clavichord. Her raven hair was bound up in a net pricked with tiny turquoises and tiffines, and her long grey skirts were arranged neatly around the stool. She smiled at the Matron of House Curram and continued to play, gracefully, though the instrument was decidedly out of tune. At the end of the next refrain she rose and gently closed the lid. Jillian set down her lamp and applauded.

'You play exquisitely, Your Highness.'

'"Manori Ro",' she said. 'A pretty folksong from what was formerly Mohan-Jaspa.'

'Not as pretty as the folksongs of Luscany,' Jillian replied, and they both laughed.

Princess Nette came around the clavichord and unexpectedly kissed Jillian on both cheeks.

'Do you remember that?' Jillian asked her. 'How dreadfully embarrassing. What can I say?'

'I was five years old,' the Princess recalled. 'It was a horrible journey. I was sick seven times. I didn't want to come. I hated

57

everybody and everything. My guardian kept telling me not to speak Luscan, because it was impolite. I said that Curram's daughter was a big girl but very stupid, and he punished me by sending me to bed without supper.'

'Welcome back to Bryland, Your Highness!' said Jillian mischievously. 'I hope this visit will be even more pleasant for you.'

'I think so,' she smiled. 'We have much in common, Jillian Curram. We are two girls condemned very young to manage great enterprises. My noble father and your estimable mother died within one month of each other, did they not? Mine of an Escalan dart, and yours of an ague on the chest. We would both rather be riding, and playing the clavichord, and dreaming secretly of beautiful men, but instead we must sit together in draughty rooms and talk soberly of war and money.' She shivered and pulled her shawl closer about her shoulders. 'How cold it is in here!'

Jillian saw that she was tired and nervous, and talking gaily to keep her spirits up. The young matron did indeed sympathise with her strongly, and found she liked her very much. Profuse with apologies for neglecting her and for her poor welcome, she tried to persuade the Princess to seek a warmer place to sit and talk, but she would consent only to return to her couch by the tiny fire in the library. 'This will do well enough,' she said.

Jillian poured her a glass of oelegen and went over to ring for Dickon, who arrived at that moment with brandy, black bread and roe, and a steaming tureen. The Princess had no hesitation about joining her. Incongruous in the gloomy grandeur of that historic room the two women balanced their trays on their knees and dropped crumbs on the tiles.

Barely out of school, Nette's talk was of boating parties and love affairs, all mixed with horrific stories of new Escalan atrocities and comic reminiscences of her first visit to Bryland, fourteen years earlier, which she remembered in extraordinary detail. 'House Curram was so bright and full of people!'

'I had no heart for all that when Mother died,' said Jillian. 'A hundred staff; grand parties every week of the season; entertaining all the Bryland notables and their entourages – it would wear me out.' Thus did she half admit she would never be half the matron her mother had been. 'Things are more difficult these troubled times. The war drains us sadly.'

Listening to herself, Jillian reflected that this was scarcely the way to put it to a rich client she was hoping to sell arms to next day, but Princess Nette's candour seemed sincere, and Jillian was glad of someone to talk to.

Next morning it was still raining, but that did not prevent a succession of carriages arriving with representatives of the Assembly, the Chambers and all Jillian's competitors seeking to pay their respects and elicit information in pursuit of their own various interests. Formerly, Curram's minions would have been drilled in intricate routines to admit the elect and frustrate the undesirables, all with a maximum of fanfares and rumours; but the three remaining servants were instructed to let everyone in, merchants and mercenaries alike. Jillian Curram had no taste for the subtleties of aggrandisement.

The Princess received every visitor with limpid courtesy, sitting very upright in bed in her shawl and tiara. On her right sat her secretary with ledgers and tables of genealogy murmuring clarifications and advice; on her left stood her bodyguard, ostentatiously motionless. Jillian wandered around downstairs nursing a headache and being feebly civil to the dignified figures drifting through her dusty halls. She wished it would stop raining. She wished she were somewhere on a boat miles out at sea. Not for the first time she thought of selling House Curram to those jewelled jackals and going to Tarnosh to look for her father.

At two there was a lull in the congregation, if not in the weather. Princess Nette came bounding downstairs in an enormous white fur. The household all sat at one table and ate rabbit pie and turnips. Conversation was stilted, everyone ill at ease; except the Princess. It seemed hardly credible that this insouciant, garrulous child, now rapidly devouring her second helping, had come to Bryland to buy equipment to expel the barbarians who had overrun the Seven Realms.

After luncheon Jillian had Dickon escort the royal visitor once again to the library, where she intended to join her immediately and begin discussion in earnest. She gave her steward instructions to see that they were not disturbed, then, consumed by nervousness, paid a swift visit to the privy.

On her way back through the front hall she chanced to look out of the window, and swore. Another visitor was making his way up the avenue. He was alone, and on foot. A sudden apprehension seized her. She moved towards the bell-rope, hesitated, ran back to the window. There was no mistake.

Jillian Curram dragged open the door and dashed out into the rain. Instantly soaked, her hair and dress clung coldly to her, and her slippers skidded on the stair. She grabbed the balustrade for support and stared desperately at the approaching figure. He was still too far away to hear her if she called out, and if she ran to him she stood a good chance of breaking her neck. There was no sense in standing there in the rain. There was no sense in going back inside and waiting for him, dripping on the doormat. There was no time to hide.

He came out of the avenue and started to splash his way across the courtyard. He looked up and saw her. He did not call out. Jillian leaned on the balustrade and watched him come.

Neither of them spoke until he was almost at the top of the steps. His face was dark and inscrutable. 'Curram,' he said, as if they often passed each other there of an afternoon.

'What do you want?'

'Come to see the Princess,' he said. 'You'll catch your death out in this weather with no coat on.'

He followed her in. Irritably Jillian rang the bell, and Bethalie Troke appeared. Jillian avoided her eye. 'Fetch me a towel,' she told her. 'The Princess is not expecting you,' she said.

'I don't suppose she is,' he said. He took his cloak off. Jillian made no move to relieve him of it, so he stood there holding it.

'The Princess is not receiving visitors today,' she said. 'She's resting.'

They looked at each other.

Bethalie came bustling back with the towel. 'Dickon says Her Highness is awaiting you in the library, and shall he bring more logs for the fire, ma'am.'

She took Karel's wet cloak. Jillian opened her mouth to forbid her, but instead said, 'Yes, Bethalie, please; and more brandy.'

Bethalie went off to the cloakroom leaving her mistress trying to dry herself with dignity. Jillian said, 'I don't know what you think you're doing. In any case, you're far too early. I've not even broached the subject of your new gun with Her Highness.'

60

He nodded. 'I can do that myself now I'm here.' He smiled sardonically. 'Do that for you too, if you like,' he offered, indicating the towel.

'I can manage, thank you.' Jillian stepped back to put a more seemly distance between them, caught her heel on the edge of the doormat, and fell over backwards, with a yell of shock and rage. She gave her elbow a painful knock, and the towel contrived to wind itself across her face. Swearing, she tugged it free.

Karel took her arm and raised her to her feet. 'Ups-a-daisy,' he said, without expression.

Bethalie came flapping back up the hallway, and stopped in surprise to see the matron arm in arm with the smith.

'Karel Jessup,' muttered Jillian, 'what game you're at I do not know, but play me false, smith, and you'll never work for House Curram again.'

He regarded her gravely, without a word, as she straightened her limp attire. She combed her fingers through her hair, thrust the towel at Bethalie, and strode off to the library, where Princess Nette rose from her couch and cried, 'Jillian, you've not been out in the rain?'

'It's nothing,' Jillian said briskly, wishing the Princess would address her formally, and pouring brandy for them both.

'But come nearer the fire,' insisted her guest, drawing aside. 'Dickon has just heaped it up again. Such a blaze!'

As she took the cup she glanced at Karel, taking him for a servant and expecting Jillian to give him an order or dismiss him. When she did neither Nette looked him over again. The mystery of his presence caught her fancy; the girl in her admired his rough looks and powerful build. Jillian sat watching her and growing angry. There was no end to this awkwardness. Princess Nette asked, 'Will your companion not take brandy?'

'This is my skilful enginer Karel Jessup, Your Highness, come on some mission to you of his own devising.' Jillian smiled sweetly. 'Mr Jessup does not drink.'

'If it's brandy I'd be glad of a drop, ma'am, Your Highness,' said Karel. 'It's bitter out, and brandy warms to the bone, I'm told.'

Jillian rang for Dickon to fetch another cup, then sat listening to their conversation and the hateful rain, washing everything away.

'I'm afraid I don't recall your name from my father's records, Mr Jessup,' said Princess Nette of Luscany.

'My name's no ornament to any book, Princess,' said the smith. 'I was only a lad when the Prince came by.' He rubbed his chin. 'Of about your years; begging your pardon,' he added, as she fluttered her eyelashes.

'While I was upstairs sobbing myself to sleep! Did you too miss that famous ball, Mr Jessup?'

'I was there a short while, Your Highness.'

'Ah! And was it the marvellous and sparkling occasion that all my servants told me, to make me envious?'

'It was quite a rumpus,' he replied. Jillian Curram glared at him.

'Then did you see my father?' asked the Princess. 'Do you remember how he looked?'

'He was very civil to me.'

'So you met him!'

'I was able to be of some service to him,' Karel said slowly, turning to nod to Jillian, 'through the good offices of my lady matron, Curram as then was.'

Princess Nette beamed at Jillian, who smiled fiercely and said, 'My mother always took an interest in the valuable work of all our artisans.'

In the ensuing pause Dickon arrived with the cup. Before his mistress could take it the Princess was there with the brandy, to pour a generously unskilful measure and indicate that it was to be given to Karel.

'And what is your work, Mr Jessup?'

'Hundred and one things,' he said, looking at Jillian for guidance.

'Karel has recently devised a way to catch the lightning in a net of brass and store it in a drum,' she announced.

'How exciting!'

'Unfortunately, the apparatus is too large to be wheeled into battle against the Escalans,' she concluded.

'You are clearly a most resourceful man, Mr Jessup,' said Nette, saluting him with her cup. 'Perhaps you have heard of Diaz Jonal, the great enginer of my own country? He too has such drums, which he sets below a waterfall so that they turn like the wheels of a mill – ' She gestured elaborately, watching their faces to see if she was expressing it adequately. 'Oh – I cannot explain! It is – ' She waved a hand in the air above her head. 'From this water he makes fire! Do you comprehend such a thing?' she asked Jillian.

Jillian could see Karel already knew all this about Jonal, and more. 'It seems you have a rival, Karel,' she said.

Karel said, 'Maybe.' He sipped his brandy, and grimaced; and coughed violently.

Jillian laughed, and said to Princess Nette, 'Mr Jessup finds fire enough already in this water.' She toasted him, unsympathetically, drinking deep; then rose at once and said, 'Karel, if you'd like to sit here and get your breath back, Her Highness and I were just about to go and inspect some sample goods I have to hand.' It was not irretrievable, she thought. If I can draw her apart now I can still secure myself as Karel's matron and make sure she will deal only with me. She smiled at the Princess, who was looking up at her inquiringly; and to Karel she said, 'Do help yourself to more brandy.'

'No need,' said Karel bluntly. 'I can say my piece now and be off. Won't take a minute.'

And now the Princess looked inquiringly at him.

Jillian saw it all. Evidently Karel resented her slighting of his storm-mill, and was making bold with Princess Nette to enlarge his commission at her expense. What a nerve the man had, to walk straight in and try to force things to his own advantage. But he was no merchant, and certainly no matron, and here she was Curram in her own House, and the upper hand was hers.

She addressed the Princess. 'Mr Jessup is very excited about a new sort of gun he is making, Your Highness.'

Nette's eyes widened. 'You are the gunsmith! Mr Jessup, please forgive me. If I had known – '

'I have seen the new gun,' Jillian interrupted smoothly, 'and it is extremely promising. It would be no exaggeration to say that this could be the gun that will win the war.' She set down her cup and put her hands together, fingers interlaced. 'But there are problems still to overcome, aren't there, Karel?'

Without allowing him to speak she went on to disparage it faintly, playing upon the distaste for his own invention he had manifested the previous evening. She deprecated the increased weight and the extra time taken in loading, while never actually mentioning what it was he had achieved. But she took care not to annoy the smith or discourage the Princess. Later, she thought, when he had gone, she would reawaken Nette's eagerness and sell her the thing anew. 'Perhaps you could bring it here and demonstrate it one day next week,' she suggested, her tone inviting him to agree and depart in short order.

If he knew he had been insulted and outmanoeuvred, Karel Jessup showed no sign of it. Slowly he stood up, and said, 'I could that. Or – begging your pardon, ma'am – ' he went on, then addressed Princess Nette directly: 'I could bring it to Luscany for you.'

There was another hiatus, a moment of complete confusion. A thick log shifted on the fire with a soft crunch.

'Karel, what on earth do you mean?'

'I'm saying I'd work for Her Royal Highness,' he answered, 'if she'll have me.'

Jillian Curram was astounded. 'What's your grievance?' she demanded.

'No grievance, ma'am,' he said. 'But I've thought on what Jonal's doing there, and what I'm doing here, and it seems plain we should be working together. You see,' he said, standing as comfortably as if they were all back at the forge and he explaining some simple principle of an engine to her, 'the miller mills when the wind blows; but when the wind don't blow, ah, what then? Whereas, now, Jonal, with all that water there in the Cathills – '

'Water? There's water enough in Bryland, surely!'

'Not pouring down off mountains, there isn't,' he said. 'Pouring down out of the sky, that's different. Unpredictable,' he said, pointing at Jillian's damp dress, which, by the heat of the fire, had begun to steam faintly. Nettled, she stepped aside.

'With his mill and my mill, we wouldn't need the wind,' said Karel, and took a sip of brandy.

'But I thought – the guns – '

He shrugged. 'Guns we can make anywhere. Anywhere there's iron.'

No one in that room was unaware that Bryland bought half its ore from Cathill mines.

Jillian was lost. She cast around for an objection to frame her anger. 'What about the forge? The rest of your work?'

'Myrn knows enough. Father can show her the rest. There's others will be glad of work.'

'And your bond to House Curram? That simply disappears, does it?'

Karel frowned slightly. 'Course not. You'd settle that atween you; if the Princess'll take me on, I mean.' He waved his hand from one to the other. 'That's not my affair. I couldn't think straight to setting a price on a man's life.'

Princess Nette stood by, waiting for them to finish. She was uncharacteristically silent, embarrassed by the Brylander matron's distress. Irregular though it was, the gunsmith's offer was a gift from heaven. There was only one answer she could make.

Outside House Curram the rain teemed on. The short winter afternoon was over. The library seemed to recede from Jillian into obscurity, as though time had run out now the money was all gone. Along the bookshelves wise old chroniclers had their backs to her. On the dull dance-floor already chandeliers lay half dismantled. Cold nests mouldered in vacant attics. Jillian turned the cup in her hand, round and round.

'Karel,' she said, and was appalled to hear the pleading in her voice, 'last night you said I was running to meet the war.' He opened his mouth, but she would not let him reply. 'Yes, you did.' She indicated the Princess. 'Do you realise that Princess Nette's people are in the middle of that war? What are you saying now – will *you* run to meet it?'

At that moment the great log settled again, and a lump of burning wood rolled out of the grate and fell smouldering on the tiles. Jillian went to the hearth for a shovel, but there was none.

Karel Jessup put down his cup, came forward and set his foot on the ember, grinding it out.

'Seems to me,' he said, 'when folk start making guns, instead of fire-irons, then they're already in the war.'

The Matron of House Curram had no more to say.

'Very good,' said Princess Nette of Luscany, and reaching up she rang the bell.

——8——
Instructions

Next day Ky varan took Bi tok into One City. Used to the bungalows of Birling canton, the boy was much impressed by paved streets and buildings of three and even four storeys. At a booth in the Gem Market he had the top of his left ear pierced with the blue steel ring that denoted his ensignature. Sore and strange as it felt, Bi tok was very proud of it. As he pushed his pony along the crowded thoroughfare, keeping close to the heels of the minister's mare, he was sure everyone was looking at his ear.

'Where next, minister?'

'The Escalan Imperial and Illustrious College of Geometry,' said Ky varan, savouring the powerful syllables.

They left the market-place by Apothecaries' Hill, crossed Temperance at the Monument, and were immediately immured in that hinterland of dusty insulæ and treeless squares that backs onto the Academic Quarter. As they entered a sunlit courtyard feeding pigeons rose up to seek the safety of the eaves. Ky varan stopped and turned his mare.

'If I were to tell you to lead us to College from here, what would you do?'

Bi tok rode forward. He peered apprehensively through the archway opposite, hoping for a signpost of some kind. There was nothing but a ladder, on an upper rung of which a pale blue pigeon had settled.

'I'd climb that ladder,' said Bi tok, 'sit on the window-ledge and look around.'

Ky varan was pleased. 'Good. But the ladder is by no means long enough. Now what?'

Bi tok shook his head. 'I'd keep going in this direction.'

'Which is?'

'North-east. I think it is, anyway.'

'Very good. Do so.'

This, thought Ky varan, was a very promising start. He followed Bi tok to a T-junction, where the boy slowed but did not stop before turning left.

'Why left?' called the minister.

'I think the College is more likely to be uphill than down,' said Bi tok decisively. He was enjoying the game. But after that he went too far up Bacon Alley and strayed hopelessly back towards the estuary.

'This *can't* be right,' he said, catching sight of Arbo Bridge once more.

'What will you do now?' asked Ky varan, reining in beside him.

'Ask someone, I suppose.'

'Proceed.'

Bi tok looked up the street. There was an old man with a broom and two young girls throwing a quoit to a dog. He looked the other way. No one.

He turned to Ky varan. 'Minister?'

'Yes, my boy?'

'Which is the way to the College of Geometry?'

Ky varan smiled broadly and told him. They set off again.

'Always take your reading from the most reliable source available,' said Ky varan. 'Always check it.'

To Bi tok the Escalan Imperial and Illustrious College of Geometry looked like a great yellow cake rising behind its walls. One day soon, he decided, he would make a drawing of it as a present for his parents. The other large buildings he could see were the Colleges of Ethics and Valuation, said Ky varan.

At the Registry two men about the age of Bi tok's father greeted the minister and were introduced to his rather nervous new ensign, who fumbled his signature and almost knocked over his stool when he stood up. Then Ky varan took him to meet a man called Lon nan, the Tutor of Novices. Bi tok greeted the man politely, staring at him all the while, for he was wearing two strange little panes of glass attached to his face in a sort of wooden frame.

'This is the invention of a woman in Nairi,' explained the

Tutor of Novices, rehearsing what was obviously a frequent speech.

'Without it my eyes are weak. But through this I can see you as clear as day!'

They each drank a cup of something slightly oily and rather strong.

'Have you introduced him at the Baths yet?' asked Lon nan.

'We have come straight from the Registry,' said Ky varan.

'You will just have time to get there before the midday rabble.'

Ky varan thought this a good idea, though slightly unexpected from Lon nan: he was never at the Baths. He had been intending to take Bi tok to call upon Gen thiri before luncheon, but found he was glad of an excuse to postpone what she would inevitably make an embarrassing visit for him.

'Will you accompany us, Lon nan?'

'Another time, Ky varan.'

The Baths proved to be all the way back down on Temperance. 'With all this riding about I shall need a bath,' observed Bi tok, who had had one the previous morning, at home. Birling already seemed quite remote to him in time as well as distance.

At the door they were given towels and escorted to a small room by a servant who waited outside while they undressed. The minister showed Bi tok how to knot the towel properly at his hip. Then the servant came back in for their clothes and knapsacks, and bowed them downstairs.

Screens draped with glistening vines divided the steam pit, the hot pool and the cold. Ky varan was the first man Bi tok had ever seen naked. Here were thirty or forty more, all older than him, all lounging or sitting in attitudes of great comfort while talking with great animation.

'Ky varan!' called someone, and several people looked around at them and waved. The Geometer gave a general salute and moved off towards the steam pit.

'Are there baths like this in your hometown?' asked Ky varan.

Bi tok shook his head, alarmed and fascinated at the prospect of walking into steam. They hung their towels on the rails and went down the steps. As they took seats on the wooden benches, Bi tok blinking and gasping, a man opposite noticed them and came over.

'Ky varan, is it not? The Senior Geometer?'

'Yes,' said Ky varan, blinking through the vapour. 'Do I know you?'

'We have met,' said the man dismissively. He was round-shouldered and uncommonly fat. 'But this young man was not with you then.'

'His name is Bi tok,' said Ky varan patiently. 'He was registered this morning.'

Still the man did not identify himself, but instead reached out suddenly and gave Bi tok's earring a painful fillip. 'Congratulations!' he cried. 'Your first time here, then, is that it?'

Bi tok nodded rather desperately, unable to speak because his lungs would boil away.

'Cheer up, boy!' said the stranger. 'It's no hotter here than in the jungles of Belanesi, you know.' And with that he bowed again and left abruptly, at surprising speed for one of such girth.

'Who was that?' asked Bi tok, rubbing his ear. 'What was he on about?'

'I don't know.' Ky varan was not accustomed to being perplexed.

They were not to find out until they reached the cold pool, half an hour later. The place was filling up by then, as Lon nan had warned, and Bi tok had been introduced to a confusing number of ministers, secretaries, clerks and officiators, all sweating profusely and wishing him well.

'At the Baths one encounters a good cross-section of the people who make One City work,' Ky varan told him. He pointed to the cold pool. 'There, you see, is another Senior Geometer, Chu tek, who sits with me on the College Council for Colonial Affairs.' He stopped then, partly because he thought it not worth bothering the boy's head by telling him Chu tek was his rival for the Chair of that Council, but mainly because he was surprised to see the fat man from the steam pit sitting by Chu tek in an attitude of cordial familiarity.

'Ky varan, my friend!' called Chu tek loudly. 'Come and introduce your curate, won't you?'

'His name is Bi tok,' said Ky varan, slipping into the cold

water with perfect self-control and helping down the boy, who yelped. 'But he is my ensign, Chu tek, as I'm sure you meant to say. Only ministers with posts in the colonies have curates,' he explained to Bi tok.

'My little joke, Ky varan,' smiled Chu tek. 'I believe you know An suixi, don't you? An suixi is an Imperial Herald. He has something for you.'

If Ky varan had not blanched at the temperature of the water, he did at the implication, and gave the Herald a look of astonishment.

'I have passed it to your attendant,' said An suixi, 'so that it wouldn't get wet.' He grinned. 'Hello again, boy!'

'The best of the day to you, minister, and to you, minister,' said Bi tok.

Both men laughed again.

Bi tok looked anxiously at Ky varan, but he was obviously bewildered too, on his own behalf.

'I haven't worked away from Escaly for nearly ten years,' he said.

'All the more reason for His Supremacy to call upon you now,' returned An suixi expansively.

'It is an honour, of course,' said Ky varan. 'But His Supremacy must be aware I am past the age for foreign duties.'

'Yet not past the strength and capacity for them, estimable colleague,' replied Chu tek with extreme deference.

Bi tok, shivering, wondered what on earth was going on. People around the poolside were looking, beginning to talk.

'Where is it His Supremacy's pleasure to send me?' asked Ky varan quietly. 'And how soon?'

'The room attendant has the scroll,' said the Herald, slipping down from his seat and bicycling his great legs up and down in the water. He puffed from the exertion.

'Even an Imperial Herald might do a Senior Minister the courtesy of letting him know the place and time of an assignment,' said Ky varan with more acerbity than Bi tok had yet heard him use, 'instead of leaving it to a menial. Especially so when more than one of his colleagues appear to know these particulars already.'

'Your keenness does you credit, worthy Ky varan,' announced Chu tek. 'Next year.' He pronounced the words separately and crisply. 'I shall endeavour to supervise the Colonial Council in a spirit that will add nothing but lustre to your memory.'

'I am not going to oblige you by dying, Chu tek,' said Ky varan pleasantly. 'Merely by going abroad.'

Bi tok looked at him in surprise. What was this?

'To the Belanesi frontier,' intoned An suixi, ducking and blowing like a sea-lion. 'To the jungle.'

'I congratulate you on your foresight in ensigning a young man to accompany you as curate,' said Chu tek.

'Where in Belanesi?' asked Ky varan, like a man who is smiling because nothing worse can happen to him.

'An suixi?' said his colleague, deferring.

'Oh, I can't remember the names of all those little places,' said the Herald. 'The room attendant has the scroll,' he said again.

Ky varan stared at them both for a moment, then waded past them to the side of the pool without the bow customary on parting from a respected colleague, let alone the salute of obeisance due to an officer of the Imperial Household.

Bi tok hurried to him, saying nothing. But when they had dried themselves and begun to dress, he asked: 'Minister, will there be mandrakes? And goblins? And crocodiles?'

'We shall discuss it later,' said the Geometer. 'We are late for luncheon.'

They bought whitebait and fried bread from a stall and ate it in a sunny spot in Time Pavilion Square. Two women with babies were occupying the bench, but when they saw the minister and his ensign approaching they rose and bowed, and sat down solemnly on the pavement.

It was the sort of afternoon when Ky varan would have been happiest to visit the Music Gardens; but now he truly did wish to see Gen thiri, and he knew where she was likely to be found.

'Have you ever been to a cat fight, Bi tok?'

'No, minister!'

'In that case I assume you would like to.'

They threw their crumbs to the sparrows and went back to collect their mounts from the Baths. As they rode along Temperance Bi tok was impatient, the Geometer noticed, but held his tongue. The cats, he reflected, would be more in keeping with the boy's spirit than balisets and bassoons. Moreover, it would be well to have him see a fierce animal or two under strictly controlled conditions before setting foot in Belanesi. Now that the first shock was past, it was correct to accept unwelcome instructions uncomplainingly, Ky varan admonished himself, especially at his age.

The sun flickered through the lattices and into the eyes of the sleepy cats. They hissed. Money changed hands. In a nasal tone the umpire chanted the ritual citation. The words meant nothing to him, clearly. He must say them twenty times a day. Impatiently, the handlers jerked on the chains. That too irritated Ky varan. There were so much more graceful ways to arouse fighting energies. But he would be charitable.

He squatted on his heels and whistled lightly through his teeth. 'Hoi-up!' he called, cheering the champion, and rubbed his hands together. He was not enjoying himself.

Then he caught sight of Gen thiri and immediately felt very relieved. He made his way up the tiers.

'Hello, Gen thiri. The best of the day to you.'

She took out her pipe. 'Ky varan.'

She had noted his manner and deduced his mood; but first, of course, she had to ask: 'Who is he?' Gen thiri was still keen on young men.

'My ensign.'

'I can see that.'

Bi tok was enchanted with the bristling cats. He propped his pad on the rail and drew them rapidly in fusain, sketch after sketch. At the first false kill, he dropped the pad in a thrill of utter panic; but he could not take his eyes off them.

'Isn't he charming?' said Gen thiri. As he had foreseen, she was highly amused by the fact that Bi tok was the son of Ky varan's disgraced housekeeper. That particular dim episode in her former pupil's career she remembered perfectly.

'Alas,' said Ky varan stiffly. 'My burden is not a single one.'

'Don't tell me. He has a sister.'

'No, of course not.'

'A *younger* sister.'

'Gen thiri, you are mocking me.'

'Dear man, no! Have some tea.' She clapped him firmly on the shoulder and signalled to the pitcher-girl.

Ky varan blew politely on his bowl.

'You won't get a decent cup of tea in Belanesi,' remarked Gen thiri.

'I see. I am the last to know.'

Gen thiri waved away his resentment, and asked directly, 'Will you take the boy?'

'Your advice would be valuable.'

Her eyes opened wide. 'Of course you must take him!'

'It was my conclusion.'

'Why do you consult me?'

Ky varan made an impatient gesture, almost upsetting his tea. 'The whole affair is quite irregular. But I must submit. I was interested to know if you would disagree.'

A gong boomed, making Ky varan jump. The loser's handler heaved the dead cat out of the pit, its entrails dangling.

'Why do you *come* here?'

'Ask him.' She pointed her pipestem at Bi tok, who sat rapt, stroking his earring.

Ky varan stood up.

'Bi tok! Come and greet Gen thiri.'

The boy left his seat and came up.

'Gen thiri is another Upper Collegian,' Ky varan told him. 'She was my first tutor.'

'Minister,' said Bi tok, and bowed. 'I wish you the best of the day.'

'You are very polite,' she said. 'I hope you won't forget your manners in the wilds of Belanesi.'

Was she teasing him? As Bi tok hesitated over a reply, she spoke to Ky varan. 'What are you doing this afternoon?'

'Preliminary grounding.'

Another match was being touted while a boy raked the clotted sand. More people were crowding in around them, but Gen thiri took no notice.

'Would you like to see my island?' she asked Bi tok.

'Gen thiri!' said Ky varan in surprise and delight.

'Bring a picnic,' she told them, rising.

As they rode up into the hills, Ky varan taught Bi tok the basic elemental clusters. They recited them together over and over, to the rhythm of the hoofs. The world was full of sunlight. There was not a cloud in the whole region.

They left the horses with Gen thiri's housekeeper and plunged on foot down the overgrown track to the lake, the basket between them. Ky varan fell silent. He wanted Bi tok to absorb the quality of the landscape. Besides, the path was steep in places, and he was rather out of breath. Bi tok lost count of the dragonflies.

Gen thiri waved to them from the disintegrating jetty. She wore a short-sleeved shirt and battered old gauntlets. There was no one else around. She was patently intending to row them out to the island herself.

She placed Bi tok in the bow, in charge of the basket. She pulled steadily and strongly. Ky varan sat upright and still on a mat in the stern. The thickness of Gen thiri's arms embarrassed him.

He had brought the scroll of Imperial Despatch with him. Later, over the remains of the picnic, he would show it to her while Bi tok attempted to sketch the lake; but for now he merely told her of the encounter with their colleague Chu tek and the Imperial Herald of the Messengers' Guild at the baths.

'My father works for the Messengers' Guild,' said Bi tok.

Gen thiri caught Ky varan's eye. Several disturbing thoughts were passing through his mind at that moment, but he said merely: 'When a minister is sent on a journey, he could not expect the good fortune of meeting a travelling companion so soon – before he has even set a foot from his door!'

'And it's a very rare and lucky young man who gets advanced into the colonial service after only one year of ensignature,' Gen thiri told Bi tok.

'We shall have much preparation to do,' said Ky varan. 'We shall study the history of the Belanesi frontier, its patterns and people. We must study the language of the jungle dwellers.'

'The junglies!' exclaimed Gen thiri with a derisive bark that scared a swimming fesset into noisy flight.

'Gen thiri laughs,' explained Ky varan, 'because like most people she thinks the Belanesi themselves are nothing more than animals.' Gen thiri was nodding agreement. 'It's true, they are not as we are. But they have buildings, and a language, a most curious tongue. My uncle compiled a grammar of it during his stay there.'

Bi tok stretched and wriggled around in his seat. 'Gen thiri's island is Belanesi,' he declared, 'and we are crossing the ocean.'

'Better not fall in then,' said Gen thiri. 'Belanesi water will poison you.'

'What nonsense!' cried Ky varan.

But Gen thiri turned and spoke to Bi tok over her shoulder. 'There are poisonous waters in Belanesi.'

Bi tok looked uncertainly at the water beneath him.

'Poisonous waters,' said Gen thiri as she pulled on the oars, 'poisonous plants – poisonous fruit – poisonous animals – poisonous people.'

A diving bird flashed into the water and was gone again.

'If the water's poisonous,' said Bi tok, 'how do they drink it?'

'Obviously they don't,' said Ky varan. 'There is other water that is not poison.' He was irritated because he thought Gen thiri was alarming the boy, and interfering in preliminary grounding; but more because only then did it occur to him he might indeed be destined to die in Belanesi.

Again Gen thiri overruled him. 'They have remedies to purify the poison water before they drink it,' she said, 'in Belanesi.'

'Elemental cluster of water, Bi tok,' called Ky varan.

Bi tok closed his eyes, concentrating. 'I'll do them all in order,' he announced.

He began to sing, in a slightly sharp treble that trembled on the edge of breaking, and Gen thiri laughed.

'To music, Ky varan! Very good! Very good indeed!'

So they all sang the elemental clusters together, to the tune of 'Lanterns in the Tree', until the shore of Gen thiri's island rose beneath them.

—9—
Cartomancy

Dickon Troke was the first of them to quit House Curram. Bryland was mustering at last, and he found himself a company of House Charne's leaving Hoven. He was very short with Jillian in those last days. She assumed he blamed her for the destruction of his ancestral way of life; some of the time she thought he was right. At any rate, she offered no defence. But he took their son, his and Bethalie's, with him when he went. Jek said he wanted to go and fight the barbarians, and Dickon said it was right that he should. 'Heaven help us,' Bethalie would say. 'A boy of nine.'

There was one brief, devastating quarrel. Afterwards they lay one either side of the bed, with a gulf between that would have swallowed any attempt at reconciliation. She lay and listened to the owls awhile, then rose, took two blankets from the chest, and without another glance at him, went into the vacant room next door. In the morning her husband and son were gone.

If she wept, then or later, Jillian Curram never knew it; nor would she pass judgement on him. Gradually Jillian came to understand that she believed, or wished to believe what he told her, that he and Jek would be back and the whole household together again after the war. Bethalie would not abandon her matron, even when there was no more money to pay her; she would not even hear of going back to her parents. By the time Jillian was in the last stages of the disposal, she found this display of loyalty more disconcerting than comforting. Setting off to deposit the last document of forfeiture at the Sovereign Assembly, she noticed Bethalie standing awkwardly by the door.

'You can come with me if you like, Beth.'

'No, thank you, ma'am,' she said.

'Well, don't just sit cooped up in there all day. Why don't you go out somewhere?' suggested Jillian, trying not to sound annoyed. 'Leave it for the burglars.'

Bethalie shook her head. 'No, thank you, ma'am,' she said.

'Suit yourself.'

Jillian turned to the road.

'Will you be wanting dinner, ma'am?' called Bethalie.

'No, Beth, I sha'n't want dinner,' replied her mistress loudly. 'I'm going to get drunk.'

They were still there, in the House, for a couple of weeks more, waiting for Jillian's papers to come through. She forbade Bethalie to dust anything. The bailiffs arrived one day, without warning, accompanied by an appreciative audience, some of whom must have trailed all the way from Hovenstok for the pleasure. It took their gang three days to remove everything, and to cover up everything they could not remove with shrouds, as though it had died. Jillian's great-grandmother's furniture stood enigmatically on the frosty lawn, scrawled with cabbalistic chalk numerals, and bound clumsily with rope, lest it run away.

That evening Jillian was saddling Pedr when Beth appeared, leaning on the front door again.

'Will you be back for dinner, ma'am?'

'No, Beth, thank you.'

From the far side of the building came a metallic crash, greeted by a chorus of guffaws. 'She won't be stubbing her toe on that no more!' someone said, obscurely.

Bethalie gave no sign of having heard.

'Are you going to get drunk again?'

'Yes.'

'Wait a bit,' she said, pulling off her apron. 'I'm coming with you.'

At the Limping Donkey in Petsdyke Bethalie demonstrated an astonishing capacity for dark ale, and flirted with three troopers, a baker and the balladeer.

'Dancing on the benches!' said Jillian Curram, heaving her up on her horse.

'I did nothing of the sort,' Bethalie gravely declared, tumbling off the other side.

Somehow they got back to House Curram, over glittering roads in a wind that sliced to the bone. Black trees wheeled nauseously against the sky. On the terrace the bailiffs had piled all the books from the library into a precarious ziggurat. Silvered with frost, the vases and the jugs stood in a long line around the edge of the lawn, marked at intervals with sticks. Bethalie shrieked with laughter.

Jillian drew her curtains and lay abed until afternoon. Bethalie came in with a mug of broth; Jillian wanted her to sit and talk, but she vanished again at once. Jillian found her in the conservatory, mopping disconsolately at an invisible stain. The rest of that day and the next they camped, wrapped in blankets, around the hearth of whatever room they could find that was not currently being dismantled.

The sale of all her emergency jewels and keepsakes on a depressed market had raised only enough for Jillian to buy herself into an undistinguished company of artillery. She had not wanted to be near guns, but the recruiting officer, a grinner called Ennigo, had promised her action before the year was out. They would be called, he assured her most confidentially, to relieve the siege of Carphale.

Jillian rode home and told Bethalie, who confounded her by seeking out Ennigo herself next day and enlisting in the ranks. 'I'm going in under my right name, Bethalie Beavon,' she said proudly.

This gesture meant nothing to Jillian. 'I am dismayed,' she wrote in her journal, 'to learn how far B. is determined to adapt her life to mine.' Yet she understood that freedom would be just as intolerable to either of them, poverty or no, and saw no reason why Bethalie should not adopt her own solution. It would be pleasant, she realised, to have at least one companion who knew her misfortune.

But Major Conroe's Artillery was not summoned to break the siege of Carphale that year. The siege of Carphale was not broken that year, or the next, or at all. Once Carphale was gone, none of Conroe's troops would give much for any of the other fortresses east of the Cathills. As no one would open a book on it, the officers held a sweepstake: How long before the news that the Escalans had Luscany entire?

Considerations of rank never prevented Lieutenant Curram and Private Beavon from ending up together on leave. Neither of them had anyone to go home to anyway. They went off and got drunk, staring at one bleak horizon or another, talking for hours about whatever came into their heads. Jillian always forgot it immediately afterwards. Bethalie tended to reminisce about House Curram, her eyes wet with comfortable tears. After two years of pointless manoeuvres, one day they actually found themselves near enough to pay it a visit.

It was the blatant inaccuracy of Bethalie's myth-making, Jillian told herself, not any real desire of her own, that drove her to agree. All she wanted was to remind herself of the exact dimensions of what she had rejected, or rather allowed to slip from her hands.

After parade they rode out of the gate and down the lane. The sky was breaking up, letting the last of the sun through. The air was moist and chilly. Cranes were assembling in the drowned fields along the Hoven Canal.

Through Seltegn they ran into quite a herd of sheep. Conroe's horses had been trained to ignore gunfire and screams, but sheep were too much for their well-bred nerves, so Jillian and Bethalie had to go round over the dykeway. Coming upon it with the sun sinking behind them, Jillian had a sudden improbable sight of House Curram with gold shining in all the windows. Drawing nearer, skirting the wild orchard and trampling what was left of the kitchen gardens, she saw it was an illusion indeed. Two years the Sovereign Assembly of Bryland had had their lien on House Curram, but had let it only to the spider and the mouse. They were too busy preparing to be invaded by Escalans. House Curram was down on a list of refuges Captain Ennigo had shown Jillian. House Curram, a refuge! She laughed aloud at the irony.

'What's funny, ma'am?'

'Oh, nothing, Beth.'

In the shadow of the west wing the great courtyard was dim, the air dry and prickly; or was it her nerves? Their hoofbeats rang strangely from the flagstones.

They stopped at the foot of the stair.

'And how are we to get in?' asked Jillian. She was utterly

astounded when her former servant unbuttoned her jerkin and produced the front door key, with great solemnity, from her bosom.

Bethalie proffered the key.

'I don't want it,' said Jillian.

Bethalie shook her head. 'It's mine to keep, but yours to use.'

Jillian indulged her. While Bethalie tethered the horses, she ran up the steps and, in a spirit of dread, opened the front door. It swung from her grasp and banged violently on the inside wall.

The House was cold, and extremely damp. In a corner of the entrance hall was a mound of mud and debris, an abandoned tano's nest. The two women wandered aimlessly through the empty bedrooms. In a dusty mirror Jillian noticed her hollow cheeks, the dark bags beneath her eyes.

'So much for mirrors.'

'What?' Bethalie was waiting impatiently on the landing. 'Oh, mirrors, mirrors are bad luck.'

'Only if you break them, surely.'

Bethalie shook her head. No, mirrors were always bad luck. 'Come on,' she said. 'Quick, or you'll miss it.'

Jillian followed her to the ballroom veranda to witness a sunset which was, actually, less than spectacular. But then she discovered that the sunset was not Bethalie's primary purpose. She was holding her old pack of cards.

'Where did you produce *those* from?'

'I must read for you, ma'am. Here. Now.'

Plainly she had had this in mind all along, but had concealed it, for dramatic reasons of her own.

'I could do with sitting down for a bit,' said Jillian non-committally, realising that she was now committed. In the last of the light she shuffled and dealt the greasy cards.

'The Five of Magpies,' said Bethalie. 'The Stag. Oh, and look: the Silver Seahorse. Put him there. That's right. Now take two more. Give them to me.' She looked at them, considering. 'No,' she said, and discarded them both. She sucked her lip.

Jillian was supposed to ask her what she could see.

'What can you see?'

'An inheritance,' said Bethalie at once. 'Silver but also gold.

What's this doing here? Oh, yes – a hoarding, but then a scattering. Um, strife. To come, there's someone else, somebody younger than you. A boy.'

'Well, I don't know about him, but all the rest . . .'

'Am I right?'

Her erstwhile mistress stared at her. 'It was a bit obvious, don't you think? All that hoarding and scattering?'

She gestured into the ballroom. Among the twigs and brown leaves the crystals of a broken chandelier lay strewn like lingering snow.

'I didn't mean – ' said Bethalie. 'I just say what the cards say. I wasn't thinking about – '

'No, Beth, I'm sure you weren't.' Jillian turned back to the improvised card-table. 'What about the war? Are we going to win? Can't you see that there?' She tapped the spread.

'No, ma'am.'

'How about this one? The Stag: monarch of the woods. Victory over the Escalan vermin,' she said, with a parade-ground inflection. 'Look at the way he's standing. Don't you reckon?'

'You're no stag, Jillian Curram,' said Bethalie, and squared up the pack.

'Is that the voice of insubordination, private?'

'Yes, ma'am.'

In the distance something exploded suddenly.

'The city!' said Bethalie in alarm. She went in to see what she could see from the gallery.

Jillian could imagine no end to the war, no end to the Escalans with their impassive, implacable orange faces. All her life, it seemed, they had been pouring army after army west over the Cathills. They captured a peak; the Hillcats took it back again; they overran a valley. Meanwhile, Bryland slumped, wearied with internal wrangling. Now its army pottered in companies from the Horneck Marches to the sea and back, preparing to meet the invader who still never came.

Jillian looked over the parapet. For the first time chickweed had taken root in the gravel. She thought of the dead. She remembered her Aunt Clotilde and her Uncle Lorenz. In her childhood, they had lived in an apartment of the west wing and were to be seen on every fourth afternoon, promenading slowly around the grounds. She remembered her mother, monumental among her receipts. She tried to remember her father. She sat down, stuck her feet out and stared at her boots.

'I can't see anything,' said Bethalie, re-emerging.

'Come and sit down.'

She obeyed; but sprang up again at once. 'What's that?'

'What?'

'That noise.'

Jillian listened. 'The wind?'

'No.' Bethalie frowned. '*Above* the wind. Listen. Sort of a moaning.'

Jillian could hear nothing. Bethalie, she decided, was just dramatising again. But Bethalie was starting to panic; then Jillian caught it, and giggling they fled through the corridors from the vengeful spirit of the House.

They rode back in an uncustomary silence, until Seltegn, where a village girl walked into the road with a lantern and stopped them, saying, 'Luscany has fallen.'

Bethalie gasped, but to Jillian it was no surprise.

'Princess Nette – is she dead?' she asked, though it was not the Princess she was thinking of.

The girl shook her head. She was, perhaps, ten, half asleep, drowsy with the dull weather, and mesmerised by the task she had been given. She knew nothing, understood nothing but that Luscany, a distant, foreign land, the name of a fine cloth, and a sort of steel too, had fallen. What that meant she did not exactly know, but she knew it was terrible; and she knew about the barbarians. 'Luscany has fallen,' she repeated clearly, and then looked aside, into the shadows, as if embarrassed.

Confused by her lantern, a bat lurched past and plopped to the ground, where it stayed crawling awhile. Jillian's horse began to tremble, so they rode on. The night drew rags of cloud between moist stars.

'Now it *will* be war,' said Bethalie.

'At last,' said Jillian. Even at the time it seemed a foolish thing to say, but she was feeling numb and singularly careless.

She thought of the messenger with her lantern.

'Beth,' she said, 'that reading – you said there was someone ahead, someone you didn't know, younger than me. That was her, wasn't it?'

But all Bethalie would say was, 'I thought it was to be a boy.' Jillian pressed her no further, for fear she was thinking about her son Jek.

Captain Ennigo was talking to the guard on the gate as they came to the camp. He returned Private Beavon's salute without even looking at her, and she went on in. That was the last Jillian was to see of her for some time. Ennigo was staring at Jillian, as usual. She stopped, to keep him happy.

'Jillian Curram, you lucky devil,' he said. 'You won the sweep.'

'I came second,' she corrected him. 'Captain Tyack had a week and a day: that's closer.'

He was visibly disappointed that she had already heard the news. 'Second's not bad,' he said. 'There's a tidy sum in that pot.'

'I should imagine there is,' said Jillian, waiting for him to tell her exactly how much. It would have been typical of Hubert Ennigo to be the one who knew that.

Instead he said, 'Enough for you to buy me a drink.'

'I don't owe you a drink.'

Ennigo raised his eyebrows. 'To celebrate your good fortune.'

The prospect of conviviality in the officers' mess made Jillian instantly depressed. Military sociability, she had discovered, made her want to bury herself in a hole in the ground.

'Celebrate Captain Tyack's,' she said.

'I'd rather celebrate yours.' The familiar inane grin appeared.

'Not tonight, Hubert. I'm tired.'

'The least you could do is come for a stargazer.'

'For a what?'

'My god, you are new, aren't you. A stargazer. You sit at the door of the tent, together, each with a drink. And as you drain them, you look up through the glass and you can see the stars.'

He pantomimed it all for the benefit of the poor girl on guard, to torment her. Jillian was sure the girl thought him as stupid as she did. 'Most romantic,' said Captain Ennigo.

'It's cloudy,' said Jillian.

'Oh, I forgot: you're one of these stolid Westerners, aren't you, with no sense of romance.'

'No interest in it, rather.'

'I could interest you.'

This, after his previous two attempts, was so unlikely Jillian realised he was quite possessed by his imaginings. Out of sheer weariness, she dismounted and flung the reins to him. 'Take my horse back.'

As she passed through the gate Jillian saw the guard smile, mocking her, she presumed, for giving in . But she thought she knew how it would be told in the morning.

'She ordered him to take her horse, like any groom, and he did, the ninny.'

But after, inevitably: *'Why does she* let *him?'*

Bethalie would be the only one who knew, and she would be much too loyal to tell them that Lieutenant Curram was lonely, and bored. Jillian had reckoned, when she threw in her depleted hand, that the army would at least give some point to her life. She could hardly have been more mistaken. The best it could do was regulate her existence.

Shivering in his tent, she crawled into bed and drew his blankets around her. Soon there was a light blooming through the canvas, and Hubert Ennigo entered, agog as ever. In her fatigue, the lamp made his face look like a grinning turnip.

'Captain Ennigo reporting the safe return of your horse, ma'am,' he said, saluting. 'The little beggar's having his oats and now I want mine.' He snuffled gleefully. Jillian assumed this must be a joke in his region.

'Where's my drink?' he asked, kissing her extravagantly.

'I don't remember where you keep the bottle,' she said.

'Course you do!'

'I don't. And I wasn't about to rummage through your smelly kit to find it, either.'

'My kit's not half as smelly as yours,' he said, pawing her crotch.

'Get the bottle, Hubert.'

Chattering away merrily, he at last unearthed two grimy beakers and a flask of oelegen.

'Hubert, let's do this and go to sleep, would you mind? I really am very tired.'

Ennigo was not to be dissuaded from his preamble. It occurred to Jillian that for him all this was a sort of foreplay, probably. But once he was ready he would, in any case, be quick. So she sat with him and had the unwanted drink, star-gazed, and allowed him to fondle her until he decided to wriggle out of his trousers and clamber on to the cot.

At first, as always, it was painful for her. He murmured thickly, 'Poor baby. Poor darling baby.' Jillian, recognising this as an attempt at tender solicitude, was almost touched.

Quite soon, as she had predicted, he was slumped across her snoring. She rolled out from under him. Now it was her turn. She curled up with her back to him and began. Suddenly, unexpectedly, her eyes were full of tears.

When she awoke, her leg was sticking out of the covers. Ennigo was outside, coming back from the lats, and behind him the field was full of cold fog. It was, after a fashion, day. Jillian had been dreaming about seals. The cavalry were all to be equipped with seals for a naval battle, so Conroe's company were sent to round some up. Jillian remembered standing thigh-deep in icy water off the frozen coast of Rhyall, calling out across a dull green sea.

'Good *morning*,' said Ennigo in a sing-song voice, as if to a child. Jillian thought of him lying beside her watching her sleep, his unshaven turnip face an inch away.

'Tea,' she said, her mouth sticky and vile. 'Send an orderly for tea.'

'Oelegen too much for you, eh?' he smirked.

It had not occurred to Captain Ennigo to ask the lieutenant where she had been the previous evening. He had heard she was from those parts; that she had been born in Hoven, into money, but had been too silly to hold on to it. Behind her back, he would call her 'the poor little rich girl', as they all did, Jillian knew. There would be bad feeling about the sweepstake. She would have to grit her teeth and go into the mess that evening, to spend every penny on drinks for them all, or they would resent her privacy, which was the only thing preserving her sanity.

'Get out, Ennigo, and let me dress.'

—10—
Aboard
the *Fighting Ray*

Bi tok took up the fine brush; hesitated; laid it down again and took a rag instead; then decided to leave the odd patch in the bottom left-hand corner just as it was. He hung the rag carefully on the side of the easel with an awkward little laugh.

'It's – done.'

'At last,' rumbled Gen thiri, and slapped her hands on her thighs. 'And now I suppose I can look at it?'

'Yes,' said the boy, getting up and moving away from the canvas as though connected to it by an invisible string of uncertain length. He had kept it from her all the while, knowing she would be unable not to interfere.

She gave a grunt of half surprise, half pleasure. 'You've made me look old,' she complained.

'Time did that, without any help from me.'

'Cheeky puppy.' She reached out a finger.

'Don't touch it!'

Gen thiri grunted again and withdrew to the far side of the room, to view it from a distance.

He had sat her here in her scrying room in the full illumination of the window, taking great care over the highlights: the grey steel of her hair; her skin, almost amber now; the monstrous rings she wore on every finger. The painting showed clearly the great mappemond and the pendula on the wall behind her, but he had also introduced a view of 'her' lake and island into the background at right. He had not been sure the Geometer would approve of this liberty with perspective.

All she said was: 'I thought you would never finish. If you

weren't leaving tomorrow, I don't think you would have.'

'Will you come to see us off, minister?' Bi tok asked, wiping his brushes and wrapping them in the damp rag.

'No,' she said.

Bi tok was surprised, and disappointed. He said nothing.

Still scrutinising her portrait, she said, 'You won't want an old cow like me embarrassing you in front of all your girlfriends.'

Blushing vermilion, Bi tok busied himself packing up, hating her. There were no girlfriends, and he was sure Gen thiri knew it. The sophisticated One City girls had no time for a juvenile provincial boy studying stuffy Geometry. The ruddy Fox-chiver girls whispered and giggled when he rode by. Ky varan had made it clear his station was far above theirs. Yet they were the ones whose mysterious bodies preoccupied Bi tok at night.

'Minister – um . . . I have to take the easel.'

'What? Well, carry on.'

'Um . . . Where can I put the picture to dry?'

'Where I sha'n't go barging around and knock it over, you mean? Here.' She prised it from the clamps with such force Bi tok winced, but she succeeded in getting it on to a high shelf without serious mishap. Still she voiced no judgement.

'Well?' he said, lingering at the door.

'Well what?'

'Do you – like it?'

'Perfectly charming, dear boy. It reminds me of you: so clever, so shiny and new, and still too delicate to touch.' The Senior Geometer sniffed, wiped her nose on the back of her wrist, and broke into a huge grin.

Blushing again, Bi tok stammered the formula for departing from a revered senior for an indefinite time, and cycled hastily away, his easel strapped to his back.

All along the ridgeway to the Shuan Hills, the pale ochre of late winter was breaking into fresh green. This is the last time I shall see this landscape for many years, Bi tok told himself; but he did not feel properly receptive to it, even so.

His tutors had many times chided him for being insufficiently grounded. His sensibilities always caused him to see a landscape as a pattern of light and shade, to scan impatiently for the spirit behind it, as if the surface detail were insubstantial and quite arbitrary. Lon nan, the Tutor of Novices, had said sharply: 'You are not satisfied with our art, ensign, and sometimes I think you never will be.' The pronouncement had shamed him then; but now, on the eve of their much-delayed departure, it seemed a stirring prophecy of great adventures.

Bi tok freewheeled down the long slope to the house, where everything was in chaos. Ky varan was in his study, taking things out of one trunk and putting them into another, while Par soo ran around earnestly, dabbing at everything with her duster and disrupting what little progress the Geometer was making.

Bi tok stole a pastry from the kitchen, ran upstairs and bounced on his bed like a child. Par soo had already packed all his various suits of clothing, from the summer shift to the full curacic dress he was dreading having to wear in the tropical heat of Belanesi. Otherwise he had few possessions: his painting things, his notebooks and tables, and a strange curio, a clock that worked by winding up a spring, which his father Kam fen had got from a messenger returning from the north-west frontier, and had given him to commemorate his ensignature.

His five statutory first-year exeats had been cut to two, because Ky varan had said there was too much extra study to be done. Bi tok's mother, Mo tai, had been angry and upset, but Bi tok himself had been secretly relieved. The squat buildings and drab people of his birthplace filled him more and more with embarrassment. On his third and last visit he had cycled all the way back to Birling in a state of high excitement to tell his parents that after months of confusion between College and Imperial Offices a sailing date had finally been set; only to find his heart inexplicably sinking a yard for every mile he drew nearer home. Bi tok did not realise it, but it was home no longer.

He kissed his father's hands, and his mother's, but not her cheeks. At supper, his appetite unaccountably vanished, he struggled miserably with the favourite dishes of his childhood. All his father would talk about were the comings and goings at his office, which he did with glee, as though they represented the ways of the entire world. His mother felt his brow and pronounced him tired from his strenuous journey, and he willingly escaped to bed, where he lay wondering how such a pair of ignorant, tiny-minded provincials had ever produced a gifted, sensitive being like him. Bi tok was aghast at his own filial infidelity.

In fact, he owed the couple more than he knew. He had, for example, inherited his mother's habit of talking to herself. Whereas she brooded silently upon her revenge against the malice of circumstance, Bi tok speculated ceaselessly about the meaning of life, always hoping to be content with the mysteries of Geometry and always failing. Conversations with his father, on the other hand, had not convinced Bi tok that human existence was a petty, shallow business, but they had led him to expect it to be simple, and so presumably explicable. For all the colours of his adolescent palette, Bi tok wished to have things black or white.

He flopped back on the pillow and devoured the pastry in a flurry of crumbs. From downstairs came Ky varan's voice, in despair: 'Not the porcelain ones, Par soo, you idiot, the *other* triangular ones!'

Next morning, it was pouring with rain. Thunder rumbled dolefully over Ku ma Meadow, and gutters overran in Bacon Alley. They rode into the city with boxes piled high in an evil-smelling cart, each of them hanging on to a rope to stop the tarpaulin sliding off. The driver knew only one verse of 'Oh! The Cruel Undertaker', and sang it over and over again, pausing occasionally to spit in the road.

As they turned into Sufferance, the pinshaft slipped, and the whole farling had to come off. The local people, in the sudden access of spite that Ky varan had frequently observed in their class, laughed and pointed at the minister and his ensign sitting on boxes by the wayside. They shuffled out in the rain to see, but none would lend a hand.

Par soo talked rapidly in a nervous, high-pitched voice and fretted about the time. 'If only His Supremacy had provided transport!' she sighed repeatedly, unable to accept that the Emperor probably knew nothing whatever of her master and his mission. Ky varan's pleas for an investigation of malfeasance had been blocked at every level. No one cared, or those who did care opposed him. It was as if his nation had turned against him that morning at the Temperance public baths; and, as if to confirm it, when they finally arrived at the dock, three-quarters of an hour late, there was the criminal himself to bid them a smiling farewell.

Ky varan brushed past Chu tek without a word, causing gossip to run around Middle College for several days. Whatever folly that scoundrel strings the Colonial Council into, he told himself, he'll not do it with a pretence of my goodwill. He headed for the *Fighting Ray* to find the captain.

Meanwhile, Bi tok was saying an awkward goodbye to his father. Kam fen stood by the railing trying to shelter them both with his tar-paper umbrella. He had loosened his hair, a sign of proud regret, and was clearly uncomfortable with it curling down his neck.

'Your mother came up with me,' he told the boy, 'but she stayed in bed. She thought it unwise to come out in the storm.' He looked scornfully at the ship. 'It's probably just as well. She wouldn't have been at all happy to abandon you to a lot of soldiers. I should have as little to do with them as possible, if I were you.'

Bi tok nodded distractedly, anxious to get away. Par soo was in tears, quarrelling with a dockhand about the ungentle treatment of a case of books.

The captain, a wall-eyed Perigian with the outlandish name of Chogra Tuy, leaned across the door in answer to Ky varan's call.

'Are you the doctor?'

Ky varan, who had been about to apologise for their lateness with full formality, bridled. 'Senior Geometer,' he said, stiffly.

'Doctor, Geometer, it's all one to me.'

Someone peered briefly over the captain's shoulder. Ky varan heard guffaws.

'My name is Ky varan,' he said, stepping gingerly aboard. 'This – ' pointing to the boy walking quickly between the puddles, ' – is my ensign Bi tok. We must apologise – '

'Loosen your collar, granfer,' said Captain Tuy. 'We can't sail till it eases – and not till our ganger shows, neither.'

The man's accent was so thick Ky varan could barely understand his rudeness. He stood blinking at him until Bi tok, hurrying up behind, took his elbow and steered him along the deck. The last of their luggage was just being carried on, and they followed it down.

In their quarters the troops were singing gloomily.

Belanesi, Belanesi,
The women are crazy,
They do it with goblins,
They do it with goats . . .

Ky varan and Bi tok were shown to a long, low cabin forward. There were three berths, one of them already occupied by a heavy-set man in his forties, an estafette also bound for New Bright Rock.

'Jo kani's the name,' he said. 'That end's all yours. You may as well stow your stuff and get dug in. We're not going anywhere for a while.'

Ky varan sat hunched on his bunk, staring through the porthole at the rain. This was all a terrible shock, a dreadful mistake. His only previous ventures overseas had been as a member of two College delegations to Salt Fan Province: three days in a swift yacht with other ministers for company, in comparative comfort and dignity. To be cramped in a dingy corner of a reeking troopship for months on end was a dismal and distressing prospect.

Par soo was the only one who understood. She came on board to receive her last instructions and say her final farewells, cringing as she ducked under the lintel of the cabin. Jo kani cleared his throat and looked away while the housekeeper knelt before her master with tears running down her face. She would have liked to embrace him, to comfort him, but that was not proper. 'What strange paths we take, Par soo,' said Ky varan faintly. 'Did you pack my pastilles?' She was at last ordered ashore by Chogra Tuy, who had a superstition against weeping women on his ship, and helped down the gangplank by a couple of sailors, burly lads with brutal haircuts, who sniggered at graphic suggestions the soldiers yelled from the portholes.

'Let us hope some of them at least will not be too unfriendly,' said Ky varan, without much conviction. 'Many, after all, will be young lads of about your own age.'

Bi tok, overhead in the upper bunk, was still trying to cram things into a tiny locker. He did not answer.

'Roll me over and stitch me up,' sang the soldiers. *'We're all going to die.'*

As it turned out, there was no one aboard within three years of Bi tok, and scarcely any with much amity for collegiate ministers actual or potential. The troops bound for the jungle scorned the old egghead and his chick. Their commanding officers apologised for the jellyfish and other marine fauna the Geometers found every so often expiring in their beds or on their seats at mealtimes, but relations did not improve. Indeed, it was one of those unfortunate creatures, all warts and feelers, that Ky varan discovered faintly phosphorescing under his blankets which finally cemented hostilities below deck. Bi tok leapt for the porthole to vomit, which he had been doing intermittently all voyage, while Ky varan marched along to the officers' cabin and thrust the dead monster into the sleeping commander's face.

'Gaze, Kien orau, upon the visage of ignorance!'

'Oh. Oh dear,' muttered the commander, inching his way up the pillow to get out from under the dripping thing, which, with its bulging sightless eyes and drooping mouth, did indeed seem to incarnate a negation of intelligence.

Ky varan waved it about.

'See how this glowing monstrosity represents stupidity and enlightenment in one.'

'Minister, I heartily regret – '

'Wrenched from its proper element to pollute my sleep, this dumb fish has finally woken me to my duty!'

From then on, Kien orau's men were divided into groups and set in rotation to study second-year Geometry and the people and patterns of Belanesi, alongside Bi tok.

Soldiers, even Escalan soldiers, are not generally known for the care they take over the cosmic harmonies. To give him his due, Ky varan did not expect them only to learn the auric spectra and the ritual observances for dawn and dusk in tropical regions. He also enlisted Bi tok and himself in their combat exercises, determinedly reviving the neglected martial arts and spiritual disciplines on which many of their routines had originally been based, and at the same time displaying an enthusiasm, if little aptitude, not usually suspected in elderly ministers. But this forced integration did nothing to enhance his own popularity, or that of his ensign.

Three years younger and a good deal smaller than the scrawniest recruit, Bi tok had hitherto shrunk from the soldiers' company. Washing, eating, or even simply idling on deck with them, he was acutely aware that he was, inescapably, their physical inferior; yet he could not afford to be thought immature. The pressure of their husky presence was intimidating.

Under Ky varan's new regime, Bi tok's difference was even more agonisingly obtrusive. In their uneasy Geometry classes he was not only the best and most knowledgeable student, he was the only one who showed any interest at all. Afterwards, pounding a circuit of the deck or fencing in strict formation, he was the most clumsy, the shortest-winded, the butt of many an unkind jibe or elbow. They called him 'fishboy'. One of the uppermen, Dep dura, bore him particular malice. He trapped him going down the companion-way and pulled his Belanesi grammar out of his hand.

'What do you want to learn to talk junglie for, kid?' demanded Dep dura, dangling the book by the corner of a page that promptly began to tear. 'Going to chat up their flea-bitten women, are you?' When such a humiliation was over, Bi tok would flee vermilion-faced to the cabin and fling himself on his bunk, shaken between misery and rage.

His cabin-companions were no help at all. Ky varan was unsympathetic. Vaguely remembering his own adolescence, he was wholly fatalistic about the discomforts of maturation, and convinced that hard work and diligence were the only way to endure them. Jo kani, the estafette, pretended not to notice Bi tok's unhappiness. His conversation was limited at the best of times, consisting entirely of monologue, usually in long, obscure anecdotes drawn from a life of military service. 'Broken Cap, that was something like it,' he would enthuse. 'Talk about disease!' When this narrative fund ran temporarily dry he could sit without speaking for a day or more, engrossed in a sheaf of pornographic woodcuts or munching salted apricots and gazing blankly out to sea.

Bi tok's only relief was when the *Fighting Ray* put into port. Then, and for a day or two beforehand, the squaddies would be too busy stoking their lust for local women to spare any aggression for the egghead runt. Watching from the gunwales at

Puruscu he saw the imminent victims come flocking out in canoes, their curious brown-skinned arms full of flowers and fruit, as though the ship bore not foul-mouthed practitioners of death and destruction, but divine beings from a lovelier sphere.

When all the hubbub was over, Bi tok and Ky varan would refuse the invitations of Chogra Tuy and Kien orau to get drunk with them in some fractionally quieter, more exclusive cellar, and walk the streets of Puruscu or Shama or Dog Chamber, still feeling the ground sway under their unaccustomed feet. Ky varan would point out how the spirit of the place was expressed in the landscape, or how the architecture exemplified the primitive mind, always concluding by discovering an illustration of the inestimable benefit conferred on the inhabitants by just and benevolent colonial policies. Bi tok was simply happy to be liberated from the prison of the ship for a few hours; happy too, if excited natives surrounded them with irrepressible curiosity, or insisted on escorting them to the governor's residence.

As a minister and ministerial ensign of Escaly, Ky varan and Bi tok tended to see the insides of places the cavorting soldiers and crew never came near, unless under arrest. In enclaves of civilisation, they discoursed in the most polished Escalan, free for a while from the monosyllabic repetition of profanities that did for conversation on the *Fighting Ray*. They varied their diet of fish and biscuits with succulent citrus and haunches of strange beasts. In a desert palace they were shown an outhouse full of blocks of ice. In a walled garden they sat on a swinging couch and were entertained by naked children performing gymnastics.

Back aboard the *Fighting Ray*, there was a day of peace while the troops basked in satiety. The sun shone brilliantly over a crystal sea. Bi tok gazed at the lithe shapes of dolphins and halicores cruising alongside. He went below to find his sketchpad. When he returned Captain Tuy, Commander Kien orau and the other officers were practising with the new revolving guns from captive Luscany in the far north-west, supporting the clumsy machines with both hands and cheering when a glossy body jerked out of the water in a flurry of blood. Bi tok watched unhappily.

A hand fell on his arm. It was Upperman Dep dura, his sneering teeth stained with liquorice.

'You wait till I get me one of those guns, junglie-lover, that's you there trying to swim with a hole in your belly!'

Things were back to normal.

Bi tok was resolved: he would endure. He could brave their taunts and surreptitious blows for a little longer. Then he would be free of his unlovely military companions forever.

At last the yellow coast of Belanesi began to thicken above the horizon, like daylight on the edge of a dream. Gulls accompanied them into Pointing In Harbour, their cries banishing the violent and oppressive nightmare. Bi tok thought of the horns of the boundkeepers, tramping the northern forests of Escaly to quell an unquiet spirit. Then he realised he was hearing a brass band. Flags were waving over the toy buildings of Pointing In, and people with brightly coloured shirts were playing musical instruments in the sunshine. How different from the dreary scene at their departure! The complementarity held a certain promise, Bi tok thought.

To one side of the crowd a strange, domed shape in green and brown was swelling from the ground, like a gigantic mushroom.

'What's that?'

'That's a balloon,' said the sailor.

Bi tok was looking at something he had only read about. This astonishing vehicle, essentially a huge bag of hot air, could apparently fly over the treetops, bearing two or three people in a basket with ease.

Ky varan came to join his ensign at the rail, but spared little more than a wary frown for the balloon before turning his attention to the troops, now forming a smart if rather perfunctory display alongside the barges that would take them upriver to Right Fist Camp. Now that was how Imperial troops should be: organised, efficient, impressive. Yet sordid memories of the *Fighting Ray* would not leave him.

Ky varan and Bi tok were to go far inland, west to the colonial capital, New Bright Rock. Once ashore, Ky varan sent Bi tok to ask what transport had been arranged. He stood in the powerful sunlight, eyes closed, imagining clean towers arising from the rich green earth, towers surrounded by young vines. In New Bright Rock, he and his ensign would be restored to their proper positions of power and respect. Already people were bowing to him. The First New Bright Rock Mission of Geometry would be designing the civilisation that Commander Kien orau and his men would be in the jungle fighting to protect.

Bi tok was coming back, with Jo kani following him. 'There's nothing, the gateman says. We have to hire our own or ride with the luggage. But Jo kani – '

As if to make up for his studied neglect of them on the voyage, the estafette was all solicitude.

'Come in my balloon, minister.'

'Your balloon?'

Jo kani seized his arm and marched him along, gesticulating grandly at the swelling envelope. 'I can't leave you here to fend for yourselves. I'm due in the Rock this afternoon.'

He waved a badge and a bundle of papers at the worried-looking man who currently occupied the basket of the balloon. 'These gentlemen are with me.'

'No, sir. No, sir. No passengers. No room.'

The basket did indeed seem to be rather small.

'What? Nonsense! Here, one of them's only a little sprout. Up you come, Bi tok.'

Moreover, Ky varan was resisting. He looked a little wan. 'If we had been meant to fly through the air,' he said rapidly, 'we should have been furnished with wings. Some years ago I made a study of avian creatures and discovered their nature to be quite different from our own. We should forbear to invade their region.'

Bi tok was already inside the creaking basket, with the pilot and Jo kani. 'Come on, minister! Here, take my hand.'

'No. No.' The pilot grew quite agitated, reaching out over the side with open hands and almost pushing Ky varan away.

'What the blue blazes d'you think you're doing?' shouted Jo kani. 'This is a Senior Minister and Envoy of the Supreme Emperor!'

But the pilot only repeated desperately, 'No passenger. No room.'

'Why, you jumped-up little monkey! No room, is there? We'll see about that.' With a vicious heave Jo kani dragged the pilot off his feet and bundled him headfirst out of the basket. He leaned over to yell at him as he lay in the dirt. 'Plenty of room now, eh? Plenty of room, ha ha ha! All aboard, then, minister, let's be having you!'

Together he and Bi tok hoisted in the reluctant Ky varan.

'Cast off there!' bellowed Jo kani.

'Can you operate this – monstrous invention – yourself?' asked Ky varan rather breathlessly, as the basket lurched upwards suddenly.

'Nothing to it!' shouted the courier, fiddling with the curious funnel-topped stove. 'If I've been up once I've been up twenty times.'

Bi tok, terrified and exhilarated, gazed over the side of the basket at the rapidly receding ground. A gust took them over the *Fighting Ray* and out to sea, but by hauling on ropes, swearing under his breath and hitting things with a small poker, Jo kani managed to bring them back round and head upriver.

Beyond the miniature buildings of Pointing In, the scrub began abruptly. The river winked up at them, slow and green between the crowding trees. Bright yellow birds darted around beneath them. The river disappeared and appeared again. The vegetation echoed with strange shrieks and whistles. Bi tok gazed and gazed. Ky varan sat rigid on the floor, staring fixedly up at the blue sky below the great curve of the bag.

Hills rose below. The balloon did not rise. The treetops were much nearer now, and as they closed to form the canopy of the jungle proper, their thick, sun-bleached foliage made it seem that they were flying over a vast tract of cauliflowers.

The estafette crumbled a fuel brick in his fingers. 'Clever stuff, this,' he announced. 'Some foreigner invented it, I'll be bound.' He laughed nervously, cramming half of the sticky substance into the diminutive furnace before giving it up as a bad job. He sucked his scorched fingers, then leaned over Bi tok, rubbing his hands briskly. 'This is all right, eh, my boy?'

They sailed steadily along, the ropes creaking as the basket swayed gently this way and that. Bi tok, his first excitement slightly faded, began to feel rather sick once more. He breathed deeply, swallowing again and again, and focusing on the distance ahead, where the sensation of motion was least. He saw a great rock protruding from the trees. There was something on top of it.

'Jo kani, what's that?'

'Eh? What on earth – ?' said Jo kani.

It was a cluster of wooden buildings, a native village.

'What? Where's that come from? What the blazes is that doing there?' asked the estafette testily.

It was obvious that he had lost his way. He dropped to his knees and poked frantically at the firebox.

Bi tok caught a glimpse of people hurrying into the open. A hillock of trees intervened. Then as the balloon sailed nearer, he saw the people again, forming a group. They appeared to be readying oddly shaped weapons.

Bi tok crouched at the estafette's side, clutching his arm. Jo kani shook off his grip.

'Can't you take us any higher?' gasped Bi tok, lurching backwards as something struck the underside of the basket.

Ky varan yelled incomprehensibly and sprawled against their legs.

'Bastard's gone cold on me,' growled the estafette, rubbing his elbow.

All at once there was a thud, and a sharp tearing sound.

The balloon dropped among the trees.

Clawed branches reached for its fabric. One snagged a rope; the basket pitched under them. Greenery whirled all around.

The furnace door flew open, scattering fire. Something snapped, heavily, and Bi tok screamed as the ground flung itself at his head.

——11——
South

Just before the sun was engulfed, Jillian Curram signalled to her patrol. They stopped among the pines and watched shadow pour down the other side of the valley.

'An aerial navy,' she said, pointing at the advancing cumulus. 'Think of it. Great boats full of warriors, sailing across the sky. Silent, unstoppable.' She nodded to them. 'The first of us to have an aerial navy will win more than the war.'

'Yes, Lieutenant,' said Private Beavon.

At the back, two of the horses began to nibble the moss on a tree.

As they moved off, Private Tofit said, 'They have airboats in Belanesi.'

Everyone laughed.

'In *Belanesi*!'

'It's true,' retorted Mollie Tofit, stung. She was a lugubrious, thin-faced individual with a prominent nose that seemed to be always red. Her hair had begun to fall out when she joined the army.

'Airboats!' chuckled Bethalie Beavon.

'Little ones,' said Mollie.

At that everyone laughed more loudly, except the lieutenant, whose thoughts were elsewhere.

'They do indeed. In Belanesi,' affirmed Mollie, stubbornly.

'In Belanesi they may have anything, Mollie!' crowed Toby Fass.

'No, I mean the Escalans in Belanesi, fathead. The Escalans have the airboats, not the Belanesi, wooden-ears.'

But they were all jeering now.

'There are no Escalans in Belanesi, Mollie!'

'What would they want there? It's all jungle.'

'Belanesi supplies us with sishfruits, goatskin, red hardwood and the principal ingredients of paint and soap,' said their lieutenant. 'Also a certain quantity of wine.'

The soldiers fell silent, looking at one another. Some suppressed laughter.

'Don't get wine in the army, ma'am,' Private Fass reminded her, after a pause.

'There has been no new wine brought into Bryland at all for three and a half years,' the lieutenant replied. 'The sole importer was House Curram.'

'Tough on Bryland, then, isn't it?' murmured Private Patt, with an unpatriotic grin.

Bryland!

Goodbyeland!

We're all bound for the highland!

They had sung; but they were not. The Orange Adversary, for reasons known only to his inscrutable self, had closed up the Cathills. There had been no news for months from north of Arons.

The response of Major Conroe, predictably enough, had been to head south.

Jillian Curram had been livid. 'They need us in the north,' she maintained, at all hours. 'Whatever's happening, they need us.'

But there were orders, he had posted them. They were being sent, all the mid-range artillery was, to Reinforce the Barrage of the Elgoe Strait.

'He swung it somehow, the old toad. I don't know how, I don't care, but he did,' said Lieutenant Curram. She was fifteen minutes off-duty, and drunk already.

'Yes, ma'am, you're right, I don't doubt it,' said Private Beavon. 'Oh, but it'll be *action*, ma'am.'

There again she was wrong; but she was not to know that for a while.

They had set out on a bright, windy day, down the Maylock Road, through Dauber Gap, and into the Greymark Hills. There Conroe kept them sitting for a week while he steeled himself to go over the edge into Upper Tarquia. Her squad seethed, but Jillian would have none of it. 'We're off the plains,'

100

she told them all continually. 'Be grateful.'

Dismissing her patrol now, she went to report to Captain Wessick. Captain Ennigo was there. He said nothing while she gave her report, but when she was dismissed he rose.

'I must go too, Franzis. I'll see the lieutenant to her quarters.'

He led her down past the woodpile.

'This isn't the way, Captain Ennigo.'

He turned, instantly furtive.

'Come on, Jilly. We can do it if we're quick.'

Jillian put her hands on her hips.

'When were you otherwise?' she demanded.

'Come again?'

'When did you ever?' she returned.

Captain Ennigo was uneasy. He recognised the jokes but he did not recognise the tone of her voice, not from her, not from Jilly.

'You can suck it if you like, that would be quickest,' he offered. 'But you don't like me mentioning that. So I won't mention it.' He grinned.

'All that was all right then,' said Jillian Curram. 'But it is not all right now. No, Hubert: take your hand off me.'

He shook his head.

She slapped his face.

He backed away, blinking. 'I hope you didn't strike a superior officer, Curram,' he said in a strange, tight voice. 'Even you could be whipped for that.'

'You really are a worm, Ennigo.'

He bounced forward again. 'But I forgive you because I adore you.'

Eventually it became pointless to resist, or rather, less agonising to yield. She knelt and tugged briskly at his buttons.

'Good girl.'

The days sloped by. Rain came down in smoky curtains, twisting thickly about the hills. They entered Upper Tarquia by the Vale of Qapsibah, where the spice trees perfumed the sodden air. Fragrances of begus and sandalwood enveloped them as they wrenched and wrestled the big guns over the soft earth. One stuck in the mud, confounding everyone. A party of three was despatched to ride downstream and commandeer barges. They never returned.

Jillian Curram sat on horseback on the hillside with the rain plastering her thick brown hair over her eyes and trickling down the neck of her cape; yet she was happy enough. She blessed the dreary landscape because she had sometimes thought she would never leave the prairies. On the march she could forget House Curram for considerable stretches of time.

The Elgoe Strait divided Upper from Lower Tarquia. Flags of Bryland, Maxava and the Treft still flew from the watch-towers, but their armies had gone. At the port half-uniformed officials gave Major Conroe contradictory information. With their impassive eyes and their solemn declarations of loyalty, they acted in every respect like quislings who had been paid to obstruct the southern campaign. In an evacuated fishing village a reconnaissance party found a hidden satchel containing a telescope of oriental design and a sheaf of papers written in a code no one could decipher. Major Conroe rolled up the pages tightly and beat them against the side of his boot.

'This proves it,' he declared. 'These Tarquian yogoes thought they had us fooled, but Algernon Conroe's too smart for them, oh my goodness yes.' He breathed heavily through his nose, staring in baffled anger at the empty sea. 'We'll head for Tarnosh,' he ordered. 'The authorities there will clear this lot up sharpish.'

There was open dissent in the echoing sail-hall the officers took for their mess.

'We've no orders for Tarnosh,' said Captain Wessick. 'What does the old man think he's doing?'

'Keeping his head down,' said Ordnancer Tyack, to a chorus of disgruntled agreement. 'The line's moved east, so he's holing up in Tarnosh to stay out of the way.'

'Don't listen to him,' said Quartermaster Aight. 'Five'll go fifty Conroe's looking at Belanesi.'

'You think the major fancies us as a jungle brigade?' asked Captain Ennigo. 'Can't say I see it, myself.'

'With those whiskers you could pass for a native, Hubert!'

'I'd rather take my chances in Tarnosh, thanks all the same.'

'Bugger Tarnosh,' grumbled Wessick. 'If we're not going east, we should stay where we're put, not traipse off to Tarnosh.'

Lieutenant Curram's squad, uncommonly enough, were all unanimous in support of Major Conroe's decision. Their reasons varied, she discovered.

'Anywhere's better than this hole.'

'No, Sar,' said Jimothy Dowel. 'Tarnosh is good. You'll like it.' Tarnosh had a certain reputation. Private Dowel was its keenest advocate. 'They're sophisticated. You can get anything you want in Tarnosh. Drugs. Sex.'

'Escalans.'

Though they still had yet to encounter the enemy from the east, they knew all about them. Escalans were ferociously disciplined, and did everything like machines. They slept in rows, in boxes made of iron, to stop themselves from dreaming. Once a week, they copulated, all on the same day. Their women were infallibly fertile. The well-known fact that they bred like flies was why they were overrunning the world.

'They'll have Tarnosh by now. Stands to reason.'

'We'll get them out.'

The coasters would take them to Tarnosh, that was no problem. As usual, the coasters were on no one's side, but recognised good coin. At embarkation, astonishingly, Captain Wessick was missing, with a party of twenty-two.

Three weeks later, Tarnosh sprawled in the sun and buzzed its soporific buzz. There was no sign of any Escalan presence. On the hill leading up to the castle, Jillian Curram finally found a market porter who could give her intelligible directions to the offices of Curram Merchandise. They were locked and shuttered. From somewhere the sound of women chanting re-echoed along the dusty arcade.

Climbing down into the area, Jillian peered through a fanlight and saw an old man with one arm, obviously one of the surviving Tarquian indigenes, sitting motionless in the corner of a darkened room. When she rapped on the mottled glass he rose with alacrity and started forwards, as if to speak to her; then, catching sight of her uniform, turned abruptly away and left the room.

When he did not return, Jillian grew angry. Who was he, and what was he doing skulking on her property? Suddenly it struck her that the building was nothing to do with her any more, and that she was probably trespassing into something she knew nothing about. As she left in confusion, she thought she heard a baby crying somewhere inside.

In the Place of Mules, quite by chance, Jillian ran into Bethalie, who was with Jimothy Dowel and the tall redhead whose name Jillian could never remember. Mollie Tofit was tagging along behind. Bethalie greeted Jillian and asked where she'd been, and Jillian felt it would be a relief to tell her. For some reason she omitted the old man.

'So you didn't actually go inside, ma'am?'

'No. I came away.'

Jimothy and the redhead looked at each other.

'Why not?'

'It was all locked up,' Jillian said again. 'There was no one there.'

'You could have broken in.'

'Oh no,' said Jillian quickly.

'Take us back there and we'll get you in,' promised the redhead. 'Wouldn't take a minute.'

Still the lieutenant shook her head, not so much from fear of breaking the law as from a disinclination to go rummaging through another empty building in search of a former self. 'I'm convinced my father's gone to Belanesi,' she said.

'Well, then, you can look for him there, lieutenant,' said Mollie Tofit.

Nobody looked at her. They were accustomed to reject what Mollie said, but she had developed an awkward habit of being right.

'Do *you* think we're going to Belanesi, ma'am?' asked Bethalie.

'It seems increasingly likely,' said Jillian.

Mollie smirked at Jimothy, who ignored her.

Jimothy was disappointed with Tarnosh. Conroe's troops, unprovided for in the city, were being forced to share inadequate barracks seven miles out of town with a legion of Kappites, also on their way to their first engagement and comforting themselves by singing interminable jolly rounds in high-pitched nasal voices and clapping their hands. Jillian, grateful for unexpected company, postponed her return to barracks.

At the scrag end of the market sat more natives than Jillian had yet seen in one place together. The men wore enormous heavy hats of split cane, and slept on their haunches. The women and children asked the foreign soldiers for money. Some offered things for sale: bottles of dubious liquid, or rough balls of fragrant wax, studded with human teeth.

'See the jungleman, ladies.' The young ruffian plucked their sleeves and pointed up an alleyway. 'See the jungleman.'

He would say nothing else, nor get out of their way. Embarrassed, Jillian threw him a couple of coins. Then the lad led them to a shed behind the butcher-house. It had a large barred window. Inside, something was crouching.

As they approached, their scrawny guide pushed past them and fled back down the alley.

'You shouldn't have given that one anything, ma'am,' said Bethalie. 'You can come here any time and see it, without paying. The poor creature,' she added.

Jillian looked inside the cage. In the shadow, she saw his teeth first. The Belanesi's grimace was almost human. His hindquarters were not. His fleece was dull and patchy where he lay irritably picking at it. His hoofs were spattered with shit. The redhead was poking him with a stick through the bars.

'Private.'

'Sorry, ma'am.'

Jimothy Dowel grabbed Mollie Tofit's arm. 'Fancy a go on that, Mollie?' She pointed to his lolling purple member, chuckling.

'Those are the real Belanesi,' wrote Jillian in her journal, 'the ones who live in the jungle. I think they are much much older than our race. The next we meet will be in the wild, face to face. They smell vilely of course.'

At next morning's briefing, Major Conroe scratched his sunburnt neck. 'It's not official,' he kept saying. 'It has not been verified.' Incredulous, Lieutenant Curram heard him say that they were not going to Belanesi, they were going to sit tight in Tarnosh pending orders. It was the same thing he had said in the Greymark Hills above Tarquia. Jillian looked at him blustering evasively. She thought of the sunken eyes of the Belanesi jungleman in the cage. She stood up.

'You have a question, lieutenant?'

'Yes, sir. Are you aware that people are dying in Belanesi?'

There was a shocked murmur. All heads turned.

'Adjutant,' said Conroe, 'who is that woman?'

'Lieutenant Curram, sir; of House Curram. Her father's missing,' said the aide, quietly, 'and believed to be in Belanesi.'

Before the major could speak, Jillian said, 'My father is the last person I have in mind, sir. I am considering the natives of Belanesi, particularly the jungle tribes. For years these people have kept us in comfort with furs and fruits and wine. Now they are being slaughtered by Escalans, just as our friends in Luscany, who sold us iron and fine cloth, were slaughtered by Escalans. We did nothing then. Will we do nothing now, Major Conroe?'

'She's distraught, sir.' Hubert Ennigo was at her side. 'Calm down, Jilly, do.' He stroked her arm.

'In time, no doubt, lieutenant,' said Major Conroe, distantly, 'if we're called to their aid, we shall go. Now will you please resume your seat.'

'No, sir,' said Jillian.

She walked past him and out of the door. When the guards came to her billet five minutes later she was not there. Next morning, shortly before dawn, a flagless clipper left the harbour. In its hold were Bethalie Beavon, Jimothy Dowel, Saraa Patt and Mollie Tofit, with a small cannon, and a quantity of guns and shot.

Jillian Curram refused to hide below deck.

'I have more authority now than I had as matron,' she noted in her journal. 'Now I have stopped feeling sorry for myself, and made up my mind, they follow me unbidden.'

'She's always writing,' said Saraa. She turned a card. 'Damn.'

'What are you writing?' asked Jimothy. She had stopped calling her madam at once, but had not yet begun to call her Jillian. She dealt the next hand, looking across at her with half-closed eyes.

'I don't know what she manages to find to write *about*,' said Mollie. Mollie was not playing. She was peeling sweet potatoes. The sea air had made her cheeks pink.

'I'm writing my war memoirs,' said Jillian.

'Mark, and a pair,' said Bethalie, who was playing not because she enjoyed it, but because it was the only condition on which she would let them use her cards.

'What war memoirs?'

'You haven't *had* any war yet.'

'Have I not.'

They were twenty-two days out, passing through the Summer Islands. The sea was slick and warm, pellucid green to a remarkable depth. There were jellyfish the size of cart-wheels, and shoals that streamed beneath the hull, a hundred thousand fish together, and not one aware of their intrusion overhead.

They put in at Delgarche for fresh water. It was here that Jillian Curram made the last entry ever in her journal. A sailor in an inn on the harbour saw her writing and tried to ingratiate himself with her, claiming, so far as they could make out, that it was himself she was writing about. He snatched the book. She snatched it back. After this and more of the same, the book fell in the harbour. A few minutes later, so did he. Officers were called, but Jillian and her companions had fled.

The captain called her to the wheel next day.

'One follows,' she announced, grimly.

'For one arrogant drunkard?' said Jillian. 'Surely not.'

'Not from Delgarche. From Tarnosh.'

Jillian went aft with a spyglass, but there was too much dazzle to see anything. All the same, when they came to Calabo they lay low for a few days in a secluded cove. They saw no ships; nor did the young goatherd tell anyone of his vision of six naked women sunbathing and swimming in the bay, for no one would have believed him.

In this way they came at last to Leopard Rock, where they left the ship and set foot on the shore of Belanesi. At once they were in thick forest, and quite lost. They struggled through the undergrowth with the gun, looking for the sun between the treetops, always heading what Jillian hoped was south-east.

One night she woke suddenly. The fire was still glowing in the middle of the clearing. Somebody was leaning over her. A man.

She almost put a knife in him. Later she would wish, sometimes, that she had.

'What are you doing here, Hubert?' she asked, trying to keep her voice level.

'Aha, I was keeping an eye on the harbour, wasn't I? You

looked so wonderful on the bridge of that clipper, so noble. I followed you.'

They follow me unbidden.

By now the rest were up, surrounding him. He gave them his best grin.

'If you're thinking of taking us back, Captain Ennigo, you could find yourself with several severe injuries,' said Saraa.

'I'm not,' he said to Jillian. 'I'm joining you.'

No one spoke. The night whirred sweetly all around them.

'The old man's daft,' Hubert went on. 'Where's the fun in Tarquia?'

'Give us a good reason not to hold your head underwater, Ennigo,' said Jimothy.

With a flourish, Hubert Ennigo patted his breast pocket.

'I've got the major's map,' he said.

Jillian looked at him, then at the women.

'No one is to sleep with him,' she said.

——12——
Flora and Fauna

Bi tok opened his eyes.

He was lying in the mud.

It was cool, and wet, and fibrous.

He lifted his head.

High above, the green canopy was so thick there was no sign of the hole through which they had plunged.

The trees were lofty and dim. Everywhere their wild crowns were interlaced with tumbling masses of secondary vegetation, clinging, festooning, dangling. Everything was very quiet. Insects chittered.

Bi tok was suddenly in pain, all up his arm and across his chest. He got to his knees. There was a bad cut on his left shoulder, scratches and bruising everywhere, but nothing seemed to be broken. His clothes were torn and he was completely covered in mud. He staggered to his feet.

Overhead he heard a shrill squawk. He looked up and saw, just for an instant, the bright yellow flash of a bird among the vines. He looked down and saw a body.

Bi tok gave a cry and stumbled towards it. As soon as he moved, his head began to spin. He fell on his knees, got up and ran clumsily on, holding his hands to his head.

It was Ky varan, face down by a puddle.

'Minister?'

Ky varan spoke into the mud.

'Is that you, boy? I can't move, boy.'

Bi tok stooped anxiously to help him.

'Careful! My side . . .'

Propped upright, his master could stand; but his right arm was useless, he clearly had a broken rib or two, and was in pain that made Bi tok forget his own. He had mud all over him, with leaves and mouldy bits of bark stuck in it.

Bi tok wiped the old man's face. It was yellow and pale. Then they ploughed their way up the bank together, Ky varan leaning heavily on Bi tok's shoulder, and collapsed on soft, damp earth, breathing heavily. Bi tok could taste the humidity.

Moments passed.

Only then did Ky varan speak. He raised himself carefully on his good arm and stared out across the water.

'There – ' he said.

Tall, smooth trunks rose from the water of a lake the colour of apricot tea. Among them was a large blob of green and brown, attached to something wooden that was floating just under the surface. Of the estafette, there was no sign. As they watched, in bleak horror, the balloon bubbled exuberantly and sank a little further.

'Jo kani!' cried the boy.

'Dead,' said Ky varan hoarsely, and a moment later: 'His luggage!'

Bi tok looked at him.

'You could swim. You could search!'

'Minister,' said Bi tok reproachfully.

'Ours was on the barge. Without his, we have nothing,' said Ky varan, desolate.

Bi tok looked around. Spiky plants and stands of bamboo leaned through the gloom. Everything smelled rich and dank.

'Perhaps we shall find something.'

Bi tok would have torn up his shirt, as he knew he should, to bandage his master's side, but Ky varan told the boy, 'Use mine.' Then they slowly left the mere and went a little way into the jungle.

Soon Ky varan stopped.

'We must stay here. Perhaps someone saw the balloon come down,' he said; but what he really meant was, I can walk no further.

'But what about whoever shot us down?'

'We shall hide until we see who comes,' directed the Geometer, looking vaguely around. In the universal dark green murk one could hardly see, or, he supposed, be seen.

'There,' he said, looking towards a tree whose buttress roots were like huge fins rising overhead. Between any two was as much space as a good-sized room, and it was full of shrubbery. He hoped none of it was already occupied.

Bi tok thought, but did not say, that whoever lived in this landscape would have to be skilful trackers and would find them easily. He helped Ky varan under cover and squatted down beside him.

By dusk he grew hungry. Several visible bushes bore glossy, unfamiliar berries, but he dared not leave his master; and in any case he did not know which might be poisonous. The ground was littered with a mulch of rotting fruit that must have fallen from the high trees; but Bi tok was not *that* hungry. The same doubt applied there too. He remembered Gen thiri, the first day he'd ever met her, saying, In Belanesi the water is poisonous. The brown lake, was that poisonous? No, it couldn't be. The trees would have died. But the trees should have drowned anyway, surely?

Senior Geometer Ky varan, who might have essayed answers to some of his questions, had fallen into an exhausted sleep. His breathing was shallow and not pleasant to listen to. Bi tok tried to make him comfortable on a pillow of ferns.

The insects grew louder as the last light failed. Later, something nocturnal howled, as if enraged to find itself waking up once again in this desolate place.

Bi tok spent a night of horror. He dreamed that Captain Chogra Tuy had come to drag them back to the *Fighting Ray*, then woke with a jump. Leaves would rustle stealthily; twigs snap unaccountably. He felt like an intruder in a hostile and predatory world. Unseen through the bushes where he crouched, animals passed all night along the secret paths of the forest floor. Bi tok hoped none of them was a crocodile, up from the fatal lake; or a tiger, walking softly between the trees. Ky varan muttered and laughed, but did not wake.

As soon as there was any light at all, Bi tok scampered out from under the tree. Something fine and sticky draped itself across his face. He wiped it away, crossed the glade and seized a bunch of berries. They were blue, and did not *look* poisonous. He ate them, testing them for Ky varan.

When, after a few anxious minutes, he did not feel ill, he resolved to take some back and try to feed them to his master;

111

but first, he had to look around and see if there were anything dangerous lurking nearby. This he could not have done, but he told himself he was searching for anything which would tell him about the place they were in, and how to get out of it.

The daylight grew stronger, but no sunbeams reached the forest floor. By exploring a little way, Bi tok discovered that the ground was undulant, with broad furrows all running the same way. In some of them, dark water glinted through the mat of vegetable decay.

Passing around a venerable mahogany, Bi tok saw a patch where what seemed to be perfectly ordinary bananas, whole armloads of them, were lying strewn around. Running forward to gather some, he surprised a tragelaph browsing on the fallen fruit. It looked much smaller than in the bestiary. The tragelaph gave Bi tok an uncertain look, then bounded into the bushes. He went after, with some mad idea of catching it with his bare hands, but only wound up jarring his ankle and falling over. Winded, he resigned himself to squashy bananas, collected as much as he could carry, and made his way back to the bush where his master lay under a gargantuan tree.

Ky varan was still asleep. A yellow and black spider the size of a soupbowl was sitting on his cheek.

Bi tok dropped the fruit with a yell. Startled, the spider bit; then rapidly scuttled away under the leaves. Bi tok could see now that the bushes were all covered with webs.

'Ah,' cried Ky varan, and kicked a little, but did not wake.

Bi tok took the lined face in his hands. Ky varan was still breathing, but his eyes remained closed. The ensign could just see two tiny red puncture marks in a wrinkle of his master's faded cheek.

Bi tok sat by him, holding his hand in a numb trance. Tears were running down the boy's face. Don't die, he was saying to himself, Please don't die. He ate bananas distractedly.

'Aha!' said Ky varan suddenly. 'What extinguisher? What priceless brass extinguisher?' He snuffled, and clacked his teeth together three times. Then he was silent.

Around noon, when even the most abrasive insects seemed to hush a little, Ky varan began to sweat furiously. He moaned for a while, then he said, clearly:

'Consider the jungle as a single self-renewing organism. As it

112

decays, the vegetation feeds itself. Also, the strong support the weak, as the tall banak allows a limb to the matapolo, an epiphyte. The fauna are so perfectly harmonic with the flora as to be invisible. Doubtless thousands are around us as I speak. We hear their voices, but we may not see them.'

'Hush, minister,' said the boy, hugging him. 'I think I hear something coming.'

Ky varan opened his eyes. He was trembling with fever. 'Ah, Bi tok,' he said. 'What a predicament, eh? Are you cold? I certainly am. Would you light us a fire, please?'

'I can't, minister,' Bi tok whispered urgently.

Ky varan misunderstood him. 'You surprise me,' he said. 'Attend. A fire is a collection of dry sticks, of various sizes, in various states and stages of decomposition by heat. Heat may be produced by friction. A fire begins with the tiniest spark, a seed of fire, and grows slowly and steadily up from the first flame. Now, consider the relationship of the burnt to the unburnt, the proportion and position of the fuel being consumed at any one moment to the fuel which is to be consumed next, and must lie adjacent.

'I shall say all this again as you proceed. Begin now. Gather suitable wood.' Ky varan frowned at the figures gathered looking down at him. 'And ask these good people to wait.'

Bi tok hoped that they were indeed good people. They were certainly the strangest people he had ever seen.

There were five, all male. They had straggling beards and curly manes that reached halfway down their backs. Their skin was not orange but greenish-brown. They had pointed ears and yellow eyes and sardonic grins on their long toothy faces. From the waist down they were as shaggy as goats, and when they moved into the bushes, jerkily, wielding blades of wood or bone, Bi tok saw that their skinny legs bent the wrong way at the knee; and their feet were cloven hooves.

Bi tok sat up.

'We-are friends!' he shouted. 'Help-us!'

The group stopped abruptly, staring at him. They conferred among themselves. Bi tok could hear from their nasal, quavering voices that the pronunciation marks in Ky varan's uncle's Belanesi grammar left much to be desired.

One, who seemed to be the leader, stepped forward and

113

dropped to a crouch, still staring at Bi tok across the mumbling body of Ky varan. The boy tried not to flinch. The native was wearing only a necklace of the carapaces of huge iridescent beetles, and the stink of him was sharp and sour.

'You-speak our-words,' he said.

'We-are friends,' repeated Bi tok slowly, though he was thinking very fast indeed. 'We-come to-help you, teach you. But – ' How on earth was he to convey 'balloon'? Were these the people who had attacked them or not? He saw that one of them was holding a large Y-shaped object that was probably a bow of some kind. He decided to be vague. 'We-fell,' he continued. 'This-one, my-chief, is hurt.'

The native leader sniffed at Ky varan's improvised sling and shouted an order to his men. One of them promptly and silently disappeared among the trees, while the rest crowded cautiously forward.

Bi tok did not know the word for 'spider'. He pointed mutely to the two inflamed puncture marks on Ky varan's cheek, then held his hands together at the wrist and wriggled his fingers, gnashing his teeth at the same time. He ducked out from under the bushes and pointed to their shrouds of white webs.

The native who had run off came back with some small green leaves which he thrust unceremoniously into Ky varan's mouth. The old man made to spit them out, but the Belanesi barked at him and held his mouth closed with the heel of his hand. Looking rather glazed now, Ky varan began to chew.

The other natives were grinning and chattering, apparently making jokes about their illustrious visitor. They were not taking this seriously, thought Bi tok. Then one of them casually reached up, gathered a sticky handful of ageing cobweb from the bush and smeared it across the Senior Geometer's face.

Bi tok jumped up with a yell, but the leader restrained him with one powerful hand on his shoulder. The boy winced, and the Belanesi turned his baleful eyes upon him.

'Rik-dikkito bit you?'

'No,' said Bi tok, rubbing his shoulder.

Their rescuer, if that was what he was, tore away the sleeves of Bi tok's coat and shirt as if they had been made of paper. The flesh around the gash was red and swollen. The man grunted, dropped to his haunches again, and scooped up a handful of red mud. This he slapped on Bi tok's injured shoulder, rubbing it gently up and down the wound. Bi tok, who had spent many painful minutes washing it clean, decided it was useless to protest. The junglemen were determined to humiliate them and soon, no doubt, would tire of this childish play and tear them limb from limb for their supper. But elsewhere, with sapling poles and strong vines, some of the group had made a sort of stretcher, to which they were now tying the limp and unresisting Ky varan.

As they set off, Bi tok ran to take his master's hand, but the old man was completely unconscious again. He made a tentative move to wipe the dishonourable mess of cobweb from Ky varan's face, but was swiftly dissuaded by the yammering of the junglemen.

There was nothing to do but go with them. They set a surprisingly rapid pace, and it took all Bi tok's energy to keep up. He decided to reserve further attempts at conversation until he saw what their destination was.

The trail led uphill. For the first time since the crash, Bi tok could see the sky between the treetops. It was a hard and brilliant blue. Shafts of sunlight transformed the arboreal dusk to luscious green and gold; and, as if in response, the sparse undergrowth began to thicken. The rescue party ploughed through broad-leaved bushes. Bi tok saw his first jungle flowers, extravagant eruptions of yellow and crimson.

After a while, the Belanesi began to sing, one of them wailing an incomprehensible line and the rest joining in with what was obviously a traditional chorus. It was the most appalling noise Bi tok had ever heard.

The slope grew steeper, but the pace did not slow. Suddenly the trees opened out ahead at what appeared to be a sheer face of rock. The natives ran straight up it, leaving Bi tok scrabbling frantically for footholds. The leader, with his permanent silly grin, hopped agilely back down to Bi tok's side and swung the boy up and over his shoulders, like a shepherd carrying a fallen kid.

'Bua-turaa,' he said. 'My-name is Bua-turaa.'

'My-name is Bi tok,' gasped the boy, clinging on for dear life as they went bounding up the vertical path. Next moment they emerged in full fierce sunlight on top of the rock. Bi tok, sliding off Bua-turaa's back, realised that this was indeed the village he had spotted from the balloon, and resolved once more not to mention the circumstances of their arrival in the jungle.

He looked down. They stood on an island of rock in an infinite sea of brilliant green. There was no sign through the treetops of the murky, inhospitable world that lurked below. Then he looked around, squinting in the sunlight. Long low buildings of shiny bamboo surrounded an open space dominated by a statue. Ky varan was being rushed into a house whose veranda was crowded with Belanesi women quite as hideous as their menfolk. Their pendulous breasts were bare. Their woolly children skipped and pranced fearlessly around the smooth-skinned strangers. The stench was like walking into a farmyard. The noise was not so dissimilar.

Bi tok pushed through the crowd, following his master. He felt weak and confused, the sun beating on his head. Bua-turaa, now carrying an infant on each shoulder, was speaking to him, drawing his attention to the huge horned figure that stood in the centre of the village. It was crudely but dramatically carved from a single tree trunk twenty feet high, and it held a plate speckled with silver over its leering head.

Bua-turaa was nodding to it. 'Well-come,' he said.

'Well-come!' they all shouted, 'well-come!', as Bi tok stopped on the steps and turned to face Bua-turaa and the statue. He felt relieved. Their worth had been recognised. They were not, he thought, to be eaten.

Bi tok made the ritual gesture for a foreign guest expressing humble gratitude, and said loudly and carefully, just as he and Ky varan had rehearsed:

'I-bring greetings from the Great-Father in-the-East to his far-children of-the-trees. Ours-together will-be prosperity, harmony and concord.'

There was to be more, but at that moment Bi tok's guts twisted sharply and he had to flee for the bushes. The Belanesi brayed in delight as the Escalan ensign wrenched down his trousers, squirming with pain and embarrassment as the over-ripe bananas exacted their price.

The spasm over, Bi tok made his best attempt to clean himself up, and took the opportunity to wipe off some of the mud they had daubed all over his injured shoulder. To his surprise, the swelling had almost subsided, the inflammation fading.

Bi tok pulled together the rags of his clothing and his dignity. He walked back to the longhouse where, in the comparative cool behind the shutters, Ky varan lay on a bamboo mat and received the ministrations of deft hands, many of them involving more rough plasters of malodorous red mud. This time Bi tok watched carefully and did not attempt to interfere. If this was jungle magic, it was nonetheless effective.

Later two native girls of about his own age led him behind the hut to a cave where they stripped him and bathed him in a pool. Exhausted, Bi tok could do little more than mumble over and over the phrases for thanks and good wishes. His excitement at being washed all over by two naked young women was amply offset by the fact that both looked and smelled not unlike goats. But in a complete village of the creatures, whose benevolence was manifest, his initial horror was subsiding.

Since nobody here wore anything but primitive jewellery and their own fleece, there seemed little point in his trying once more to reassemble the filthy ruin of his own clothes, so Bi tok improvised a loincloth from the fabric of his trousers, and went back indoors.

Looking around inside the longhouse, he now saw that it seemed to be a place set aside for the most ancient and infirm of the village. Ky varan would be safe here. He was sleeping peacefully now, his face and side swathed in poultices of mud and slices of fruit laid across his battered face. Bi tok's escorts showed him a mat laid next to his master's, and left him to sleep.

When Bi tok first woke, in full darkness, the village was so quiet he could hear the jungle throbbing away below. Ky varan had not moved. When Bi tok woke next, it was early morning by the light, and fifteen children of various ages were standing around them in a circle. Two ran away at once, and a third, squeaking, 'Enemy! Enemy!' in some distress. Bi tok silently shooed out the rest, lest they disturb Ky varan, and lay himself down again to sleep. When he woke the third time the sun was high, and Ky varan was awake too, and talking quietly with an elderly native.

'Minister!' said Bi tok gladly. 'The best of the day to you!'

'I am happy to see you in sunlight, Bi tok, my boy,' said Ky varan, with more feeling than was customary.

The woman came over to sniff Bi tok's shoulder and stare inscrutably into his eyes. 'You-are-well,' she assured him, nodding, and went out.

'The harmonies are everywhere, even at the ends of the earth,' said Ky varan, triumphant but pale. 'The cure for the poison of the spider is in her web. The rock cuts, but the mud heals.' He coughed drily, six or seven times, pain evident in his face.

'How is your arm?' asked his ensign.

'Not too old or too broken to mend,' replied Ky varan. 'They believe.'

'Blossom on the branch, sap in the stem,' said the old woman, returning with fruit husks abrim with their own juice. She indicated the ones who occupied the other mats in the longhouse. Through slats of split bamboo the sunlight fell in stripes across their motionless faces. They seemed to be smiling; but then they all always seemed to be smiling.

Bi tok recognised her proverb. Ky varan's uncle had been uncertain of its meaning. Bi tok was none the wiser. Ky varan drank half of his juice, then fell asleep again with his red-stained mouth wide open. Bi tok sat by him most of the day.

In an animated interval, the Geometer told his pupil: 'These people are nearer nature than us. We have lost their instinctive sense for the organic harmonies.' He looked sad for a moment, then brightened. 'What a study all this will make, on our return! And you, Bi tok, shall illuminate it with your brushes.'

Bi tok found charcoal and a flat smooth stone. He tried to sketch Ky varan asleep, then the nearest native, with equal lack of success.

Towards evening Bi tok was summoned to dine with the tribe. From the door he looked back at his master dozing in the violet light, and at the few old natives who were his master's mute, unmoving companions. He could scarcely tell which was which.

He went across to the largest hut of the village, guided by the smoke billowing from the middle of its roof, and found the whole tribe assembled in a cheerful din. What with the noise, the heat and smoke and the ever-present stink, it was with some

118

difficulty that Bi tok picked his way between the reclining bodies and scrambling children to a space by Bua-turaa, who greeted him.

'How-is the man?'

'Healing, Bua-turaa, honoured-chief, thanks-to-you,' said Bi tok, with a wholehearted salutation.

'Sit-eat,' said the Belanesi chief; and, as Bi tok obeyed, 'A puzzle. You-people kill us, yet we-heal you.'

Bi tok tried to explain. 'We-Escalans kill only bad-jungle-people who attack us-people,' he began, feeling himself blushing. Bua-turaa's smile remained as mocking as ever, but Bi tok had the impression the jungleman was toying with him. 'We-Escalans wish to-live-in-peace with-you-jungle-people,' he affirmed, solemnly. 'With-all-Belanesi.'

All Bua-turaa would say was, 'Eat.'

Two young natives, apparently the chief's sons, bounded around helping Bi tok to a great array of spicy dishes. He gave his attention to them willingly, for he was famished as well as embarrassed.

There was a salad of cucumbers with a sesame dressing, fried fingerlings with yams and fresh limes, murena poached in a brown bean sauce, and a crisp breaded gourd, and those were only the ones Bi tok managed to remember later. During the meal he drank freely of a tangy fruit juice that he discovered, rather too late, to be quite alcoholic. He dearly wanted to use this social occasion to enlighten Bua-turaa further about the benevolence of the Supreme Emperor of Escaly, but his ears were deafened with the chatter and clatter, his tongue would not obey him and his Belanesi vocabulary had fled his befuddled brain.

In stark moonlight he stumbled back across to the longhouse. The statue seemed to be striding after him, menacing him with its ridiculous plate.

Ky varan was still immersed in dream. Bi tok collapsed at his side into a tangled, seething confusion of sleep.

They were awakened at dawn by a shout, three loud cracks as of large branches broken sharply, and hurrying footsteps. Then someone began to wail, a high warbling cry of inhuman misery.

The minister and his ensign looked at one another in uncertainty. Bi tok rose and went towards the door. Before he could reach it it was kicked open from outside.

Upperman Dep dura burst in. He was brandishing a Luscan revolving gun.

He hit the floor, raised the unwieldy weapon and loosed four shots into the huddle of natives at the far end of the hut. Bleating, they slumped where they sat, one of them squealing and convulsing, the rest perfectly still. Then the barrel swung round towards Bi tok.

Dep dura was panting and grinning like an overexcited dog, but his voice was a purr.

'They told us this lot were harbouring Escalan renegades,' he said. 'But they didn't tell us it was you, fishboy.'

Ky varan raised himself on his damaged elbow, his other arm flung out, fingers spread.

'My boy! You're making a dreadful mistake!'

Dep dura climbed to his feet, smiling.

'No, granfer,' he said. 'The mistake is yours. This is the correction.' And he shot Ky varan in the head.

'*Father!*'

Bi tok threw himself on the body of the murdered man, then fled back to the shadows as the cumbersome muzzle sought him again.

'I can still see you, kid,' came the voice of Dep dura. 'Traitors I can see in the dark. And I'm looking at one – right – now.'

He fired.

There was a click.

The five chambers of the gun were empty.

Bi tok did not know what had happened. He crouched whimpering on the floor. The pain of shock in his heart was as if he had been shot after all.

Upperman Dep dura stepped through the maze of sun and shade to stand with his back to the door. Leisurely he knelt down there and began to work at the gun.

'I told you I'd get myself one of these, didn't I, kid?' he said conversationally. 'Beautiful thing, isn't she? Trouble is, she does need feeding once in a while.'

Bi tok heard the rattle of the shot falling into place.

'There,' Dep dura went on. 'Only takes a second.'

As the upperman locked the wheel back into the barrel, the

silhouette of a second soldier appeared behind him in the bright doorway.

Dep dura turned and spoke over his shoulder.

'All done here,' he said. 'This last one's mine.'

Then he coughed. His hands went to his throat.

The gun clattered to the floor.

Dep dura toppled over backwards, a slender dagger protruding from his neck. He spouted blood like a dying dolphin.

The soldier stepped into the hut, went down on one knee and jerked the knife free with one hand while reaching for the fallen gun with the other.

Bi tok scrambled in terror to Ky varan's side and seized the dead hand in a fierce grip, as though the minister could still save him. Glaring up in defiance, he was amazed to see that the soldier was a woman.

The woman had an expression of bitter sorrow on her face. Yet she was looking not at any of the six dead bodies in the room, but at the Luscan revolving gun. She wore a threadbare uniform Bi tok did not know, and spoke to him in a language he did not understand.

'You'll be safe with me,' said Jillian Curram.

——13——
New Arrivals

The Escalan boy was quivering half naked by the body of the old man. She couldn't leave him there, whatever was going on. And with him and the unexpected gift of the revolving gun, Jillian Curram reckoned she had about all she could manage. She cleaned out the soldier's ammunition pouch and took the boy outside, intending an early exit, when two more Escalans appeared out of a hut on the far side of the village, heading her way.

Jillian and the boy swerved hastily into a sort of lean-to roofed with palm and housing several large vats of some pungent, frothy mixture. The natives were no doubt planning to eat or drink it at some future stage of its decomposition. For her part, Jillian would be only too happy to leave its vicinity as soon as possible.

She motioned the boy into the space between two vats and, leaning the clumsy gun on the sill, peered cautiously out. She did not believe the two Escalans had seen them, but they were still approaching. Fortunately all the villagers were cowering indoors.

Where were their archers?

She fired a single shot and ducked, massaging her wrist. Karel – or somebody – had improved the thing since the first time she had tried one, but the recoil was still hefty.

Two balls whistled harmlessly through the fronds above her. Not having expected armed resistance, the Escalans were jumpy. She had drawn fire from both of them, as she had hoped; and they were carrying only pistols.

Jillian looked out again. They were kneeling back-to-back to reload. Very disciplined. She emptied the rest of the charge at them and saw them both go down.

She took the twenty seconds to reload, then seized the boy and fled, almost barging into Mollie Tofit who was staggering grimly uphill with two gourds of water.

Jillian brandished the revolving gun exultantly. Mollie was startled to see her with a young Escalan, but too sensible to start asking questions.

'You go on,' she said. 'Beth and I'll put the fire out.'

Jillian glanced back and saw black smoke soiling the clear blue sky. She slapped Mollie encouragingly on the arm and took off.

Hubert, meeting her by the tapang a few minutes later, was considerably less restrained.

'Bloody hell, Jill, we're not taking prisoners!'

'He's not a prisoner,' she said shortly.

'What, then? A recruit?'

'A refugee.'

'Jillian, I don't suppose you've examined his skin? He's only from the other side, you know.'

'Then why was an Escalan going to shoot him? With this.' She held out the revolving gun.

Hubert at least recognised it.

'Does it matter?' he demanded. 'They're all vermin.'

Jillian looked at him. He was tired and dirty. He had lost ten pounds in the last few weeks and his left hand was still bandaged from a previous skirmish. She took pity on him. 'You can carry it,' she said, offering him the gun.

'Great!' enthused Jimothy and Saraa, arriving at that moment. They caressed the captured weapon with something that looked disturbingly like love. 'Ammo?'

Jillian showed them her pocketful.

'We'll need more,' was Saraa's only comment.

Jimothy said, 'Who's your friend?'

'I didn't ask his name,' Jillian admitted.

The boy was staring unhappily into the trees. Jimothy waved to get his attention. 'Jimi,' she said, pointing to herself, and the others: 'Saraa. Jillian. Hube. What's *your* name?'

He seemed to understand. 'Bi tok,' he said quietly.

'What? Pardon?'

'Beetle?'

Jimothy and Saraa fell about laughing.

'Okay, Beetle, what's your excuse?'

'I think she fancied him,' said Hubert, but they ignored him.

'There were a lot of bodies,' said Jillian. 'Old people. They'd been shot. One of them was an old Escalan. The boy seemed to have been looking after him. The soldier with the gun was reloading. What could I do?'

'Odd,' said Jimothy. 'Well, Beetle, what was all that about?'

He stared back at her, uncomprehending but patently unafraid.

'He might know something,' said Jillian feebly.

'He'll have to earn his keep,' said Saraa. 'Like Hube.' She and Jimothy exchanged sly glances.

'I like your earring, Beetle,' said Jimothy. 'It's really sexy, isn't it.'

'Did anyone see Beth and Mollie?' asked Jillian suddenly. 'They were taking care of a fire, but they should have been here by now.'

No one spoke, but they all looked at each other, suddenly sober.

The raid had been typical. They always struck from cover, without warning, ambushing a patrol or defending a settlement, then melted back into the jungle before they could be identified, much less caught. It was possible to stay reasonably safe when your enemy didn't know you were there; nevertheless, they had been lucky. So far.

'We'll wait,' said Jillian. 'Fifteen minutes. Then one of us goes to look.'

They all fell silent, leaning against trees, listening. Over the incessant churning bass of insect life and the chaotic chorus of a thousand birds high up in the canopy, the gibbons were singing their pure, sweet song. From the distance came the imperious squawk of a toucan. A humming-bird went drilling past suddenly, startling Jillian. But there were no human sounds. There seemed to be no place for humans here at all.

She looked around the little gang: Jimothy sitting perfectly still; Hubert too, hunched up with his eyes closed and his arms folded; and Saraa licking her dirty fingers and rubbing someone else's blood off her shin. Beth and Mollie were probably dead,

124

and now she was endangering them all with this boy. Yet they accepted it, even Hubert, whose function was to provide the note of discord that kept them all together. They trusted her. But she didn't know what she was doing.

She certainly didn't know anything about children. He was, what, fifteen, perhaps sixteen. She looked at him sitting beside her, arms around his knees and his curly head bowed. Jillian realised he was crying silently.

What did she know about Escalans? You were supposed to think of them as insects, mindless but for their own communal will, spreading like a plague. In a moment of crisis, she had made the mistake of letting one become human. Well, perhaps it *was* a mistake. It was certainly no way to win a war. The wisest thing would be to slip the knife in now, while he wasn't looking, put him out of his misery. Her hand hesitated at her belt.

Sudden footsteps shook her from her trance. It was Mollie, also in tears, out of breath, her tunic scorched.

'It's Beth,' she gasped.

'Did they get her?'

She shook her head frantically. 'A spider. Bit her. I think she's dying!' she wailed.

Jimothy seized her with an arm about her shoulders, hugging her, letting her cry.

'I'll go,' said Jillian, in fright, animated.

As she moved the boy, sensing her his only sure friend, ran after her, not wanting to be parted from her.

'Mollie, show me where!'

The three of them raced back up the trail that was no trail at all, stumbling through tangles of rattan, bamboo and vines, edging between saplings and large oaks, slipping on the damp rug of dead leaves that covered the mushy earth. Barefoot, the boy tripped over a root; Jillian reached out to steady him, then turned and there was Bethalie, slumped against the tree, her eyes staring wide, her teeth chattering.

'Beth!'

Jillian wanted to scream and back away. She bit her knuckles. The boy looked up at her anxiously. She clutched at him as if he were in danger too.

Bethalie had managed to take off her boot. Jillian forced

125

herself to squat and inspect the swollen ankle with its two tiny punctures. What the hell did you do for spider-bite anyway?

The boy was leaning over her shoulder. He gave a little gasp and swung away to beat hurriedly at the bushes, as if he had lost something.

Jillian and Mollie stared at him.

'What's he doing?'

Jillian shook her head.

Not finding whatever it was he was after, he came up to Mollie with an urgent, excited expression. He held out his hands, pressing his wrists together and wriggling his fingers.

'A spider!' said Jillian.

Mollie looked at him dumbfounded.

He pantomimed searching the bushes again, came back to her enquiringly.

'He wants to know where it is.'

'It ran off,' said Mollie.

'Well, show him where!'

Bewildered, Mollie went a few yards further up the trail and pointed vaguely at a clump of qamat. The boy crawled under it, rummaged around, gave a small cry of triumph, and backed out again quickly, brushing at himself.

'Look, he's got cobweb all over him. What on earth is he doing?'

Impatiently the boy scraped the furry strands together, ran back to where Bethalie was lying and wiped them on her wound. She cried out, the first sound she had made.

'Oh, stop him!' shouted Mollie.

Jillian started forward, but something made her hesitate. Now he was digging in the mouldering leaves, coming up with a pat of thick red loam and smothering Bethalie's ankle in that too. Then he sat back on his heels, smiling at all three of them and patting his patient's hand.

Ten minutes later, Bethalie arrived back at the giant tree with her arms around Mollie and Jillian's shoulders. She was hopping on her good foot and dangling the other wrapped in a bandage of fresh leaves. The trio were preceded by Beetle, happily carrying Bethalie's boot.

'He's just earned his keep, Saraa,' Jillian said.

126

The camp was in a cave high on a bluff in a fork of the river. The approach was extremely difficult, which was why they had chosen it. First they had to scramble down the slippery bank into the gorge, then inch one at a time across the slimy fallen tree that bridged the river, before climbing sixty feet of tangled creeper to the narrow ledge that led to the cave mouth.

For a time they all stayed at home, going out only to gather food, and clustering ineffectively around Bethalie, the first of them to be incapacitated.

Her swelling had gone down at once, but she remained feverish for a couple of days. The boy kept by her in the back of the cave, wiping her sweat and squeezing fruit for her to drink. He was plainly capable, and happy to have something to do. Hubert kept an eye on him, but never mentioned him without an unpleasantry. Mollie too was having trouble accepting the idea of a nice Escalan. But there was no way to reduce him to a prisoner after he had saved Bethalie's life.

While she recuperated Beth formed a firm friendship with him. Immobile still, she talked quietly with him for hours, repeating everything again and again until he understood. 'He's a quick learner,' she said, with unconscious pride. Although she never once compared him to Jek, Jillian was sure the Escalan boy was replacing the son she had lost.

One afternoon, struggling back from a fishing expedition, Jillian was met on the ledge by a gravely smiling Beetle, who said carefully, 'Good afternoon, Jillian, have you caught fish?'

'Well, yes I have, Beetle,' said Jillian with delight. 'So many I have had to leave some across on the other side of the river.' She spoke slowly and distinctly, pointing. 'Would you like to help me fetch them?'

Beetle looked at her, concentrating for a moment until he had worked out her meaning, then said simply, 'Yes,' and led the way back down. Bethalie, hobbling to the edge on a crutch, stood shading her eyes and watching him every cautious step of the way there and back with the nets of tiny carp, already beginning to dull as the fierce sun dried their scales.

After that, though Saraa and Jimothy still teased the young Escalan, it was not with much malice. Only Hubert kept his distance, talking sarcastically about the boy in his presence, using words he could not possibly know. 'The little nurse is becoming a formidable linguist,' he grinned.

'More than you know, Captain,' said Bethalie. 'He can talk jungletalk too.' She nudged the boy's foot with her stick. 'Go on, Beetle: say what you said to me today.'

All eyes upon him, the boy looked away self-consciously. Rapidly he said, *Deëko-deëko u aängi einu ngaä-tat.*'

Jimothy and Saraa spluttered with laughter and began bleating at each other. Ignoring them, Jillian said, 'What does it mean, Beetle?'

'It means,' he said carefully, 'At the proper hour the thin ox will kick.'

'And what does *that* mean?'

'I don't know, Saraa.'

Hubert raised his eyebrows. 'Hidden talents, my, my.'

'Only from those who keep their eyes closed!'

Now they all looked at Jillian. It was the first time she had actually shouted at Hubert since the night he tried to climb into her hammock.

Instantly calm, she asked the boy, 'Where did you learn that?'

'My master had a – '

Stalled, he looked to Bethalie, holding his hands out palm up, side by side, and opening and closing them.

'A book.'

'Book, yes. And in the village, Bua-turaa, he said that too, *Deëko-deëko u aängi – *'

But Jimothy and Saraa were laughing again.

'Shut up,' said Jillian. 'Beetle, do you know more?'

'Oh yes,' he said, and began reciting words and phrases of Belanesi at random, translating what he could. When they had trouble repeating them, he said, 'Wait. I write,' and went and got the Gunners' Manual whose margins provided their only stock of blank paper. Here he wrote the characters in a precise, graceful hand, and told them how each was sounded. Looking through them later, Jillian turned back a page and found neat little drawings he had made of everyone when no one was looking, while he sat by Bethalie's bed. His tiny study of her own face occupied her for a time.

Next day Jillian asked him to go with her to the village on the rock. Perhaps with an interpreter, even an inexpert one, they could at last start to talk sensibly to the Belanesi. Beetle seemed willing enough to go, but perhaps he had misunderstood her purpose, for when they reached the hills and, through a gap in the vegetation, saw the rock for the first time, Jillian realised that the boy was in the grip of a silent sorrow.

'Beetle, whatever is it? What's wrong?'

He did not answer. She put her arm around his shoulders and he looked at her with tears in his soft green eyes.

'I am sorry, Jillian,' he murmured at last. 'It is hard for me.'

Suddenly she understood. 'The old man.'

'Yes. Ky varan.'

'Your master.' She felt desperately guilty. 'I should have thought . . .'

'Also – he was my father.'

'Your father!'

Jillian was aghast, mystified, but could see that this was emotional quicksand. She thought of her own lost father, could not even recall his face. 'I didn't know,' she apologised.

The boy smiled sadly. 'Nor did he,' he said.

He did not say more, and she did not press him.

They left the hills and went back to the river. It had been raining, and in a bend where the bank had fallen in, a small pool had formed.

'Look, Beetle. Shall we stop and swim? Would you like that?'

'Yes,' he said and, kicking off his homemade sandals, slipped into the light brown water just as he was, in his tattered loincloth.

Jillian envied him his simplicity and directness. She took off the belt that held her gun and her knives, unhooked her boots and unwrapped her leggings. She stepped out of her breeches, which she had cut down to shorts, and pulled over her head the battledress tunic that had long since lost its arms. After that it was a relief to untie the halter that protected her breasts and plunge naked into the tepid water.

'Oh, this is marvellous!' She swam towards Beetle, who had been studiously looking the other way.

'Hello!' he cried. He pretended he had been waiting a long time and was surprised to see her. 'If you had clothes like me, much more comfortable, I think,' he said; then, apprehending from her outraged laughter that he had expressed himself amiss, blushed hotly and swam quickly away into the mainstream.

Darting in pursuit, Jillian dived and made a playful grab at his loincloth, as though to pull it off; and felt him beneath it, firm and full. She drew back, laughing to cover her shock. What am I doing? she asked herself. In that instant she knew what she had been ignoring since she had rescued him: that at sixteen, he was no child.

Should she stop and apologise, or swim away again carelessly as though nothing had happened? What if he had mistaken her foolishness for flirtation? 'Beetle –' she said – that idiotic name. But he was not attending to her. He was staring downriver, frowning. She floated to his side.

Then she heard it. Men's voices, drifting to them on the water. In the distance, through the foliage, a boat appeared: Escalans, without a doubt. They were singing. And to judge from Beetle's look of dismay, it was a song he knew and did not wish to hear.

Keeping her head low Jillian swam some yards downstream to peer cautiously through a clump of sweetrushes. There was activity on the river-bank, and square shapes, huts or tents, in a clearing surrounded by ungainly, blue-leafed trees. She swam quickly back again, and found Beetle on the bank, guarding her clothes. He had pulled them under cover of a bush; the gunbelt was uppermost, near his hand. She squatted beside him, squeezing water out of her hair, heedless now that she was naked.

'A new camp,' she said. 'Another advance.'

'Yes.' He rubbed his shoulder. 'They guard against the Belanesi.'

'I think you have the wrong word,' said Jillian. '"Guard" means defend. The Escalans attack the Belanesi.'

He did not accept this. 'Belanesi attack my people. For no reason.'

'No reason!' Suddenly she was very angry with him. 'Beetle, it was Belanesi who saved your life. You: one of the people taking their land.' She pointed to the river. 'That camp has just taken a piece more.'

The boy looked upset. 'We are not taking. We will share with the Belanesi. We will help them. We will not harm them.'

'Tell that to the dead people on that rock,' said Jillian. She regretted it instantly; but she was too enraged to apologise. 'Beetle, you were in that hut when the Escalan soldier shot four old and unarmed natives. Then he shot your father. If I hadn't rescued you, he would have shot you. How can you talk such nonsense?'

The boy bit his lip. After a moment he said, with an effort, 'It was not as you think. That man, the man you killed, he did not like us. He made a mistake.'

She gazed at him, obviously disbelieving his attitude, but he would not explain. Instead he said, 'Killing is bad. The soldiers are wrong, I think. We should talk to the natives.'

'You should go away and give them back their country. And *you* should go away and let me dress.'

Unabashed, he said, 'I shall watch the river.'

When she rejoined him, he said, 'Jillian, it is so. The Belanesi need the Escalans. They are the goats, we are the goatherds.'

'You sound like a missionary.'

But he did not know the word, and she, disgusted with him and with herself, would not explain.

—14—
The
Peaceable Land

Jillian led Beetle back along the river. When huge boulders blocked the way or pools were too deep to ford, they had to detour into the forest. The sunlight hit the stream in patches, making moss and rock look like burnished felt. The vegetation was extremely wet and spectacularly lush just here, with purple growths like giant aubergines; orange and pink and violet flowers; and fungus, tan and frothy, that clung in enormous swathes to trees along the bank.

Snails inched across leaves, brown snakes with turquoise heads slept on stumps, and broad-winged butterflies flapped in and out of the shade. A large frog hopped straight past the boy's ear, making him cry out and almost lose his footing. Jillian laughed.

She made him go in front of her across the creeper bridge. He looked down once, forty feet on to rocks and wild water, and after that gazed determinedly and rather apprehensively straight ahead. When they came to the fork a couple of miles further on, she found the rising river had swept their own rotting log bridge away.

Saraa and Bethalie were watching from the cave as Jimothy dangled up among the vines, fifteen feet out on a branch with no hope of getting any further. Hubert sat on the near bank, shouting instructions.

'Bloody hell,' he said. 'Hello, you two. Been for a nice little walk?' He smirked.

'Hubert, are you on watch?'

'No, Jill, Mollie is,' he said, 'as usual,' and laughed nastily. 'Why?'

'The Escalans are on the river, about three-quarters of a mile past the bridge.'

'Good news.' He cupped his hands and shouted: 'Bring the cannon with you, Jimi!' Then he said to Jillian, 'Meanwhile, what about all this, eh?'

High above there was a scream and Jimothy came crashing from the tree. She clutched and caught at a skein of vines, some of which broke. She hung spinning for a time, with foliage raining down around her, then began to swing, whether on purpose or by accident Jillian could not tell. Back and forth Jimothy swung across the water, shrieking gaily.

The river was deep but not fast. She dropped, eventually, and was carried downstream a way before managing to swim awkwardly towards the bank. Jillian climbed down and swam out to help her. Hubert handed them his oelegen flask.

Jimothy was shocked and exhausted, but was soon laughing. 'I can't believe I did that,' she said, over and over again. When Mollie came back out of the forest, she didn't believe it either. The two started bickering until Jillian took them all to look for a suitable fallen tree. They found one and managed to drop it into the gorge. After quite an effort they succeeded in lifting it again to fall roots-first against the foot of the bluff, where Saraa and Bethalie jammed it with rope and a rock.

Suddenly the crown of the tree, which everyone had thought perfectly secure, rolled out of its lodgment and fell into the river. Held by its roots on the far side, it started to swing round in the current and was immediately in deep water out of reach.

With the yell of a demon, Saraa leapt on to the trunk with a rope in her hand. She fell over directly and almost off, but steadied herself on all fours and scrambled up to the other end, where she tied the rope to a branch. All the while the current carried her slowly back away from them. Jimothy whistled and clapped as Saraa dived heavily into the river with the rope over her shoulder. They helped her haul in the tree and wedge it properly this time.

The next day Bethalie, Jimothy, Saraa and Mollie went to look at the Escalan camp. Hubert had been already, alone, at dawn. They took Beetle with them, but he was little help. He had never seen an army camp before, though he did recognise a number of faces from the *Fighting Ray*.

'I thought you came in an airbag, Beetle.'

'Not all the way, Mollie,' said Beth, protectively.

Men carried large boxes from place to place and marched in circles. One group sat sharpening swords. The only things Beetle could overhear were orders, routine abuse and, once, a song.

'What are they singing, Beetle?'

'It is a song they sing when they work, Bethalie. It means nothing.'

'Yeah, but what's it about?' Saraa wanted to know.

Jimothy put her hand on his knee. 'Aren't you going to tell us?'

'They sing about women of Belanesi. They sing the women – make sex – with animals.' He shook his head. 'It is a stupid, wrong song.'

'Typical,' sniffed Mollie.

But Saraa said, 'Tell us the *words*, Beetle.'

'Teach us the song,' said Jimothy.

Embarrassed at first, but then beginning guiltily to smile, he complied. By the time they got back to the creeper bridge, they were all singing lustily through the catalogue of improbable sexual congress attributed to Belanesi women by Escalan men.

'Hey, Beetle, what's Escalan for "insects"?'

'Shut up, Jimi,' said Mollie. 'In fact, you'd all better shut up. You don't want to let Jillian hear you singing that.'

'She wouldn't mind,' said Saraa.

'She would,' said Bethalie.

'She would,' said Jimothy. 'She's a prude.'

'Oh she isn't!' said Mollie, whose admiration for their former lieutenant was large.

'No, it's not that she's a prude,' said Bethalie. 'But she would say we were insulting the jungle people.'

'Oh, it's only a bit of fun.'

An inky-blue gecko skittered up a sish tree. Herons quartered the river. The day was growing hot, and hazy.

'Here, Beetle,' said Jimothy. 'Is Jillian a prude or not?'

'What she means is,' said Saraa slowly, 'what's she like in bed?'

'Don't, Sar,' said Bethalie. 'You mustn't talk to him like that.'

'He doesn't know,' said Mollie, patronisingly.

'Doesn't he?'

'Of course he doesn't.'

'Oh. Well, Beetle,' said Saraa. 'When you find out, will you tell me please?' She gave a low gurgle of laughter.

'All right,' said Beetle, innocently.

'Oh, Beetle!' cried Bethalie; and they all laughed.

That afternoon, while Bethalie was doing some laundry, Beetle began to build a raft, in case anyone was ever stranded again. It could be kept in the lower cave, with the cannon.

Among their rather haphazard supplies they had, in fact, a small bag of nails. Precious as they were, Jillian would unhesitatingly have offered them, but the boy's design used only logs, sticks and creeper. She found that characteristically Escalan. She thought of Escaly as built entirely of wood. They were conquering the world with weapons stolen from their victims. They had stolen Karel Jessup's revolving gun when they stole Luscany. And they did it with such assumed moral superiority. Beetle was not free of that either; yet in him it was oddly touching, even attractive. And he had curly hair, like the smith's.

'Is that the work you would have done in New Bright Rock, Beetle,' she asked him, 'making rafts?'

'Not rafts,' he told her, 'buildings – or pictures for make buildings. And pictures to send home, to show Belanesi. And readings for all Escalan people who come, for them to know what must.'

Bethalie's cards, which she still had with her, fascinated the young Escalan. He had learned all their names from her, shuffling them and dealing them out in mnemonics she could rarely follow. 'Oak-Apples,' he would mutter: 'Hubert's moustache-comb,' or, chuckling throatily, 'The Brown Seahorse: Mollie lights fire under an empty pot!'

Left alone, he quickly finished the raft, caulked it with mud then dragged it up the bank to dry. The day was overcast and sultry. He climbed up to the cave, but Bethalie was asleep and all the rest out. He wondered what to do next. Jillian's clean shirt, spread white and damp upon the ledge, was like a prepared canvas. It gave him an idea.

With the paints he had mixed up from tree-gum, red earth and crushed berries, and the sticks whose ends he had chewed to make brushes, he began a picture on Jillian's shirt. The clumsiness of the media precluded any technique but the crudest, yet he was content. There was something about these blobs and streaks of flat, muddy colour that seemed just right for depicting the primitive jungle. A harmony of means and purpose, he told himself.

He painted splashy green foliage and tall brown trees. In the branches he put a monkey and a killing bird, and hanging down, a blue snake and a black and yellow spider, and lots of fruit. The animals did not seem unhappy with each other's company. Below, he painted a spindly tragelaph and a great pard lying side by side. In the background orange people smoking pipes held out huge coins, one each, to other people who had big yellow smiles, fuzzy grey legs and black hooves.

'Very pretty.' Bethalie looked over his shoulder. 'But I don't know as Jillian will think so. Did you have to use her shirt?'

'We have not paper.'

'Hmph.' Bethalie held out her hand. 'Coming for my "patrol"?'

Bethalie's foot had healed completely, and now she was exercising it strenuously: along the ledge, down the vines, across the log, up the bank, then a short stroll in the forest, where they sat under a kapok tree. Large pink butterflies skittered in the still air. Overhead a flying squirrel soared, landed on all fours on its chosen tree, and scurried off headfirst down the trunk. Small, anonymous-looking birds moved assiduously across the forest floor.

Suddenly, without so much as the crack of a twig by way of warning, a jungleman sprang from the trees. The birds scattered, chittering with alarm.

He squatted five feet in front of them, his nostrils flaring. Bethalie stifled a shriek. He scratched his flank slowly with a long, supple hand.

The Belanesi was unarmed. It was impossible to tell what he intended.

'*The-best of the day to-you*,' said Beetle.

The native had a rich, golden coat, unlike any he had seen so

136

far. His hair curled thickly from nape to hoof. He panted, drooling slightly, but did not speak.

'*What do-you-want?*'

Bethalie had no gun, but she had a knife. It was in her hand.

'Ask him what he wants,' she said, her voice low.

'I have,' said the boy.

'Ask him again!'

He repeated the phrase, his intonation just as before.

The man came forward, stepping high. His eyes flickered with what could have been unease. The smell of him stung their nostrils.

'*We-are your-friends,*' said Beetle clearly. He could see ticks hopping in the man's fleece. 'I have told him we are friends to him,' he explained.

'Do you know him?'

The boy shook his head.

'Draw your knife,' she said.

At first he did not understand. 'Draw?' he repeated, and then, understanding, 'Oh. No. Wait. *What-is your-name?*'

Were there, he wondered, wild junglemen that had no names, no power of speech?

Without a reply, he went on. '*I-will-not harm-you. She-will-not harm-you. Speak with-us.*'

Then the Belanesi laughed. '*Kei-eën rik-dikkito.*'

'What's he say?'

'Spider weather,' the boy translated.

'He knows who you are!'

'Perhaps. *I-am Bi tok, she-is-named Bethalie.*'

He made such a bleat of her name she gave him a sharp look. But the Belanesi was ignoring him still. He said something else, something that made Beetle look up, as if he had forgotten he could not see the sky for the trees. Unmistakably, the man beckoned. They followed him.

'Where are we going?'

'I don't know. All he said was, Next the rain. Three days rain, he said.'

The native pranced along, rarely looking back, until they came to the river. Then he stopped and spoke again, waving at the blue trees that grew all along the river-bank. As they looked

137

to see, he spoke a fourth time; and when they looked back, he had disappeared.

'Where's he gone?'

'I don't know, Bethalie.'

'Are we supposed to follow?'

'No.'

The boy was looking carefully at the trees.

'Well then?'

'He said, Three days rain, the flowers fall. I think those flowers.' They were large, darker blue than the leaves, with a fat trumpet of pale yellow. 'Then he said goodbye.'

'What did he want?'

'Perhaps to warn about the rain.'

'And the flowers?'

'I don't know, Beth.'

Back at the cave, Jillian was sitting on the ledge. She had her shirt on her knees and she was looking at it. Before she could speak, Bethalie said, 'We met a jungleman.'

'When?'

'Just now.'

'From which village?'

They shook their heads.

Jillian looked at Beetle. Her eyes were hard. 'Did you speak with him?'

'He did not answer. But he said it will rain three days.'

'When? Tomorrow? Today?'

'I don't know, Jillian.'

'You don't know much about the Belanesi, do you, Beetle?' She crumpled the shirt in her fist, cracking the rough paint. 'You spent months learning their language. They rescued you in the jungle and you lived in their village for two days. You made friends with their chief and you feasted with them, but you don't know much about them.' Her mouth twitched.

The boy watched her master her irritation.

She sighed. 'Perhaps it's yourself you don't know much about.' She spread the shirt on her lap, and pointed to his painting. 'What do you call this?'

'"The Peaceable Land",' he said.

She reached behind her and picked up the revolving gun. 'And what do you call this?'

'Gun,' he said.

She lay the gun across her thighs, next to his picture. 'I don't see this in here.'

'It is my picture,' he said. She waited. 'It is not my gun,' he said. 'I did not bring here.'

'Nor did I, Beetle, though it probably belongs to me more than anyone else. Your people brought it. The Escalans. They tried to kill you with it. I can understand you hate it. But you cannot pretend it does not exist.'

'Some of my people have guns,' he said urgently. 'I have not gun. If I could, they have not guns too. I cannot, Jillian!'

She shook her head.

He went on. 'If I and father arrived at New Bright Rock –'

'You would have changed things.'

'Yes!'

'With your architectural drawings, and your fortune telling, and your paintings of "The Peaceable Land" to attract more colonists, you would have changed things.' Her voice was bitter. She jabbed at the picture again. 'What's this your orangers are giving the Belanesi? Poison?'

There was a pause.

'I'm sorry about the shirt, ma'am,' said Bethalie. 'I fell asleep while it was drying.'

They both ignored her.

'Come and sit down,' said Jillian to the boy. He sat beside her. Bethalie gratefully drifted away.

Coloured birds, maal and duraquara, darted in and out among the vines. Huge faint clouds swirled in the sky, the exhalations of the jungle.

'I wish *I* understood the Belanesi,' said Jillian. 'I wish I could make them see the danger. They do not believe anyone could want to hurt them. They have no idea of war at all. You've seen those hunting bows they carry. Lethal things. Where were they when your soldiers attacked?'

They stared at each other.

'All the Belanesi seem to do,' Jillian concluded, 'is eat and drink. They're happy. Why don't you all leave them alone?'

'They need us,' he said. 'To help and guide them.'

'They do not need you,' she said. 'But all the while you are here, they need us, and this.' She patted the gun.

139

'Guns need more guns,' he replied. 'Is that your symmetry? The killing is wrong. I swear it! But it is not for you to kill my people who kill Belanesi. Your people are not my people. Your people are not Belanesi. You – do not – belong here.'

It was the strongest repudiation he could have phrased.

Evidently she did not realise this, and merely said, 'If we hadn't been here, Beetle, you would have been dead.'

'It might be better,' he answered, sullenly.

This was so ludicrous, so adolescent, it made Jillian laugh, though not unkindly.

'Cheer up, Beetle, you'll sort it out yet. Why don't you go and get us both some melon? And here – you can keep the shirt.'

He took it from her without a word and walked away, not into the cave but back along the ledge.

'Beetle?'

'My name is Bi *tok*!'

Eventually she saw him below, crossing the log and climbing up into the forest. She supposed that he had gone to cut a fresh melon, but he did not return, then or for supper. Jillian went to bed and fell asleep. She had dissuaded Bethalie from searching for him in the dark. If he wished to be childish, he must take the consequences.

The boy sat in the forest as the sun went down and the creatures of the night arose. It grew chilly. He put on the shirt.

Eventually he got to his feet. He followed the sound of the river and found the log. Stars bobbed beneath him on the dark water.

He skirted the vines and made for the lower cave. There he reclaimed the little raft with its unfinished paddle. He looked at the shadowy bulk of the cannon and wished he could take it and drop it in the deepest part of the river. Then he turned, and cast himself adrift among the wavering stars.

——15——
At Right Fist Camp

Bi tok paddled down to the fork of the river and let the current take him into the mainstream. He lay prone on the raft and watched the shaggy silhouettes of overhanging trees glide slowly and smoothly across the polished sky. The murmurous insects calmed him, and he slept.

When he woke, a hornbill was yelling, and everything was blue. All motion had ceased. Rubbing his eyes and peering around through the mist, he discovered himself aground on a great bend of the river, and surrounded by sweetrushes. By the time he had shoved himself free, the sun was chasing off the last of the vapour, and the water was glittering.

He knelt on the raft in his shirt with the tableau of peace across the back. He paddled with firm strokes to one side and then the other, just as Gen thiri had taught him at the Escalan Imperial and Illustrious College of Geometry. And he began to chant, self-consciously at first, then more boldly, in time to the paddle, the long-neglected formulæ for a traveller greeting sunrise in a foreign land. A troop of monkeys hooted furiously at him as he passed.

The river widened. Bi tok was uncomfortably aware that some of the long, gnarled shapes he saw floating were not logs. Then, far ahead, he caught sight of the liana bridge, and remembered the rocky stretch it spanned. He began to be grateful he had run foul of the rushes. This terrain he preferred to navigate in daylight, and awake. There was nothing on the bridge but an old crow-pheasant as Bi tok swept under it.

His raft was well built, and sturdy. Bi tok was pleased with it, unlike the one he had been obliged to build at College. That had behaved perfectly until the elderly Colonial Tutor climbed on to it. Then it sank directly, bearing the reverend gentleman, in full robe and dignified posture, swiftly beneath the surface.

Bi tok thought of Jillian, and Bethalie. He wondered if they had noticed him missing yet, and if so, who had been first. They would not look for him long, he supposed, with a sad pride. ('Let the little perisher drown,' Hubert would advise.)

Bethalie, he thought, was a good woman. She deserved better than this half-life of wariness and violence. He wondered what their home was like, that featureless netherland beyond even the north-west frontier. Jillian, Jillian seemed to be happy here, in her predatory habitat. Yet he could not think of her without a strange, hollow feeling. If ever he met a woman of his own age like Jillian Curram, he would not so quickly be parted from her, for all her impatient spirit.

The raft swung around in the stream and floated into a pool, where it lingered awhile surrounded by spiky bushes and blue trees. Then the boy paddled on. The day had grown very still, and very hot. He blinked sweat from his eyelashes and took off his shirt.

He wondered how advanced the morning was. He knew he should be hungry, but instead felt a tremulous unease. The sun no longer seemed to be shining quite so brightly. The air seemed to thicken about his head.

All the animals of the jungle roared at once.

The treetops began to pitch and sway. The bushes rustled. Abruptly the sun went out, and everything fell horribly still.

He heard the rain begin, like a million tiny drummers in the distance. Then blue light sliced the forest in two about his head, and the wind flicked at the raft and pushed him into the water. With a crash of leaves, the whole jungle leaned over one way. The air was full of dust. Great trees threshed with tension. And another river fell whole out of the sky and landed on Bi tok.

Just before he drowned, the wind dropped as abruptly as it had risen, and the rain resolved itself into a monstrous downpour. Vicious blue flashes continued to dazzle him, and thunder, crackling as it broke.

He dived to get out of the rain and at once saw his raft floating above him some yards away.

His first impulse was to reach it; then he remembered a

142

lesson: It is better to be wholly in the water than coming out of it, when lightning strikes. So he stayed as he was, floating after the raft when it spun away, letting the rain fall on his head, and wondering how long he could endure.

At last the storm seemed to have moved off a little, or Bi tok convinced himself that it had, though the rain did not actually ease. His raft drifted towards him, and he collapsed on it, exhausted.

The raft had suffered. A log had broken, a creeper sprung, and there was not a trace of mud left along the seams. He had lost his paddle, his clothes and one of his sandals. He had no idea how much further there was to go. He lay on the raft and floated in the rain, careless of crocodiles.

He thought, This must be the first day.

Because of the poor visibility, the raft was almost on top of Lighterman No kiu before he spotted it, so he pulled it in himself and then sent someone to tell the watch. He knew he would be reprimanded for this breach of procedure, but not as severely as for reporting the raft in person, then failing to apprehend it. That was the army for you. Reporting a raft which turned out to be a harmless clump of flotsam would not win him any commendations either.

Nor was it a harmless clump of flotsam, though gradually becoming one in the battering rain. Word went quickly round the camp that a boy had been found, floating down the river with nothing on him but a single sandal and an earring. Those who had been there longest told wild stories of the northern women who lived all alone in a cave, with no men, but with an Escalan boy as their slave. Newcomers remembered the boy on the *Fighting Ray*, the minister's solemn little catamite, and winked at each other.

Dressed in a plain uniform shift, Bi tok sat near the edge of the clearing, in a bamboo hut. He was under armed guard. His stomach was growling. The rain had stopped as suddenly as it had started, and he could hear the eager screeching of the forest creatures as they snapped up what it had flushed out. Then the door opened, admitting watery sunlight and a Secretarial Minister, hitching up the skirts of his gown above the wet grass.

143

The boy rose and performed the correct obeisance. The secretary fished a pair of eyeglasses from his satchel and made a note in his book.

'Your name is Bi tok?'

'Yes, minister.'

'You were formerly ensigned to the renegade envoy Geometer Ky varan?'

'I was his ensign. But he was not a renegade.'

The secretary lifted an eyebrow. 'Do you deny that upon arrival in Belanesi you and he concealed yourselves in a village of the enemy?'

'Our transport crashed,' said Bi tok. 'We were injured, my master very badly. The jungle people rescued us and took care of us.'

He pushed up his sleeve and showed the secretary the long pink scar on his shoulder.

The man glanced at it, but said only, 'What transport was this?'

'The balloon of the Imperial Estafette, Jo kani.'

The secretary paused in his writing. He regarded Bi tok as though revising his estimate of the magnitude of mischief involved in his mysterious reappearance.

'Do you know the whereabouts of the missing estafette?'

'He was killed when the balloon fell.'

Bi tok's interrogator looked annoyed, and suspicious. 'This is altogether irregular. How did you and your master come to be in the balloon?'

'We travelled with the estafette by sea from Escaly. At Pointing In he invited us to ride with him to New Bright Rock.'

'And then you crashed, you say. Can you be more specific?'

'The estafette was not wholly familiar with the operation of the balloon. Natives shot us down.'

'Killing the estafette.'

'Yes.'

'And you and your master then took shelter with these same natives.'

'Yes, minister.'

The secretary put down his pen and folded his hands on his knee. He looked at Bi tok sternly but with pity.

'I must urge you to think most carefully about your testimony, boy. Was it the case that you and your master Ky varan were held prisoner by the Belanesi?'

'Oh no, minister,' said Bi tok, concerned. 'We would have left for New Bright Rock as soon as my master was well enough to travel.'

'How would you describe your stay in the village of the enemy?'

'They were kind to us,' said Bi tok. He thought of what Jillian had told him the previous evening. 'They are a peaceful people. We should study them more, and learn to live harmoniously with them. Then they would not be our enemies.'

'All who oppose the progress of the Empire are our enemies, Bi tok,' said the man patiently. 'Some no doubt may attempt to disguise their hostility.'

This reasoning escaped Bi tok. 'Why should they do that?'

'To influence the unwary,' replied the secretary promptly. 'Did you perhaps see it as your duty, amid all this peace and kindness, to teach them of the Emperor and his bountiful goodwill?'

'There was scarcely time, minister. My first duty was to nurse my master, and we were in the village less than two full days before the army arrived and he – died.'

'Ah yes.' The minister nodded, showing little sympathy. 'And what happened to you then?'

'I was taken by a party of Brylanders to their camp in the jungle.'

'Are you aware, Bi tok, that these barbarians also impede us in our progress?'

'Yes, minister.'

'The enemies of our Emperor seem to be making strenuous efforts to protect you,' observed his interrogator.

Bi tok did not reply.

'So, boy: do you now see it as your duty to lead us to this camp of Brylanders so that we may destroy these enemies of our Emperor?'

Bi tok had known this was coming; and that he would be unable to answer.

'Must I record your silence as a refusal?'

Bi tok stared dumbly at the ground.

'Very well.'

The Secretarial Minister wrote quickly and decisively for a while, then rose and opened the door. Bi tok thought he was about to leave and began to make his valediction; but the minister said, 'Come in, upperman.'

In walked Dep dura.

Bi tok gasped and shrank away.

The apparition's head was bowed, its neck deeply scarred and puckered.

'I believe you know Upperman Dep dura, Bi tok,' said the minister mildly.

Dep dura's voice gurgled harshly in his ruined throat.

'I'm a ghost, fishboy. Come back to haunt you.'

Bi tok sat trembling, his hands crossed on his chest.

'Upperman,' said the interrogator smoothly, 'would you please identify the prisoner and tell me where you met him first?'

'His name's Bi tok, minister. He shipped with us on the *Fighting Ray*, along with his master, an old Geometer.'

'And how would you describe their conduct on the voyage?'

'They spent all their time learning junglie language, minister. And they tried to make us learn it and all.'

'Did this strike you as an appropriate subject of study for a Senior Minister of the Escalan Empire, upperman?'

'No, minister. I reckoned then they were traitors. We all did.'

'It's not true!' cried Bi tok.

They ignored him.

'There was some talk that the old man, what's-his-name, was sent out against his will,' Dep dura continued, hoarser than ever, but happy to go on like this all day. 'I reckoned he was out to do the dirty.'

'Where did you see Ky varan and Bi tok next, upperman?'

'I was ordered to take a squad and discipline a village where there was Escalan renegades hiding, minister,' he said. 'It was them.'

'And what, in your opinion, were they doing there?'

'Telling military secrets to the junglies, minister, and helping them plot against us. I lost five men on that job,' said Dep dura.

Bi tok shook his head slowly from side to side.

'What action did you take, upperman?' asked the minister.

'I executed the old man, and I'd have had him too,' Dep dura croaked, pointing at Bi tok, 'but a northerner bitch came for him. She put her knife in me, and if she hadn't been mean enough to want it back – ' he leered sideways at Bi tok, ' – then I would have been a ghost, wouldn't I?'

'Thank you, upperman,' said the Secretarial Minister quietly. 'Now please fetch the commander.'

Dep dura left. The minister sat tidily finishing his notes. From the trees, birds called.

'What will happen to me?' asked the boy desolately.

The minister looked up. 'They'll flog you for the whereabouts of the cave. Then I dare say you'll be shot.'

'I am innocent.'

'You are contaminated,' said the minister emphatically. He sought some way to mitigate it. 'If you were not so innocent, you would know that.'

He signed his name with brusque slashes of the pen.

Upperman Dep dura returned, followed by Commander Kien orau, who looked at Bi tok as if he were a specimen of something unpleasant.

'That's the one, isn't it?' he said. 'Devilish how they turn on you, these metaphysicians.' He spat, and wiped his mouth with a kerchief. 'Shoot him,' he said, and turned to go.

The secretary proffered his notes.

'Keep them,' said Kien orau. 'Write them up. Do whatever you do with them.'

The strangled voice of Dep dura arrested their attention.

'Commander, permission to make a suggestion.'

'What is it, upperman?'

'Well, commander, it was through him we lost five men and one of the Luscan guns. Why don't we save him up and use him for target practice when this new consignment arrives?'

'What?' The commander looked at Bi tok speculatively. 'Oh, I don't think our friend here will need more than one bullet, upperman. But you have an idea there. The ship's in, apparently,' he added, 'lying to until this filthy weather dies down.'

'Another two days at least, commander, so I'm told,' put in the Secretarial Minister.

'Hold him till they get here, whenever. Make a bit of a show of it. That'll cheer the men up a bit. And it'll show the gun merchant what happens to people who think of cheating us. Just in case.'

'Surely though, commander,' said the Secretarial Minister, 'two days – well, surely you'll examine him first?'

Kien orau looked blankly at him.

'He knows the barbarian women's hideout.'

'Will he tell us?'

'Not willingly.'

The commander grimaced, sucking air through his teeth.

'I do hate torture, secretary. Such a vile practice. Give me the quick clean kill every time. The boy will die. The women may be wild, but they're only women. They won't elude us long. Satisfy yourself.'

The three men left the hut and walked out into the sunlight. Everything was steaming.

An orderly brought food to Bi tok, but he could not eat much of it. He sat in the hut, shivering.

Prisoners with death sentences were excused parade. Bi tok sat alone all night, sleeping fitfully. In a lucid interval he wondered why he did not walk out of the door and let the man on guard kill him. He was giving his consent to an absurd conspiracy for his own delayed execution. Yet he did not move. He was paralysed. He dreamed Ky varan and he were digging for potatoes in Kam fen's vegetable garden. Large birds of midnight blue sat on the pergola, cawing restively. They spoke in the voices of girls, praising his 'bone structure'. He was a child again, and ran for his mother, but could not reach the door handle. Through the lattice she mouthed at him, urgently.

The gong sounded, and it was morning. Breakfast was brought to him, meagre enough, and he wondered why he should still eat; but the rations were familiar. The dried fruits of his childhood were delicious to him again, and he wept, without hope.

Before long the trembling, nervous sensation of the previous morning began to steal over him again. He sweated, and felt a lull settle on the jungle. And then the roaring came. It was not, he now realised, the roar of animals, but a great rupture of the air. It sounded like a gigantic stone ball, studded with iron, being rolled down an incline from heaven.

At last it was done, and an uncanny silence fell once more. It grew dark. He heard the guard cough, and swear. A stray draught stirred Bi tok's curls. Next moment the wind was bashing at the bamboo walls, raking the earth up into his eyes. He felt the shock of pressure on his chest.

A strange inversion sucked Bi tok off his feet. He hit a corner of the roof, and felt it give. He grabbed at the slats, but failed to gain any purchase. Then he was soaking wet all over, he was on the ground and the ground was awash. Sheets of water were pouring in between the canes. Through the gap at the bottom of the door, Bi tok could not see the boots of his gaoler, only wildly splashing water. He thought the man must have run for shelter.

The gaoler, however, was still out in the open. He was lying face down in the mud some yards away. Jillian Curram had hit him on the back of the neck with a club. Now she tore open the door of the cell hut and leaned in.

Rain cascaded about her. She yelled at him. *'WHY AM I ALWAYS SAVING YOUR LIFE?'*

Bi tok could not hear her. He flung his arms about her neck.

In the rain she could not see his tears, or anything at all, much. But someone saw them as they fled down the track to the river, and three shots were fired. They ran on into the storm. At every instant Bi tok felt his back snapped by a bolt of hot iron.

Jillian hacked her way into the bushes. Beyond, the river foamed.

He followed her into the water, clasped her hand: 'Jillian. Wait.'

'What?'

'The raft.'

'Where?'

He pointed vaguely upstream.

'We search.'

Everything was green, dank, buzzing. Lightning webbed the smoky distance. Anywhere there might be danger. She shook her head.

Bi tok insisted on going alone, prowling through the water-plants. He knew he would not be seen. Evidently Jillian Curram overestimated the vigilance of the Escalan army. By the time he found the raft, however, he was almost too exhausted and rain-battered to bring it to her; but he managed.

It was sagging somewhat. His knotwork was sound as ever,

but the vines had been too fresh. They had absorbed water and slipped.

Jillian climbed aboard, squatting uncomfortably with one knee up. She gave him a look of amusement, almost admiration.

'Paddles,' she said.

'No.'

A momentary tightening of the lips.

'Stay here.'

He clung on to the branches, the raft bucking under him in the wild water.

Soon he heard more shots.

In a while she was back, with two paddles. She lay down, letting the rain drum on her back. 'Barges,' she explained, and laughed, and coughed. Jillian Curram was enjoying herself.

One corner of the raft dipped considerably now that both of them were aboard. They paddled past the anchored barges, huddled in the gloom. Someone spotted them and shouted. A pistol was fired; they saw the ball hit the surface. Then they were in clear water. Agonisingly slowly, they headed upstream.

'Aren't they following?' asked Bi tok.

'Will they?'

'Perhaps.'

It was murky, they could see nothing.

'Better things to do than chase a woman and a boy,' Jillian said. Bi tok did not attempt to dissuade her from this conjecture.

Together they fled across the lagoons of the drowning forest.

—16—
Afloat

The rain stopped. Everything seemed to sigh. The sun came out and brightened the overhanging grove. It was near noon, and the wet air boiled.

'We'll wait.'

They sought ground and shade, and contrived to wedge the sodden raft on a shaded mudbank between two bushes.

'What do we now, climb a tree?'

Jillian said she thought they should stay on the raft in case the river rose and it drifted.

Bi tok lay down. Exhausted he slept, but dreamed of clinging nets and swiftly woke. He found Jillian asleep now, her back to him. The boy felt strangely alert. Her proximity excited him. Quietly he freed his penis from his clothing.

Soon Jillian, without turning over, asked: 'Is that good?'

'Yes,' he said, guiltily. He had been remembering her undressing by the pool.

She did not speak again. Bi tok strove to continue, but his appetite had fled. He felt suffused with shame, not that she had heard him, but that he had been masturbating at all. Yet Jillian's tone had suggested that she did too. He would have thought her too old. He cursed himself for not begging her to take hold of him, at least. He slept again, it seemed for a blink only, before Jillian was crouching by him, one hand on his shoulder, another lightly over his mouth.

'One of yours,' she murmured.

'Mmh?'

She mouthed the word 'boat', and let him sit up.

It was one of the lighters from Right Fist Camp. It passed

151

several yards away. He heard the voices of two men discussing cats. He recognised one voice.

'Dep dura,' he said, when the boat had gone well out of hearing.

'What?'

'The soldier,' he told her. 'The one who shot my father. The one with the revolve gun. He is alive.'

'No, I killed him.'

'No. His neck is – is – ' He imitated it for her.

Jillian looked mortified. 'Oh Beetle, oh no.'

'They asked questions. Dep dura said to kill me.'

'I told you!'

'They think, I am a traitor.'

'You are. You must understand, Beetle!' She hugged him, aggressively. 'And I was congratulating myself on saving your life again. I should have been more thorough the first time, shouldn't I.' She spoke for her own benefit.

The boy peered uncomfortably through the foliage. 'We go now.'

'No.'

'He has gone by.'

'We don't know which way. We might meet him.'

'Yes: upstream?' he persisted.

'He may turn back any time.'

'Why?'

'He may think he's passed us. He would be right,' she pointed out.

But at last she had to agree to continue cautiously. As they dragged the raft from the bank, however, a log slid out of it and everything came undone. Bi tok looked at it in dismay.

'It was a good raft,' said Jillian. She seemed relieved to be back on foot, cutting them a path. She followed the river, but kept well away from it.

The sun was still high. Where the foliage thinned, Jillian sought shade.

'Tell me your real name again,' she said suddenly.

'Bi tok,' he said.

She repeated it. 'I'm sorry I called you Beetle.'

He now knew what the name meant, but he said, 'Beetle is good for now. Now I am Beetle, certainly.'

152

She heard a flatness in his voice which was worse than bitterness.

'Why did you run away?' Jillian asked. 'Was it because we argued?'

'It was part,' he agreed. 'I thought I – did not – belong with you.' The words were difficult for him to say. 'But I do not belong with Escalans.'

She could say nothing to that.

After a pause he said, 'Jillian: why do you come after me?'

'Because they were going to kill you!'

'Why do you care?'

She hesitated before replying. 'I told myself that if you asked that, I would say I didn't want you to tell them where we are.' She laughed ruefully. 'It's true, but it's not important. We would have moved.' She turned suddenly, wiping sweat from her face. 'You didn't tell them, did you?'

'No.'

Nothing more was said for a while. Bi tok tramped on in her wake, swatting the mosquitoes that landed on his arms and legs.

'You're an idiot who shouldn't be walking around on his own,' she said. 'And I'm an idiot for wanting to protect you.' Her voice was light, flippant.

Along green colonnades of palm they saw something blue: the Escalan boat. Jillian stood for a moment staring at it, and then at nothing.

'Shall we take it away from them?'

She was gratified to see his eyes widen.

Lighterman No kiu was not best pleased to be assigned to Upperman Dep dura. Dep dura stood in the bow, scanning the forest for this barbarian woman who gripped his mind like a sorceress. Where the boy fitted in, No kiu did not know.

Dep dura spoke lazily of violent things. No kiu had heard the men laughing about him behind his back.

'No one said it was the same woman,' No kiu pointed out for the twentieth time.

'It was.'

'What if they've left the river?'

Dep dura merely glared coldly at his subordinate. His jaw

was growing stiff. His neck ached from holding his head up so long.

'I'm all in,' he said. 'Keep your eyes open.' He lay down on a sack.

Soon No kiu surreptitiously slipped a line into the light brown water. He was sure the upperman would have forbidden it as a distraction of attention. But No kiu had seen a shadowy school of mothfish, and where they went, waxari usually followed. No kiu reckoned at least one of them should not go back empty-handed when this was all over.

Waxari there were, sleek and stupid, their nacreous mottlings growing dull as they ceased to flop around his feet. The upperman had not moved. No kiu was sure he was asleep. He was straightening up from shipping his fourth fish when he saw the woman.

She was a slip of pink in the distance, sitting on the bank. Yet he was sure it was a woman, not a man, nor a junglie.

No kiu half rose, looked round at the tiller to check its set, looked back and she was gone.

He almost shouted to the upperman, thought better of it and went forward to wake him.

'The woman.'

Dep dura was instantly awake. 'Where?'

No kiu pointed to the tiny bay.

'I can't see anything.'

'She was there.'

'What was she doing?'

'She was sitting on the grass. She must have gone into the trees. Perhaps she saw us.'

The upperman cursed him, as if for failing to make his boat invisible. The wound on his neck flushed red.

'Take us there.'

'Upperman, she was naked.'

'That's an order!'

No kiu went back to his tiller. 'It's a trap.'

Dep dura took offence. 'You think a naked woman could harm me? A woman? You think she's going to strangle me, with her bare hands?'

They went curving in under the trees.

'No woman is clever enough to trap two men,' rasped Dep

154

dura. 'Except in bed, eh?' He grew excited. 'I'll tell you what to do with a naked woman.' He did, briefly but graphically. 'Take us closer in. And shut up.'

To their left the mud plopped languidly. Green fronds brushed their faces. No kiu felt the boat bump and rebound, and he threw the anchor over. Dep dura jumped down into the water and staggered around until he had his balance.

'Shall I come with you?'

'No. Stay here. Guard the boat.'

Dep dura waded ashore through a cloud of tiny gnats. The greenery crunched wetly beneath his boots. The trees, a mixture of white copal and ugly blueleaf, opened before him like an inviting maze. A macaw squawked and was silent.

Dep dura squatted to look at the ground. Broken leaves and stems: someone had run this way. He loaded his pistol, primed and cocked it. Then he rose, and saw, between two trees, something brown and crumpled, lying on the ground as if discarded. Naked, the lighterman had said. Had she been bathing when she saw them, and dropped some piece of clothing in her flight?

The Escalan upperman turned to the boat. The lighterman was leaning over the side, watching him apprehensively. Dep dura gave him a cocky wave and stepped into the trees.

Bi tok hurtled from the undergrowth, flung himself at the soldier's legs and brought him down. The gun flew away and landed with a bang among the leaves. Dep dura shouted, heaving himself up. Bi tok clung to his neck and hit him over the head with his club, and then again, afraid the first time had not been hard enough.

On the boat No kiu heard the report, the commotion among the leaves. He felt a bump of something against the far side and whirled around. He saw a naked woman, streaming with water, coming at him with a knife. She was the last thing he ever saw.

Still staring numbly at the motionless Dep dura, Bi tok heard the splash of the lighterman's body hitting the water, and ran to the edge.

Jillian smiled at him broadly. 'Our boat.'

Bi tok looked nervously behind him. 'Dep dura,' he said.

'What?'

He pointed. She understood.

'Is he dead yet?' she asked.

'I don't know.'

Jillian vaulted over the side and came running ashore. She cuddled the anguished boy and kissed him, then ran on into the trees. A minute later she was back, carrying her clothes, her gun, her knife and machete, Dep dura's jacket and boots and his gun.

'He won't be needing these.'

Bi tok looked at her appalled.

'Cheer up,' she said. 'We did win.'

'Yes,' he said.

He waded into the water, clambered up the side of the boat and tipped himself aboard.

There were no rules here. He had knocked down a man of his own race and beaten him viciously about the head, all to gain possession of a boat which was in no sense his. He was preserving his own life, for no reasons he could name.

Jillian came across with the pile of clothes on her head, the weapons held on top. He reached down to take them from her, then gave her a hand up.

She rubbed her hair. 'Put them in the sun, Beetle. Those boots could dry before we get home. I'll see to the anchor.'

'You enjoy this,' said Bi tok.

'What?'

He shook his head. He would not repeat it. She had killed two men, then hugged and kissed him. All upstream he obeyed her without speaking.

At last she came and put an arm around him, pinning his arms to his sides.

'Is something wrong?'

He would not look at her. He felt the sting of tears. 'You enjoy this,' he repeated, accusingly.

'What? Cruising in the sun, alone with an exotic young man, through the most beautiful land in the world? Certainly I enjoy it.'

She squinted into the low sun. The aisles of the forest were filled with rich golden dust. Flowers blew.

'A shame about the boat, though.'

'What do you mean?'

'We'll have to wreck it.'

'Can't you hide it?'

'Not for long, I fear. This is becoming a busy corner of Belanesi.'

After a minute or two, he asked, 'Did you see the man?'

'What man?'

'The boat man. In the water.'

Jillian shook her head.

'I saw.' He stared at the trees. 'Fish were eating him.'

She shrugged. 'He ate fish.' She pointed to the little heap of waxari in the stern. Then she took Bi tok's hands, holding him at arm's length and scanning his face. 'Is that what's upsetting you?' she asked. 'It's death, Bi tok.' She laughed wearily. 'The enemy. The one thing you can depend on. Everything runs out.'

'You kill,' he said. He placed a hand on his chin. 'I kill,' he said, unhappily.

'He was a soldier, for goodness' sake. Being killed is a hazard of their, of our, profession. Would you rather they had killed us?'

'Yes,' he said.

'You do talk nonsense, sometimes, Bi tok.' Jillian shifted uncomfortably on the bench.

'Of course! My life is nothing. A mistake. My future is only to die.'

'Like your father before you, I suppose,' she said with irony.

'Certainly.'

She lay down with the sun on her back, head resting on her folded arms.

'Why are you all so arrogant?' she asked.

He did not know the word.

'You think you know everything,' she amplified. 'Your Emperor wants to conquer the world. What does he know about the world? Nothing. All he knows is that if he sends out enough soldiers he can kill everybody else, and then it will be easy. All the things they taught you, all those "harmonies" and "formulæ" you were trying to tell Beth about – what have they got to do with how things are *here*?'

She slapped the wood of the deck.

His green eyes were grave.

'I made the raft,' he said.

Jillian laughed. She sat up with one leg under her.

'Yes, you made the raft. And you painted that idiotic picture.'

Bi tok frowned. 'The picture – you did not understand, Jillian. I know is not how Belanesi is. It is how it should be. The true way. You see only the army. Are violent men. They do not obey the Emperor.'

'No, Bi tok,' she said firmly. 'The reason you were taught to paint "The Peaceable Land" is because the army is doing exactly what the Emperor commands. Don't you see? Don't you see how it works?'

He bit his lip.

'As long as you obey it, as long as you even think you should obey, it will keep working. Life doesn't stop because your plans don't work out. Life only begins when you stop planning.'

She had begun to sound rather foolish to herself, but she was in the mood for philosophy, a mood of triumph and temporary peace in the glorious late afternoon.

'Look at me,' she said. 'I was born rich. My mother was one of the wealthiest and most important people in Bryland. Then she died, and all the power and the money and the House were mine. I was to follow her. That was the plan for me. Then your Emperor sent his soldiers, and everything – fell apart. My mother died. My father disappeared.' She waved her hand. 'Instead of being rich and powerful, I ended up without a penny. Then I joined the army, because I thought I could fight back against these terrible orange people who had ruined my life and killed my friends. And also – ' she laughed ' – because I had nothing better to do. So I joined the army, and guess what we did. Nothing. Marched all over the place, never fought a battle. I wanted to fight Escalans. I wanted it so badly I ran away from the army, and came here. Without a plan in my head. And then for the first time in my life I knew I was free. I know who I am and what I'm doing.'

She laughed again, stretching her arms over her head.

'I'm sailing on the river with an Escalan, one of the people I hate so much. And I don't mind at all.'

He sighed.

'Look at you,' she went on, relentlessly. 'You're thousands of miles away from home. You're travelling with your father but he doesn't even know he *is* your father. He's supposed to take you to New Bright Rock and look after you, but there's an accident and then he's killed before you get there. You're helped by the people who are supposed to kill you, and nearly killed by the people who are supposed to help you. Nothing you've learned fits the facts. Your life isn't over, Bi tok, it's just beginning. You must understand: you're free.'

'Am not free,' he said sullenly. 'I am not free of you. You save my life. You say all I think is wrong, you wish me think all you think. You are outside me, inside me. I run away, but you follow. I want free of you, but without you I die. With you I don't know what to do!'

Tears of anger filled his eyes.

'Don't cry, Beetle, oh don't.'

She drew him close and began to wipe his face with her sleeve. She kissed his cheek, then his lips, then his lips again.

Bi tok, hardly knowing what he was doing, put his arms about her. She held him tightly to her breast. He could feel her bones, hear her heart.

The sun was setting. A lull settled on the forest. He felt weak, empty of everything that was not her.

In a while she left him and went to see to the sail and the tiller. The boat turned aside under the trees. She stood behind him, and held him to her.

'Is there a girl, Bi tok? At home? In your mind's eye?'

He turned in her arms. 'There is you,' he said.

'Dear me,' said Jillian, and laughed.

'Yes,' said Bi tok.

She unfastened the cloth from around his loins.

He was eager, and uncertain. He clung to her. He discovered instincts he had never known. He felt illuminated, incorporeal, then suddenly, too soon, exhausted, and sticky.

Jillian seemed to be highly delighted.

'Was it good?' she wanted to know.

'Yes!'

'It will get better,' she told him. 'Would you like that?'

'Of course.'

His eyes seemed to glow in the twilight.

'And you will help me talk to the jungle people?' she asked.

The relevance of this escaped him. 'Yes,' he said.

'Then you are not proposing to die quite yet.'

He realised that she was teasing him. He felt extraordinary. Her thigh lay across his belly. His mind seemed to float independently of the boat, images like bright bubbles bursting on its surface. He saw himself in prison again, wondering about the guard outside, but not going out to him. He saw Dep dura and Kien orau nodding at him, having settled a time for his demise. *'Our friend won't require more than one bullet, upperman!'* He saw Dep dura kneeling in a doorway full of sunlight, reloading a gun.

'The guns!'

'Which guns?'

'The revolve guns,' he said.

'Oh.' She yawned. 'Those guns.'

'There are more.'

'Where?' Her voice was a degree more alert.

'Not here. At the sea, the harbour.' He searched his memory again. 'They come when the rain stops.'

Jillian Curram sat up.

'Tomorrow,' she said.

——17——
Hubert Ennigo Makes His Stand

Next morning the storm began early, waking everyone. Pale in the sick green glow, they came to the mouth of the cave and stared out at the lightning.

Below them the rain poured from the hull of the beached lighter.

'I don't see what's wrong with that,' Saraa was saying.

'She stole it from the orangers,' said Jimothy. 'If they see us in it, they might not be very pleased. They might want it back.'

'We can sail as far as the camp,' Mollie pointed out. 'If we stay out of sight.'

'Exactly,' said Jillian, 'but we must have one scout on foot, just in case.'

'Mollie,' said Hubert acidly. No one laughed.

'When we stop,' Jillian continued, 'we unload the cannon and load it . . .'

Saraa and Jimothy laughed. Bethalie smiled.

'You know what I mean. Load it and secure it. Then I'm afraid we sink the boat.'

'What?'

'I mean it. If they spot the boat – '

'We can hide it.'

'We can take it further downstream.'

'We can *carry* it.'

'All that way in the rain? Not likely.'

'We can do it. We don't have to take it up into the village.'

'No, we don't have to climb the rock with the bloody thing.'

'For goodness' sake,' snapped Hubert. 'If we were to carry it anywhere, it would be to a point halfway between the village and the camp. Don't women understand geometry?'

'Prick,' said Saraa.

'What my friend is trying to say, *Captain* Ennigo,' Jimothy explained, 'is that women don't get taught strategy and everything. They just get orders.'

'We're working this out for ourselves, Hubert, in case you don't realise it.'

'If you've good advice, best give it early, Captain,' said Bethalie.

'I did! I said we should just go and do it, and to hell with the natives.'

'Who do you think we're doing it *for*, Hubert?' asked Jillian coldly.

'Six of us to take a boat full of guns from the Escalan army?' said Mollie. 'Great strategy, Hubert. Truly inspired.'

'I don't like it any more than you do,' Hubert Ennigo said. 'I simply say we're wasting our time. The Belanesi can't fight. They just don't know how.'

'They could stage a diversion,' said Jillian. 'They know the jungle.'

'They can give you a scare when they pop out of the grass right in front of you,' Bethalie commented. 'A lot of them could be very frightening.'

'A bunch of goats?'

'Why didn't you stay in the army, Hubie?'

'I want to fight, damn it, not run about in the jungle trying to control a bunch of bloody goats.'

Jillian looked at him with disgust. 'You make no sense at all, Hubert.'

'*I* make no sense? *You* can say that?' He was almost rigid with contempt. 'All right, Lieutenant Curram, all right. Just let me hear you answer a sensible question. When have the natives ever taken the slightest notice of what we say or do? They sit there singing silly songs until they get killed.'

'We've never had Bi tok with us before,' said Jillian.

Involuntarily, all the women turned to look into the cave.

The boy was standing in the shadows. He had been listening.

'Breakfast is ready,' he said.

'We're talking,' said Saraa.

'We'll talk anyway, so at least let's eat.'

Jillian went in and they followed, but for Hubert who stayed leaning against the cliff with his arms folded, barely in the dry at all.

'Hubert.'

'I'm not hungry.'

'Hubert, we need to talk with you.'

'But you don't want to listen.'

Saraa ate most of a squirrel. She belched. 'This is your big day, Beetle,' she said.

'You can be a hero, like us,' said Jimothy.

'Stop it, you're confusing him,' said Bethalie.

Jillian put her arm around him.

'Bi tok, what could you say to the Belanesi to make them understand what's happening?'

The boy thought for a little. '*Many soldiers . . .*' he began. 'No. Will think I mean you. Perhaps *I-wish you to-come . . . Come-with-us to-water . . .* I don't know,' he said. 'I must see first, then speak. The formulæ have no precedent.'

'Eh?'

'What's he mean, Beth?'

'Talk Bryle, Beetle, eh?'

Jimothy held up the revolving gun. 'What's this in Belanesi, Beetle?'

He uttered nine or ten quavering syllables.

'Yes. Well, I can't say that, but why don't you say – ' She held up the gun and pointed to it: 'Do You Like This? You Can Get Lots Of Them Over There.'

'I can say that, Jimi,' said Bi tok, shelling more nuts.

'All right, say it then. Not to me, to them.'

'Will do no good. The Belanesi not like guns.'

'These are good guns, Beetle.'

He smiled. 'Are no good guns. Jungle people are not soldiers.'

'Hubert was right, eh, Jillian,' said Mollie.

'Hey, Hubert!'

'Shut up, Sar.'

'Hey, Hubert, you were right! Where's Hubert?'

Hubert was not there.

They rushed to the edge and looked down. Hubert was

wheeling the cannon aboard the boat. The rain was easing to a steady drizzle, but the river was still rising. Soon he would be able to refloat the lighter with ease.

'Hubert, what are you doing?' Jillian yelled.

He looked up, the rain splashing his face. 'Somebody's got to take charge here,' he shouted. 'I'm taking the cannon because you're not fit to command it. And I'm taking the boat because it's a damn sight more valuable with a cannon in it, whatever Jillian Curram, in her expensively tutored wisdom, would have you believe.'

'Those are ours, Hubert!' she shouted. 'They belong to all of us!'

'Ennigo, you rat,' yelled Saraa.

'We'll all go by boat until we sight the camp,' said Jillian loudly. She walked out along the ledge. 'Then we'll see how it looks. Jimi will scout.'

'What about him?' shouted the man in the boat.

'He's coming with us.'

'Not with me, he isn't.' Hubert had the sail up. 'He's no responsibility of mine. He's nothing to do with us at all. He's a son of the bloody enemy. How do we know he's not a spy?'

'Hubert!'

'Let her risk her neck for him if she wants to. I know what she wants with him, and I think it's pretty sick, frankly. Who's coming with me?'

Saraa threw a stone at him.

'Where's your crew, Captain?' shouted Jimothy.

'One of you go with him,' said Jillian. 'Make sure he doesn't do anything foolish.'

'No one's going, Jillian.'

'Not with him.'

'You can go,' said Saraa, 'if you want.' She sniffed.

'Hubert,' shouted Jillian. 'Listen to me.'

'Make it quick.'

'If you take any risks, we lose the cannon, the boat – and one of our number. Think about that.'

'I already have. Get rid of him, or I'm off. Now.'

'Why should we accept either?' Jillian demanded.

'Goodbye, Lieutenant,' said Hubert as he bobbed into the

river. He grinned, instantly merry again, and gave a bold salute. 'Give my love to the natives, won't you?'

'Hubert! Keep to the right bank! The right bank! We'll find you before it stops raining!'

The wind and the water took him away out of hearing, and out of sight.

Jillian swore and kicked a stone over the edge.

Bethalie shook her head.

'How could he do that?'

'He's a man,' said Jimothy. 'Men always want to be Captain.'

'I hope they sink you, Ennigo!' Saraa was roaring. 'I hope the crocs get you!'

'They're on our side, the crocodiles!' cried Mollie. She and Saraa began to laugh.

'We could ambush him at the bridge, if we're quick,' said Jimothy.

'He's got the cannon,' said Mollie. 'He'd shoot us first.'

'He'd never.'

'He would.'

'He'd miss.'

'No,' said Jillian. 'The Escalans would hear the shooting, then we wouldn't have a chance.'

Bethalie had gone back into the cave. Jillian followed and found her finishing off her breakfast.

'There's no time for that now, Beth.'

'We'll need all our strength, ma'am. Here,' and she handed Jillian her bowl. Jillian ate, distractedly.

'How's the weather?' she called. 'Does it look like stopping?'

'No.'

'Never,' said Mollie.

'We must go.'

They all came inside and began picking up weapons.

'If we all turn up with all this gear they'll have to take us seriously,' said Jimothy.

'Belanesi don't like guns,' said Bi tok, who was watching.

'You'll explain it to them,' Jimothy told him. She held out a pistol. 'Here.'

He drew back. 'No.'

'Not to fight with,' she explained, 'to protect yourself. In the jungle.'

'No.' He would take only a sharpened stick. 'Guns protect nothing.'

'Don't tell the natives that, Beetle, will you?'

But he was gone, hand over hand down the vine like a strolling ape.

Under the high canopy, the apes themselves were sitting it out. Brightly coloured birds still perched among the lianas, unruffled by the continuous rain, but the hollow trees were full of eyes. The ground was sodden and all the rills were running.

The five women and the boy padded swiftly across the forest floor. They crossed the river by the hanging bridge, and saw no sign of Escalan occupation, or of Hubert Ennigo either. The river ran golden, dark and deep, turbulent with rain. The crocodiles were all beneath the surface.

'Wake up, crocodiles!' called Saraa. Mollie hushed her.

'Look at that.'

They were moving through a grove of blueleaf. They stared curiously up at the flowers, which were pendulous and engorged with water. Green veins bulged like the veins of stricken animals.

'Ugh.'

'They smell nasty.'

'Come *on*, Mollie.'

Bi tok thought as he ran: The native he and Bethalie had met in the forest had said something about flowers. What was it? But he could not remember. He was wet through, and had a pain in his side.

They toiled uphill, and caught their first glimpse of the rock through the treetops ahead. Above it the wet sky was as grey as ever.

'Jillian, can we rest a minute?'

'A minute. No more.'

They sprawled between the buttresses of a huge ironwood, panting and gasping. The ground was hardly wet at all. They had been there a moment, no more, when the grasses parted and a lithe brown pard was among them, striding through, head low, looking neither to right nor left. It was heading away from the river. It was there, and it was gone. The grass closed over it.

'What did he want?'

'She,' said Mollie.

'What did she want?'

'Nothing.'

'Good.'

They ran on. They reached the foot of the rock. They had seen none of the Belanesi; nor did they see any now, though they craned their necks.

'How are we going to get up *there*, Beetle?'

'I don't know,' he said. 'Bua-turaa carried me.'

'She's teasing, Bi tok. There's a path. This way.'

They climbed. Monkeys sheltering in the canopy trees shrieked at them as they went by.

There was no one at the lintel stone. The village was closed against the rain. Water dripped constantly from the thatch. It ran off the plate the totem held and splashed over its head.

From the hall came the sound of many people moaning, repetitive and low.

'What's wrong?'

'I don't know,' said Bi tok.

They moved closer.

It sounded to the Escalan boy as if all the villagers were inside the hall. Amid their assembled reek there was another smell, fruity and at the same time earthy. It meant nothing to Bi tok, or to Jillian. They all held their arms across their mouths as they approached the veranda.

Saraa paced swiftly to the fore.

'Saraa!' said Bi tok.

They looked at him, then her. Saraa had her dagger drawn.

'We're on their side, Sar,' said Bethalie.

'Sorry,' muttered Saraa.

It came to Bi tok that the continual moaning was, in its own harsh way, harmonic. He wondered if it were music.

There came a loud thump and, unmistakably, laughter. Discord ensued.

The door was open. Bi tok stepped inside.

The heat and stench were extreme. The hut was full of smoke. Confusion prevailed. The natives were lying in piles, crawling over and under each other.

Bi tok wondered whether some strange mass sexual rhythm had peaked, but all the children and old people were here too.

Nor did the Belanesi seem particularly excited. Torpid, rather. As he tried to go forward into the pack, he realised that many of the people on the floor were unconscious.

In the Foreign Room of the Nightingale Library at College had hung a large piece of bark decorated by a primitive of Stone Eye. It had been framed and displayed as a curiosity because it depicted the ancient artist's odd belief in another life *after* life. This second life was to be murky, violent and grim, evidently. Now Bi tok felt as if he were walking into that painting.

The women came into the longhouse after him, except for Bethalie, who stayed out in the rain, feeling sick. Mollie gave the scene one look of complete revulsion and said: 'I'm staying with Beth.'

'Mollie!' appealed Jillian.

'What's the *point*, Jillian?' asked Mollie, her voice unusually shrill. She went out.

The natives writhed, wailing and groaning.

Saraa gaped.

Jimothy sniggered. 'It's a good job Hubert's not here, isn't it?'

Jillian did not reply. She looked extremely disturbed.

'Shall we go?'

'No,' said Jillian. 'Follow Bi tok.'

'Oh, *look* – ' protested Jimothy; but Jillian ignored her, and she followed. Saraa followed her, covering her nose and mouth.

Assuming the origin of the mêlée to have been a tribal feast, Bi tok was squeezing his way through towards Bua-turaa's place. Around it were slumped some elders who were somewhat conscious. They were still moaning, deeply and rhythmically, and occasionally laughing in high-pitched bleats. Bi tok realised they were very drunk on something. As he stumbled over an outstretched hoof, they recognised him.

'*Bii toöök! Biii toööök!*'

'*Little-enemy!*'

Long hands reached lazily for him, jostling him lasciviously.

'*Hairless-boy* . . .'

The musty, sweet smell ahead increased suddenly. Bi tok glimpsed people sprawling around a bowl or a vat of some kind.

'*Bi tok.*'

It was Bua-turaa, bleary but still focusing, supported by his sons.

'*You-are-here. Good-good.*'

The Chief seemed to regard his presence as only just.

'*The-best of the day to-you, Bua-turaa.*'

'*Have-you-drunk?*' asked Bua-turaa. He waved a supple arm. '*Your-friends. Have-they-drunk?*'

'What's happening?' asked Jillian.

'He asks us to join their meal.'

'Meal,' said Jillian faintly.

'To drink,' said Bi tok. 'That, I think.' He pointed. Bua-turaa wobbled his head encouragingly.

'Tell him we haven't got time.'

'*We-greet-you, Bua-turaa, but we-go,*' said Bi tok. '*We-go but you-go-with-us to-water.*' He heard the nonsense he was speaking. '*We-wish* – ' he said.

The Chief interrupted him.

'*Drink! Drink-now! All-drink!*'

'He wants us to drink.'

'He seems quite persistent on the point,' said Jillian, shivering. There was water dripping down her neck, she realised suddenly, and looked up. The rain had soaked through the thatch.

'*Yes! Drink-now!*' Bua-turaa followed her gaze, pointing with an infirm finger at the dripping thatch. '*All-drink-now!*'

'Not likely,' said Saraa.

'We'll drink, Saraa,' said Jillian.

'Why should I?'

'Because if you don't they won't even listen to us, much less help. Bi tok,' she grabbed his arm, 'do you know what this is?'

He looked at the vessel Bua-turaa's sons were conducting him to. It seemed to have been made from a large slice of palm tree. It was almost empty of a scummy, shiny brown liquor that stuck to the sides in greasy curds. Even the little there was stank profoundly of oleaginous decay.

Bua-turaa's left-hand son thrust a coconut shellful into Bi tok's hands.

Bowing automatically, the boy sniffed the contents, then wished he had not. He took a sip.

It was bitter. It tasted powerfully of milk, and mould.

169

Bi tok gagged, but turned it into a peculiar growl, rolling his head and rubbing his stomach in appreciation. The Belanesi pawed each other and snickered.

The boy had hoped he would now be allowed to pass the cup, but he saw that Bua-turaa and others were pressing a shellful on each of the three women, while pointing occasionally at the roof. They were clearly in the grip of some befuddled misapprehension.

'*Driiink!*' they chorused.

Bi tok held his breath and poured down as much of the vileness as he thought would not at once come lurching back up again. Others, he noted, had already failed at this. Their beards were matted with yellow, their fleece splashed and soiled. They lay as if stunned. How could they be enjoying this?

Behind him he heard Saraa choking and Jimothy wheezing exaggeratedly and saying: 'Wonderful.' Jillian was still looking at hers.

Bua-turaa's right-hand son suddenly pointed to the doorway.

'*Two-women drink,*' he called, over and over again.

Cheerful hands seized the skulking pair and dragged them through the ruckus. Bethalie looked as white as bone. She had vomited already. Mollie held her shell with eyes averted.

Bi tok took another gulp, swallowed it in a spasm, then tried to begin his speech again.

'*Many soldiers are by-the-water. They-come to-kill you.*'

Bua-turaa tipped his head to one side. His yellow eyes were bloodshot, his teeth huge and awful.

'*Drink!*'

They all drank. Bi tok sucked so desperately at the last of his that it trickled out of his mouth and down his chin.

'*For flowers,*' he dimly heard Bua-turaa say.

Nothing looked as it had before.

Balls of coloured light began to float leisurely from one side of the hut to the other. Faces spun in the air. The smoke was fluorescing. Somehow Bi tok understood that no one else could see any of these things.

Soon some of the women could see many things that were quite similar, however. Jimothy could see a cone of sparkling darkness above her head that threatened to rush down over with a roar. Mollie saw everything as through water, and kept rubbing her eyes. Jillian saw foot-long caterpillars with bright yellow fur squirming rapidly in and out of the piles of people. Whenever she looked directly at one, it vanished. She wondered why Bi tok was standing there so long without speaking. She wondered how long she had been standing there. She sat down, feeling rather ill. The smell of the drink seemed to rise up her throat and sicken her.

'Poison,' said Bethalie, and fell over.

Before Bi tok's astonished eyes Bua-turaa turned into an antelope with curling horns of jet; into a man with a huge backside and skinny legs; into a woman with a flower in one nostril. He felt immensely cheated.

'Where is my father?' he demanded. 'My dead father. What have you done with his body?'

He realised he had spoken in Escalan.

Bua-turaa was speaking. His voice came booming from an immense distance, and Bi tok forgot what it had said as soon as he heard it.

He made a supreme effort to gather his shattered wits. There was a request to be made of Bua-turaa, and it was most urgent. The boy looked behind him for help.

Bethalie lay unmoving on the floor among the other casualties. Saraa had collapsed on top of her. Jillian sat crushed up against a helplessly laughing Belanesi. Her lips were working silently and tears coursed down her face. Mollie sat with her arms around her knees, her face hidden as she rocked to and fro to the rhythm of the groaning chant.

Only Jimothy was on her feet. Her face was a mask of disgust. She was obviously struggling not to retch. She said some words of Bryle Bi tok did not know and dropped her shell on the head of a comatose old woman. Jimothy and Bi tok stared foggily at each other.

Suddenly Bi tok was out on the veranda in the sunshine. Jimothy was with him. The din at their backs was even greater, but they were listening to different music, livelier music, played on a pair of pipes by a single mouth.

The golden-haired piper sat on the shoulders of the totem, leaning back on the upraised platter at an insouciant angle. His lips curled meatily about the reeds. He looked wilder than ever, all woolly knees and elbows, but his fingering was faultless. The music he played was swirling, stirring, a music to heed and follow. Bi tok wanted to float up and away.

The children were waking. They came rushing out of the hut and through the puddles. They too carried pipes. They skipped around the statue in a savage dance. High they leapt into the air, threw back their heads and leapt higher.

Bi tok looked at Jimothy.

She seemed to be trying to tell him something.

'Beetle! Beetle, it's stopped raining!'

A face loomed leering in Bi tok's mind.

'Hubert,' he said. 'Boat.'

He made to run into the crowd spilling out of the longhouse.

'Beetle, where are you going?'

He was going nowhere. His feet would not obey him. He pitched into darkness. He did not hear Jimothy laughing scornfully as she tottered after him, or the bamboo rail that broke as she, too, fell.

—18—
The Kicking
of the Thin Ox

Bethalie, first down, was first awake. She remembered instantly, with complete clarity, where she was and what had happened. Bethalie had had no illusions, no visions. Nor had she ever had a megrim, though she had an aunt who regularly did. She thought what she was feeling now was what her aunt felt like just afterwards.

The heavy thing lying across her was Saraa, she discovered. She managed to wake her left arm enough to lift her a bit and squirmed free; sat on the floor scowling and blinking, rubbing her arm.

The longhouse was full of sun and damp air. Jillian and Mollie were out cold, just like Saraa. Otherwise, the place was deserted.

There was no sign of Bi tok or Jimi. And she wondered where all the natives had gone. Some of them had looked fit to sleep a week.

Perhaps the music had been real. Perhaps the music, and all the people getting up and leaving in a great tumbling, trampling rush, clambering up on one another's backs, fighting in the doorway, keening as if in imitation of the pipes: perhaps all that had been real. It had felt like a dream. She had forgotten it till this moment.

She looked down at Saraa, then shuffled over to Jillian, who lay on her side, curled up, grey beneath her tan. Bethalie winced and reassured herself that she was still breathing. 'Madam,' she said, and then, 'Jillian.'

She spoke softly, but somehow woke Mollie, several yards

away. Mollie sat upright and immediately burst into tears. Jillian did not awaken, though she opened her mouth slightly, and began to dribble.

'Jillian. Shut up, Mollie, do.'

Mollie continued to sob.

'Jillian. Wake up. They've all gone.'

'Whuh?'

Jillian had never felt so weak. The afternoon light was too bright for her eyes. She held her arm up over her face.

'Beth?' She lifted her head. 'What happened? Where's Bi tok?'

Bethalie could not say.

'Mollie? Is that you?'

Mollie snivelled incomprehensibly.

'What's wrong with her?'

'I don't know. She's just woken up too. Mollie, what is it?' Bethalie went over to her.

Jillian got to her knees. She felt drained. Faint, tiny lights went floating up her spinal column, and fizzled out in her head.

'Sar's coming round,' she said. 'Sar! How do you feel?'

Saraa sat up, groaned, and swallowed audibly. She looked at each of them in turn with unsteady eyes, saying nothing. Then she clambered to her feet and leaned against the vat, breathing hard, before setting out determinedly for the door, her feet crossing and weaving at every step.

They heard her break into a run along the veranda and clatter urgently down the steps. Then they heard her being sick.

She came back in more normally.

'Oh that's better.'

Her eyes were bright and her cheeks pink.

'Jimi's outside,' she said cheerfully. 'And Beetle too.'

'How are they?' asked Jillian, getting up at once.

Saraa stared at her. 'Not very well, Jillian, I think!' she bellowed, and roared with laughter.

Jillian staggered out into the full glare of sunlight splintering on the wet treetops. She saw the snapped rail, and Jimothy sprawled below, her arms stirring feebly in the wet dust. Jimothy was swearing, fluently and low.

Jillian knelt and held out a hand. 'Can you reach?'

Painfully Jimothy pulled herself up. She was lavishly

bruised, but nothing appeared to be broken. 'I was quite floppy when I went over,' she said, complacently.

Bi tok had come running up the steps.

'The boat! Hubert!'

'Are you all right?'

'Yes! Of course! The boat!'

Jillian hugged him. 'Hubert will have to wait,' she said.

'But the other boat! With the guns!'

He was positively hopping up and down.

'I don't think we're all quite ready to travel yet,' said Jillian. 'Where did they all go?'

'I don't know. Went when the music was, when the rain stopped,' said Bi tok impatiently.

'How long ago was that?'

'I don't know!'

'I don't suppose you know which way they went.'

He had not seen. Jimothy had. She pointed.

'Away from the river,' said Jillian.

Jimothy nodded, still not speaking. She clutched her elbow.

'All the animals go that way,' said Bi tok. His enthusiasm seemed to have abated. He was gazing down into the jungle. A troop of gibbons was crashing by, making the branches shake. They could hear hoots of alarm, and the squeals of pig.

'Something's frightened them. I suppose the people felt the same,' said Jillian. She sounded disappointed.

Saraa grinned from the doorway. 'We could try another village.'

'The next is that way too,' said Jillian.

Jimothy was checking her guns. 'Well, I'm going,' she said, and ran.

Saraa lumbered along the veranda and leapt smoothly through the break. Bi tok ran down the steps after her. Jillian whirled around and yelled into the hut. 'Beth! Mollie!'

Bethalie emerged, supporting Mollie.

'Mollie, are you all right? Do you want to stay here?'

'Not likely.'

They ran past her. She ran too.

It seemed as if exertion brought back, in half-formed eddies, the mental effects of the potion. Bi tok did not know how he got down off the rock. He only ran, towards the ripe black smell of the river. Once he thought they passed through an overgrown tiltyard dominated by a defaced statue of Tem nekis the Navigator; and another glade seemed to be full of the huge blackened sunflowers that he remembered terrifying him on winter visits to his great-grandfather's grave in Foxchiver. To either side the bush appeared to thrash ceaselessly, as though there were creatures continually coursing through, unseen, but then probably there were.

There was no evidence, no fearsome sound or ominous light ahead to explain this gregarious impulse to higher ground. It seemed impossible that the great organic sponge of the forest could really be flooded after only three days' rain. Bi tok felt the shift of vast territorial energies, flowing heedlessly through and beyond him as he ran.

A branch hit him in the face. He skidded, fell; got up and ran on. Mollie, he thought, was behind him, and Bethalie and Jillian he had just seen, over to the right. Saraa he had lost sight of; she was limping one moment, the next away at speed.

When they heard the blast of the cannon they all instinctively drew together again. Even Jimothy turned back to join them.

'Did you hear that?' she asked, nonchalantly, but only just.

Jillian was white. 'The idiot. The *idiot*.'

The sounds of returned gunfire came to them clearly across the water, like cracks of a rope.

Jillian ran ahead, attacking the hanging thickets with her machete. She cut herself halfway through to the watercourse before she realised how high they were. She peered down, clinging on to the vines while she got her breath back.

The air was full of pollen. It was sickly sweet and sticky. There was a positive cloud of it down on the river.

Jillian hung there and looked down at all the men running around and jumping into the water. Then she saw the stolen boat, with Hubert and the cannon aboard. They were out in the middle of the river, spinning carelessly round and round.

Jillian greatly resented what he had done; but at the same time she knew that her resentment was insignificant. Because Hubert had sunk the gun barge; but even more because Hubert was dead. Hubert was folded up across the breech of the cannon with blood all over his back and his head. This tableau revolved gently beneath her on the turbid water in a haze of adhesive dust.

Escalan soldiers were still being marshalled hastily and sent into the river. Some of them seemed to be having difficulties. They waved their arms and shouted.

All around, unperturbed, millions of fish were coming up to scour the surface of what had been washed from the trees. Some of them nibbled at the large blue flowers floating everywhere. As Jillian watched, a diver rose gasping amid a clutch of the flowers, pitched forward and then began to float quietly on his face.

In the centre of the chaos, the gun barge was sinking steadily. Its decorated prow protruded from the water at an absurd angle, like the snout of an outraged arapaima. Astride and clinging to its nose sat a man in black, clutching the last box of guns and bellowing at the soldiers, who were having no luck retrieving the ones that had sunk.

Jillian turned. By now all the others had cut themselves windows in the green wall.

'I must get lower.'

Alone she worked her way on to a limb of rock and dropped down to a ledge that ran out directly opposite the capsized boat. The pollen clouds were all about her now. The grains clustered in her eyelashes, gummed up her nostrils. Jillian rubbed her eyes, watching the stranded merchant.

He was not an Escalan, that was evident; nor was he any native of Belanesi. The darkness of his skin showed that he was a southerner, though, or had been a long time living there. As his footing became more and more perilous, he shifted about, always clutching his precious box, and called for help. His face was amply shadowed by his broad-brimmed hat, but something about him seemed distantly familiar. Jillian stared down at him perplexed, cursing the veil of dust.

The boatman he was shouting at edged his craft up closer. Around the two lapped a floating mess of the great, greasy flowers. They were the flowers of the blueleaf, Jillian could see that now, their distended coronas burst and limp. Presumably this was all their pollen in the air. There were also now several dead orangers afloat, wherever she looked. Nor did the boatman himself appear unafflicted. His movements were

177

increasingly spastic as he stood up and leaned out towards the armourer, who was fighting for breath and whining hideously, though that might have been from fear or from the exertions of his ordeal. He crouched on his wooden berg, holding out the box to be rescued first.

Perhaps her faculties were still awry from the violent potion. She may have been reminded of, or even believed she saw, her mother presenting the first box of Karel Jessup's guns to Prince Dolo at the parade; or the smith offering a second box to the Prince's daughter. Perhaps she saw simply a hired servant of death the enemy, or perhaps it was the man himself. Whatever, or whoever she thought he was, she shot him twice.

He threw up his hands as if exasperated at this further indignity. The last box of revolving guns toppled into the water. The man turned to face her as he fell backwards, two sudden scarlet blooms enlivening the black of his jerkin.

Jillian was already scuttling along the ledge when the Escalan Army fired back.

The Escalan Army, that afternoon at Right Fist Camp, was in complete and dishonourable disarray. Their lungs felt full of water, their muscles turned to string. Nevertheless, and notwithstanding the loss of the cargo, many of them were armed, and some of them were still able to see the northerner woman shooting from the ledge. Some of those succeeded in pointing their guns in her direction and a few in actually pulling the trigger. Since they were on the opposite bank at the time, it was a futile gesture.

The women fired back anyway. There was no response whatsoever from any of the boats.

But in the Escalan camp itself, across the river, there were still many men running around with wet bandannas over their mouths.

'We'll have to go over there.'

'Why are *we* all right?'

'Perhaps only Escalans get it.'

'Beetle's all right, aren't you, Beetle? *He's* all right.'

Jillian led the way down to the point where they would all have to jump into the water.

'I'm not going in there.'

'It's all right for us, Mollie, it doesn't hurt us.'

'Crocodiles do.'

'Crocodiles?'

'The crocodiles will be miles away!'

'Crocodiles also not like guns.'

As if on cue, more shots and shouting sounded from the camp.

There were Belanesi coming out from the trees.

Everywhere. Along the far bank, on all sides of the camp, behind and all around them.

There were hundreds and hundreds of them, whole tribes, of every colour fleece, some with skin that was spotted or streaked. Many had painted their faces and arms, daubed fierce animal shapes on their chests. The reek of them had been masked by the humid, sickly air. They had moved up completely silently, but now they made a raucous and terrifying noise. They screeched, and yelped. The children blew loudly on blaring horns. Older ones whirled stone bolas. Everyone held a sharpened stake. They came flowing into Right Fist Camp and overran it in a minute.

Bi tok looked over his shoulder at a group of black-legged men. Each was holding a Y-shaped hunting bow with both hands, ready to cock it with his hoof. He saw that some of the children's pipes and whistles were equipped to blow showers of thorns. Everyone was yammering, wide-eyed, watching the battle across the river.

'Come on, then!' said Jimothy.

The Brylanders and Bi tok leaped into the water and converged upon a rowing boat, whose asphyxiated occupants Jimothy and Saraa unceremoniously evicted. Bi tok sat on Jillian's lap. They bumped free of the jam of boats and bodies and struck out rapidly for the other side.

'We're all right, and they're all right,' commented Mollie. 'Only the orangers have got it.'

'Of course,' said Bi tok. He looked astonished at the implications of his own deduction.

No one had anything to say about the apparition of the Belanesi nation as an army. Jillian had said nothing at all, not a word, since the shooting. She looked more shocked than anything. She gazed at the spot where the cross-eyed gun barge and its fatal cargo had gone down, but there was no sign of it, nor of

179

the man in black, only maleficent flowers, bobbing on the waters of Belanesi.

Saraa was first out of the boat, scrambling on to the pontoon and shoving bodies impatiently into the river so that she could tie up.

Mollie shouted a warning. An Escalan was staggering down the path to the jetty in a ridiculous fur coat. Jimothy made a noise like a strangled bark, lifted her pistol and shot him. He spun, blood flying out of his mouth, and fell among the undergrowth.

Bi tok screamed at Jimothy, at the world, but everyone ignored him.

The women tore into the camp in a ragged posse, shooting and knifing any Escalan they found still moving. It was a relief to them to be able to be soldiers again, acting without thinking, taking refuge in destruction.

Only Bethalie hung back with Bi tok. He looked at her in anguish and horror. 'No need!' he cried. 'Make them stop, Beth!'

She merely looked glum. 'I can't, love.'

She could see he was right. The jungle people were hardly even bothering with weapons. They trampled, they kicked, they ran down their incapacitated enemies in a pack. Where an Escalan gunner fired from cover, they hurled themselves bodily over the obstacle. He could shoot, and kill, but at most he could kill only five before they had him; and what were five? The noise was monstrous, and appalling, and unending.

Bi tok turned from the carnage, terrible things written in his face. He went back and sat quietly in the boat, staring away down the majestic arcade of the river, while the waterlogged corpses sank all around.

Later, when the tumult faded, he heard voices ashore and looked back. The other four had rejoined Bethalie and were chattering, subdued but still excited. Once again, but for Hubert, they had all survived. Saraa was rehearsing the circumstances of a kill, with all the actions, while Jimothy watched indulgently, her arms folded. Mollie was counting, and pointing this way and that for Bethalie's benefit. Jillian was adding comments, smiling and scratching her head. She looked satisfied, he thought, in a very physical way he could not share. Suddenly she was a stranger, and he was an ignorant boy.

Mollie announced that she was exhausted, and sat down on a stump. Jillian drew Bethalie aside.

'Did you see the merchant?'

'Him in black? I certainly did.'

'Did you get a good look at him?'

Bethalie mused. 'Fair enough.'

'But not to say if you'd ever seen him before.'

'No.'

Jillian nodded. 'I've seen him before.'

'Where? In Tarnosh?'

'No. He'd already gone from Tarnosh.' Jillian looked at her steadily.

Bethalie, puzzled, stared into her eyes; saw something there; jumped. 'Oh ma'am, you're never thinking – '

Jillian made an odd, meaningless movement with her left hand. 'I am, though. I am, God help me. Beth – ' Her composure broke, and her voice with it. 'It was, wasn't it, Beth?' She clutched at her friend.

'No, it was not,' said Bethalie stoutly. 'The idea. That your poor father would serve Escaly! You must be tired, ma'am. The sun tricks the eye.' She was babbling, nervously. 'He had a noble carriage, your father, ma'am, and a noble brow. This was nothing like.'

'Bethalie, when did you last see my father?'

'The same afternoon you last did, I'll be bound,' rejoined Bethalie, on her dignity. 'I always used to go and see him into his coach when he was leaving. We all did. We all lined up. He would give us each a penny or a plum, or once a precious nutmeg wrapped up in a swan's feather.'

This sounded so unlike anything Jillian could remember of her father's infrequent visits that she could only look askance at the solid, sunburned woman with the bloodstained hands.

'Beth, Beth . . .' Jillian shook her by the shoulder, turned her face to the battlefield. 'Does nothing get through to you?'

'Oh, it gets through, Jillian. It gets through.' And Jillian could see that indeed she was exhausted, running on frayed nerves. By the green twilight Bethalie looked ten years older, and weary of coping.

181

Bi tok saw Bua-turaa and several youngsters with bows and javelins coming down the track behind the women.

During the massacre the natives had turned into something, followed some enigmatic impulse that frightened Bi tok very much. Yet he felt safe now, felt grateful; he could not help it. He was caught in the updraught of their triumph.

Seeing the jungle people approaching, restored to their habitual semblance of humanity, he knew that his people should not be slaughtering the Belanesi, nor talking to them particularly much, but rather listening to them attentively, and observing them constantly. For they were beyond all calculations. The tables of Geometry, Chronology and the Five Bloods could all be torn up. These people looked like animals, and could fight like them, without mercy. Yet they had language, architecture, cookery, music and medicine. Bi tok wanted to go back in time and sit beside Bua-turaa at the feast once more, to ask him a million questions, and have none of this to have happened. He hesitated to climb out of the boat.

But when Bethalie called him to come and translate, he went straight away.

The bodies were being gathered, and would shortly be burned in a pit of fire. The Belanesi wished the Brylanders to be present at the celebrations. Food had been brought from all the villages and cached at the edge of the jungle in readiness for this. Dishes had been weeks in the preparation, they stressed. Their smiles had never looked more ferocious.

Bua-turaa praised the women's courage. *But you will-not-survive long here if you do-not-learn from-us*,' he warned.

'Tell them we thank them, but we sha'n't be around much longer,' Jillian told Bi tok. 'Tell them we must go deeper into the jungle to hide from the soldiers they will send after us.'

Bi tok relayed the message without reaction.

There was a shout from the camp. The fire was almost ready. If the women wanted to take anything from Right Fist Camp for themselves, now was the time.

They began to move off up the slope towards the hanging smoke.

Bi tok stood aside, looking out across the water as before. He gave a cry, and pointed.

Some of the natives were trying to sort out the jam on the

river. They were unused to boats, and nervous to be on water. One Escalan boat, the one he and Jillian had stolen, had got away from them.

The current had caught it; Hubert, still crouching protectively over his cannon, was floating placidly away downstream.

For an instant Bi tok expected someone to jump into a boat and row furiously in pursuit. Even if they did not want to honour Hubert's remains, there was still the cannon they had lugged all the way from Tarnosh. But no one moved. They were all too fatigued; and now they had the whole arsenal of Right Fist Camp for the picking.

'Say goodbye to Hubert,' said Jillian, lightly.

But two of the young Belanesi were in animated conference. One of them set his foot on his bowstring to cock it, and the other passed him a painted arrow, which he slipped into the slot. Then he aimed up into the violet sky, high over the dwindling boat, and flicked the catch. With a deep *thunk* the arrow left the bow, and as it met the air, burst into flame.

They all lifted their heads and watched it trace its perfect parabola of golden fire against the deepening twilight, to land with an audible knock in the planking. The natives clapped and cheered, then fell silent, straining their eyes, for nothing seemed to be happening. At last, just before it was lost to sight, the boat suddenly blossomed with flame. The powder caught. There was the dull smack of an explosion; a scream of wildlife that had scarcely recovered from the din of the massacre; then bubbles, black debris, and nothing more.

Jillian tried to persuade Bua-turaa to take guns and swords for his people, but he would not, just as Bi tok had promised. The women began to sort out what they could carry and what they could not. Hastily they made up slings of arms and ammunition to be laid up in concealment in the forest all around. They knew this was only the first battle. They threw away their rags and dressed themselves in bizarre assortments of Escalan finery to feast with the Belanesi by the light of the blazing pyre.

Not that they could contrive more than a token appearance of celebration. They could harden their hearts, but they could not secure their stomachs against the stench of burning flesh. They drank more than they ate, then slipped quickly into the dark to finish the looting of the camp. Jillian was surprised to see that Bi tok stayed put, apparently, for the whole of the grotesque festival, neither eating nor drinking but talking intently with Bua-turaa and other elderly dignitaries of the tribes. She was glad of it, for she knew she had nothing to say to him herself.

Jillian Curram woke at dawn. It was a Belanesi dawn, unique and complete as any other. The birds in the highest branches began to call, and then, out of the ebony dark, a sliver of white appeared, a creeper, catching the light like a white cord let down from heaven. Next, behind it and off to either side, the texture of the trees began to coalesce in light, more blue now than white. Then the dusky green emerged, filling the forest gradually like liquid, from the bottom up. The monkeys screamed, the hornbills screamed, and it was day.

Jillian stood at the edge of the camp, watching the transformation. If you looked steadily enough in the wrong direction, it was perfectly possible to imagine that the holocaust had never happened.

Bethalie came to her.

'We must be moving,' Jillian said. 'Is everyone up?'

'Saraa's still snoring. I don't fancy the state of her head this morning! And Mollie's helping breakfast. We'll be an hour yet, at least.'

Jillian looked at the ground, scuffing the toe of a new boot to and fro.

'Talk to him, Jillian. You must.'

She smiled to think she was so transparent.

'I must. Where is he, Beth, have you seen him?'

'Down by the water.'

He was, sitting hunched under a blueleaf. She bit her lip and approached him. As he turned she was amazed and relieved to see he had found paper and a pencil and was sketching the vista downstream.

'The best of the day to you, Jillian.'

'Bi tok!' she cried gladly. They embraced and kissed; then Jillian forced herself to move away a little so as not to touch him, not to compromise him.

'We have to be going,' she said.

'Do you go far?'

'Far,' she echoed, a trifle foolishly. 'Far.' She opened her arms wide. 'Right out of the region. Hit, and run. It's the only way.'

She thought he would speak, but he did not. His green eyes regarded her solemnly. He was so young.

'You must tell them, tell Bua-turaa, that they ought to move the village too. They're so exposed, up on that rock. Do they understand? Understand, I mean, that destroying this one camp doesn't mean no more Escalans. Probably it means many, many more Escalans.'

'They will manage. As yesterday.'

Jillian was doubtful. She looked up at the deflowered branches. 'How often do these things bloom?'

'They manage other things. Know other things, things Escalans do not know, cannot know.'

'Is that what Bua-turaa was telling you last night?'

'Part of that.'

'You understand them so well,' she said; and then, quickly, 'Come with us. We need you.'

'No,' he said. 'I need to stay.'

She felt the loss of him already, and spoke, without thinking, to shun the emptiness inside her. 'Do you want me to stay?'

He looked almost startled at that. 'No, of course. What do you mean?'

In confusion she retreated. 'I thought – you might . . .'

Coolly he turned away to look again at the scene he was drawing; but he moved too slowly. She saw the tears standing in his eyes then, and cursed herself silently for a fool.

'You're being much more sensible about this than I am, damn you,' she said.

She sighed, reached out and took his hand.

'I want you to come with us. But you're right. This is not going to work. I . . . I have to fight. I couldn't face myself if I didn't go on fighting. Whereas, you . . .'

'I stay,' he said firmly. He even smiled slightly. 'I learn. Always, always I learn. I think I know nothing but to learn! Shall learn all I can from Belanesi. Shall learn to heal.'

'You healed Beth's ankle,' said Jillian. She was feeling better already.

'Yes. The bite of rik-dikkito is one thing. No Escalan knows to heal that. But to protect from a poison, before the poison comes!'

He shook his head, excited by a concept he could barely grasp.

'Knowing that, people might never be ill ever.'

Jillian grimaced. 'And we thought *we* were protecting *them*.'

Far off among the blue trees someone was calling. '*Jillian* . . .'

'They need you,' he said.

'They do,' she said. 'But they must wait a minute. There are some things I wanted to teach you first.'

'*Jill-ian!*'

Bi tok was a little anxious. 'We will meet again,' he said. 'When one is hurt or ill, you will bring to me.'

'No,' said Jillian firmly. 'Now.' She seemed urgent, embarrassed, amused. 'And not here, either.' She looked across the amber river to the sheltering trees. 'Over there.'

Then their eyes met, and Bi tok began to smile too.

'Always I learn,' he said. He put his arm around her, and they kissed. Then they went out along the pontoon and took a boat, though it was not their boat, and rowed off across the river, the sun sparkling on the water all around.